THE UNINTENDED

THE WATCHER SERIES BOOK ONE

ROBIN WOODS

Second Edition

CONTENTS

Epic Books Publishing

First Edition 2011, Second 2012; Version 2.5 2022
Editors Edition 1: Katie Isaacs & Alexis S.
Editors Version 2.5: Beth Braithwaite and Tamar Hela

Translation Rainer Maria Rilke's "Second Elegy," from *Duino Elegies* expressly for Robin Woods by Irene Gillis.
The Holy Bible, New International Version®, NIV® Copyright © 2011 by Biblica, Inc.™ Used by permission. All rights reserved worldwide.

Cover Design & Slayer Tattoo illustrated by Vera Walker.

Summary: After breaking up with her boyfriend, seventeen-year old Aleria Hayes finally feels liberated. Unfortunately, her ex's buddies are not making it easy on her. When his friends harass her one night, a mysterious stranger, Bowen, steps in to rescue her. But just as this new relationship seems to be taking off, Ali is attacked by something far worse than spiteful high school boys. When she awakes, her eyes are opened to a world where gods still walk the earth, where vampires and other immortals fight for supremacy— and where fate may be stronger than free will.

[Fiction-Fantasy, Fiction-Young Adult, Fiction-Paranormal, Fiction-Vampires]
Paperback ISBN-10: 0985454253
Paperback ISBN-13: 978-0985454258
Hardback with Dustcover ISBN: 9781941077238
Hardback Laminated Hard Case ISBN: 9781941077320

To my honey—
You are my rock.

A smooth sea never made a skillful mariner.

—Anonymous

1

THE END IS A NEW BEGINNING

The drive home from school had done little to calm me down. Entering my room, I flicked on my stereo and fell back onto the bed. The music was a perfect blend of yearning and contempt to fit my mood.

After a moment, I probed my cheekbone. It hurt enough that I decided to drag myself from bed to inspect it in the mirror. There was only a faint pink mark; thankfully, it didn't look like it would bruise.

Anger surfaced when I pictured Mark's stupid face after he'd slammed my locker shut, hitting me in the cheek. He hadn't meant to physically hurt me, but his behavior since I'd broken up with his best friend, Robert, was inexcusable.

It was bad enough having my last class with Robert every day and facing the constant can-you-see-how-much-you-hurt-me eyes. I should've waited a few more weeks until school was over to break it off, but it felt like I was living a lie.

I just couldn't fake it. He wasn't a bad guy, but he *was* smothering me—and more recently, pressuring me.

I plopped back on the bed, staring blankly at my bag full of homework on the floor. It seemed to be mocking me. I looked away, and my eyes settled on the framed prom photo on my dresser. Then I glanced around the room at every other reminder of Robert. I grabbed a plastic bin from my closet and decided that it was time to box anything that had to do with him. Within five minutes, I had over two and half years' worth of memories shoved under the bed. It made me feel better, but there was still a weird sense of unease that made me tense, like something bad was going to happen.

One thing was apparent: there was no way I could concentrate in my room. I heard my mom in the kitchen, so I bounded down the stairs.

Before I could open my mouth, she asked, "Do you know what your plans are for tonight?"

"The girls are carpooling to a movie from Campbell Perk. I thought I could hang out with them for a bit, then stay behind to get caught up on homework."

She raised her brow while she contemplated my answer. I was in *huge* trouble for letting my grades slip after the breakup.

When she still hadn't answered, I added, "I promise I'm gonna ace my unit tests on Monday. There won't be a C on my report card."

"Then you can go. You think you'll be out past dark?" She had that pinched, worried look.

"Um hmmm, but they have to pick up their cars afterwards. I'll see if they'll meet me for dessert after the movie so we can walk to our cars together." I tried to look convincing so she wouldn't insist on driving me there and picking me up. That would be entirely too humiliating.

"Check with them. If you go as a group to your cars, it's okay."

"K. I'll check." I started a group text as I went back upstairs. I had my answer in under a minute. "Mom!" I yelled downstairs. "They said they can walk me back to my car."

"Okay, sweetie. Do you want me to pack you some food?"

"That would be awesome, thanks."

I started throwing supplies in my bag. The groan of the garage door opening made me realize it had to be close to 5:30—my dad was home. I darted into the bathroom to touch up a little and headed downstairs.

My dad was already seated on a barstool at the granite counter, chatting with my mom as she cooked. They were both giggling about something that had happened at my dad's work, but I wasn't curious enough to ask.

Mom handed me my food as I gave my dad a huge hug from behind. We chatted for thirty seconds before he stopped to call my younger brother from his comics to set the table. I wanted to get to the café, so I said my goodbyes and mussed my brother's hair on my way out.

It was a short drive to the café. I pulled into the free parking garage two blocks from my destination and walked the remainder of the distance. A little extra studying, and I would be back on track.

I strolled into Campbell Perk Coffee Roasting Company and was pleased to find my favorite overstuffed leather chair in the corner available. I dumped my stuff on the table next to it to reserve it for my friends while there were still plenty of vacant tables. The café was laid out in a long L shape, with mustard-colored walls and a huge fireplace. Large mismatched rugs kept the sound from echoing as mellow music mingled with the aroma of coffee and sweet cream.

I looked around to see whether it was safe to leave my stuff unattended while I ordered; it was. When I got to the counter, my favorite barista was working. Becca already had my zebra mocha ready for me.

"I saw you come in," she greeted, grinning.

"I guess I'm that predictable, huh?"

"It's not a bad thing to be predictable."

"Yeah, I guess not. It's kind of fun to be able to order the usual. Not that anyone besides you would know what that is."

"Miles would," she whispered, glancing over her shoulder. "Pretty sure he has a crush on you."

I rolled my eyes. "Don't let him get his hopes up," I grumbled. *Soooo not ready for boys with crushes right now.*

"He's a nice guy." She shrugged.

"I'm sure he is. I mean, he seems nice. I just don't know him."

"Okay, no pressure. But, I haven't seen you in here with your boyfriend in a while. I think Miles has noticed too."

"Yeah, that. Hmmm. You probably won't see him much anymore," I added, not wanting to go into any more detail. I didn't think my local coffee shop employees needed to know all the details of my messed up love life.

"You okay?" She frowned.

"Yeah, things are good. I gotta get to studying though," I said, then went back to get the studying over with.

Sitting down, I curled my legs underneath me and scanned my to-do list. I decided to finish the last chapters of *The Great Gatsby*. Afterwards, I wasn't exactly happy with the tragic ending, so I contemplated my mixed emotions.

I liked Gatsby's ability to hope, and I couldn't help but like Gatsby. His purity of love for Daisy was earth-moving. Too bad he had wasted it on her—she wasn't worthy of that type of love. I still had a hard time with the fact that he went after her when she was married. I wondered how it would feel to have someone love you so much and have it be illicit?

I closed the book and sipped what was left of my mocha. The girls would be arriving any moment now. While I waited, I picked at the food my mom had sent with me.

As I debated whether to start my next project, I leaned my head back and closed my eyes for a moment, smelling the leather chair and espresso. When I had cleared my head enough to pick up the next project, I heard Breanna laughing outside through the thick, plate glass windows. Her laugh was better than a homing beacon.

The bell on the glass door jingled as two girls entered, and Breanna practically bounced across the room, her straight, dark blonde hair swooshing back and forth with each movement. Her denim shorts were a little too short, and her t-shirt strained across her chest I moved my bag to the chair I was in and slipped into a seat at the table to join my friends.

"How's it going, sexy?" April purred, lifting her brows suggestively.

"Good. I finally completed *Gatsby*. I only need to finish reading a play and do some review."

"So, what are the chances that you will go to the movie with us?" she asked hopefully.

"Sorry, I promised my mom I would get caught up. *Believe me*. I would rather be with you guys. I promise I'll hang out more after finals. So much, you'll be sick of me." I winked. "We're doing a study session tomorrow, right?"

"Yes, and you better," she threatened.

Just as I was about to add more, Marie and Kaela strolled in. They were my two closest friends in our group. Marie was about to open her mouth and ask me something when April interrupted.

"Nope, already asked her."

"Just dessert later tonight then," Marie confirmed.

I nodded.

"Okay, but you better be here after the movie. Don't you *dare* walk to your car alone. Did you see that another girl went missing in the North Bay two days ago?" Kaela said, driving home the point.

I swallowed. "No, I hadn't. Where?"

Marie answered, "Pacifica. We are serious. No walking to your car alone. I'm blonde, so *I'm* totally fine. But *you* ain't so lucky." She flicked her waves comically. She was joking, but at the same time, totally serious. That was the fourth girl in the in the Bay Area to go missing. All of them were average height, fair skinned, light eyed, brunette, and between the ages of sixteen to twenty. *So* not good for me.

Both Kaela and April were brunettes, but Kaela was just five feet tall. April had olive skin and huge brown eyes, so I was the only one who fit the profile.

Marie pushed my shoulder. "And, by the way, we are splitting lava cake later."

I saluted Marie, and with pursed lips, she dismissed me in a return salute. Since the breakup, I 'd become a hermit. Marie was leading our group in my absence, even though she hated it. I was grateful, and as soon as school was out, I was sure I would be ready to take over again and things would get back to normal.

The five of us bantered back and forth for the next forty-five minutes. The girls ordered their coffees to go and gleefully left to watch the movie, promising to see me in a little over two hours.

I decided to stay at the table and cleared my stuff from the leather chair. Flipping open *The Tempest*, I let Shakespeare's words saturate my brain, getting lost in the vocabulary and wishing we spoke as articulately today. My vocabulary was larger than normal; consequently, my friends were always teasing me about my word choices.

I stretched and glanced up at the counter just as Miles shot a jealous look towards the door. Confused, I peeked over at the entering customers. Robert, Peter, Tyler, and Mark were weaving their way to the counter.

Furious didn't begin to explain how I felt. This was *my* hangout, *my* safe place, and Robert knew that. Was he checking up on me? Why would he choose to come here? It wasn't like it was anywhere near his home. I tried to keep calm, hoping that they would get their drinks and leave, but I wasn't that lucky.

They settled in two tables away. Tyler looked at me contemptuously every so often. I could see the veins running over his lean muscles, his skin already glowing with a fresh tan. He would have been good looking if it wasn't for his personality. I growled internally. He was wicked smart, but he always used it to manipulate others. I was sure he'd been talking trash about me to Robert every moment he could. And Mark was easily swayed by Tyler's negativity. Mark was the reason people stereotype jocks.

Peter was my only ally in the group. I missed him more than any of the others, but I understood that he couldn't be my friend anymore. He couldn't bear being split in two; he was my oddly charismatic, yet introverted poet friend.

Peter stood at a few of inches shy of six-feet tall and was a water polo player at our school, his light brown hair perennially sun-bleached, even in winter, and his skin always golden. His eyes were like dark-chocolate and always seemed to shine, like they were a beacon showing his kind soul. He loved me, but his loyalty was to Robert, and I could never begrudge him that. He had apologized profusely to me, but he couldn't handle hanging out with both of us.

After a while, Robert stood up and disappeared into the restroom. Mark and Tyler took advantage of his absence. Mark started tossing bits of a pastry at me, crumbs scattering all over my table. I tried to ignore them, staring intently at my book, gritting my teeth. My jaw started to throb, so I relaxed my mouth.

A larger chunk landed on my shoulder and debris went into my hair and down my dark button-down shirt. I still tried to maintain my cool, but shot them a disgusted glance. I could see that Peter was trying to dissuade them, but Tyler was prodding Mark.

Tyler hissed "slut" through his teeth, and I saw Peter smack him on the shoulder. This only encouraged Tyler, and a whole string of derogatory comments meant for me slid through his teeth.

Cussing was never my thing, but some expletives were definitely coming to mind. I sat, deciding whether to fight or to flee—wavering back and forth. They were acting like I had committed some unspeakable crime, like I had cheated or purposely tried to hurt Robert. I was not guilty of either crime, yet I still felt guilt the size of a small planet.

I didn't know if it was worse to be the dumper or dump-ee. I had never said anything bad about Robert, nor was I planning on it, but his friends were making my patience wear thin.

I slipped the books I wasn't using into my bag and looked at the clock on my phone. The girls wouldn't be back for at least a half hour, and it was now very dark outside. I could have called my parents, but I didn't want to bother them. I was sure I would be safe for two blocks by myself, even though warning bells were going off in my head.

Or, I could just walk over and punch Mark in the face and return the favor from earlier today. My anger started growing, and I clenched my fists until my nails began biting into my palms and my knuckles turned white.

Mark laughed at me goadingly, his ruddy face infuriating.

Robert returned, and the boys seemed to settle down a little bit, but it was too late. Mark was going down. All four of them looked at me as I stood up. My chair popped back loudly from behind me. But at that exact moment, I felt a light touch on my elbow and an unfamiliar voice charmingly said, "Hey, honey, are you ready to go?"

I looked up, bewildered, my adrenaline pumping and ready for confrontation. And then I felt even more baffled, as I had no clue who this guy was, but he was...*beautiful*.

2

WHITE KNIGHT, WORST ENEMY

I sat, blinking up at the complete stranger with his outstretched hand. He was tall, with flawless pale skin, and blue eyes so piercing that they made Paul Newman's look mundane. Every feature was perfectly balanced on his chiseled face, his blond hair tousled like he had just walked off a runway in Paris.

It took me a second to realize what he was doing; he was saving me. I was the damsel in distress, and he, the heroic prince, was swooping in for the rescue. This made me both blush and feel irritated. I didn't need saving, but nothing good could come from my current course of action. I unclenched my fist and replied, "Ummm. Okay..."

His smile made my heart quicken. I lifted my bag and headed towards the door. He guided me out, lightly placing his hand between my shoulder blades. As I passed Robert's table, I noticed that all four of them sat speechless. Peter held food halfway up to his mouth, watching me exit with probably the hottest guy I had ever seen. I couldn't deny that it thrilled me a little.

Once outside, the night air seemed especially sweet, with the jasmine spilling from the flower boxes along the street. I paused when we were out of view of the café windows and turned to look at my own personal rescuer. Once again, I felt my heart race when I looked at him.

"Thank you," I said timidly, hit with unexpected shyness, my cheeks burning.

He grinned at me. "As amusing as it would be to see you punch the big one, I didn't think the end result would be favorable."

"That obvious, huh?"

"To anyone paying attention. And, I was paying attention…to you," he added, still smiling.

"I could have taken care of myself, but this was probably better."

"Yes, *probably*."

"Well, anyway. Thanks again." I started to turn and walk towards the garage, feeling awkward.

"Do you mind if I walk you to your car? It isn't exactly a safe time of night to be out alone." He sounded concerned.

My eyes narrowed in mock suspicion. "How do I know that *you* aren't the one I should be wary of?" I teased, grinning.

He stepped towards me, looked at my face, and changed the subject. "What happened to your cheek?" he asked as he touched my cheekbone. His hand was cold and felt good on the injury. There was a strange warmth that seemed to follow the initial coolness.

"It was an accident, but let's just say I would have loved to have punched the big one at the table," I answered.

"Mmmmm," he murmured, not liking my reply as he glanced back at the café.

I took a few more steps towards the garage, because it looked like he was contemplating going back inside. The last thing I needed was for someone I didn't even know to get caught up in my battles. He turned his attention back to me and was instantly by my side. "So again, may I be a little old-fashioned and walk you to your car?"

"I guess I'm okay with old-fashioned," I replied, still a little flushed.

"My name is Bowen Reynard, by the way. I just moved here a few months ago," he said, easily making small talk.

"I'm Ali."

"Yes, I heard the boys at the other table. Is it short for Allison?" he inquired.

I paused for a moment and chuckled. "No, it's short for Aleria." He grinned, so I added, "Don't laugh. I know it sounds like an allergy medicine or something. My parents went on some vacation in Europe and visited a place named Aleria and...voilà." I curtsied. "It means 'Eagle.' Not that you need to know that. Anyway, now that you know the complete history of my name—" I cut myself off and shook my head, a little embarrassed by my babbling. *Shut up*, I cringed.

"No, I think it is beautiful—unique. Good for an independent person."

"An independent person who apparently needs rescuing," I grumbled a little sourly.

"Is that so bad? I rather enjoyed it."

"I guess not."

"May I carry your bag? Sorry. Again, I'm a little old-fashioned. It's how I was raised. It by no means indicates that you are incapable," he amended quickly.

I shrugged. "I guess if you already *rescued* me, you might as well carry my bag."

He chuckled once more and took my bag as we crossed the street. "We all need a little help now and then. Look, you just rescued me from a dull evening at the coffee shop."

"I suppose I did do that," I replied, polishing my fingers on my shoulder. We walked past the last storefronts chatting easily, all awkwardness gone. He was confident, reassuring, and almost—intoxicating.

I fished the keys out of my pocket as we arrived at my car. He smiled and opened my door for me. I was about to tell him to put my bag on the backseat, but he placed it there without prompting. Now I felt awkward. I looked at him again and was in awe that he was being so attentive to me. I know I'm not bad-looking, but *wow* was all I could think.

He leaned in towards me with an odd expression when a vehicle driving into the garage noisily scraped on the speed bump. The car was packed with what looked like college students, and it bounced up and down, flashing headlights all over the garage. Boisterous laughter boomed from the car's open windows. They pulled into a spot a few spaces down and piled out, effectively breaking the spell I was under.

Bowen retreated a couple of steps. For a half second, it looked like anger flashed across his face, but when I refocused, he wore that infectious smile.

"Maybe I'll see you around?" I asked, sliding into the

driver's seat. He seemed to be distracted by the antics of the college students, who apparently were in no hurry to vacate the garage.

"Most definitely," he replied.

"Okay then, until later."

"It was nice meeting you, *Aleria*," he complimented, breezing his fingers over my cheek once more, his hand still icy. Then he shut the door and turned his attention back to the frolicking college students. Another car pulled into the lot, and they cheered.

I carefully backed out and waved farewell to the beautiful boy now standing at the end of the parking space. He grinned, his eyes smoldering. I couldn't place the expression on his face.

I pulled down the ramp, easing over the speed bump, and looked in my rearview to gaze at him one last time, but he was already gone. A little disappointed, I made a right turn onto the side street, and then another right onto Campbell Avenue.

The drive felt extra-long after the unbelievably long day. It seemed like yesterday when I had been at school.

Filled with conflicting emotions, I pulled into my driveway. I was still annoyed that Robert had gone to my favorite study haunt, knowing that I went there all the time. *Was he trying to annoy me? Make me feel guiltier? Or did he want his friends to harass me? Maybe he wanted to punish me.* It wasn't like I hadn't punished myself enough. He probably just wanted to talk to me.

I turned off the engine and sat in the dark while the song on the radio finished. As soon as it was over, I got out and reached for my bag. It had fallen over, the contents dumping all over the floor. I grumbled and started tossing books, gum wrappers, and scraps of paper back into my bag.

I noticed something shiny and silver gleaming in spite of the dim light, tucked under the driver's seat. I carefully plucked it from its hiding place and was filled with a warm rush of relief. It was a silver locket that I thought I had lost at the beginning of the school year.

Joshua, the boy who used to live across the street, had given it to me the very last time I had seen him. He had walked across to say goodbye two days after his parents' funeral. He had told me that he was flying back to Penn State and didn't know when he would be out again since his family was gone. I had always felt some type of special bond with him; his leaving again was painful. He'd handed me a small, black velvet drawstring bag. I remember looking at him a little confused.

He smiled his comforting smile and said, "It was my mother's. I just wanted you to have something of hers. She loved you very much. They always wanted another kid, and she always thought of you as a daughter." He paused and didn't look at me. "I'm going to miss you, Als. Keep your chin up and don't break too many hearts, okay?" He glanced at me, kissed the top of my head, and glided down the porch steps. "Please say goodbye to your parents," he said, without turning, holding back emotion, and then disappeared from my life.

I traced my finger across the scrolling and inscription on the antique locket. On the backside the initials, "JMC," Joshua Michael Copeland, looked a little worn. I carefully opened it, and there were two pictures inside, both of Josh. One of when he was around five, and the other when he was seventeen, about to go away to college. I palmed the locket and walked to the porch, trying to hold onto warm memories of Joshua instead of how much I missed him.

As I put my house key in the lock, I suddenly felt like I had to get the door open *right away*. I was completely creeped out, like I was being watched, or something was coming for me. Not one to doubt my instincts, I pushed the door open, hurried through it, and swiftly closed and locked it. I leaned against the large white doorframe, not sure why I suddenly felt so panicked. I thought I had heard something on the porch, but when I looked through the peephole, I didn't see anything. Taking a deep breath, I dropped my bag at the bottom of the stairs and proceeded down the hall to let my parents know that I was home.

I ducked my head through the doorway of their room. "Mom. Dad. I'm back."

"Okay, sweetie. Did you have a good time?" my dad asked.

"Oh, yeah, studying is the greatest! Can't get enough of that," I answered with a bleak smile.

"You doing okay?" my mom added.

"Yeah, I'm fine. I'm just going to read over my notes one more time and get to bed early. We have a study group tomorrow."

"Okay. Night, baby."

"Night."

I trudged back down the hall and dragged my stuff up the stairs. The steps seemed steeper than normal. My brain felt so tired. Then I realized I had left Campbell Perk before Marie and the others had gotten back. I dug through my disheveled bag for my phone and sent a text to our group thread.

"Had 2 go home. Robert showed up. Got an escort to my car. No worries." Then I put my phone on "Do Not Disturb" and placed it on my nightstand.

Tossing my *Complete Idiot's Guide to Shakespeare's Plays* on the bed, I picked up my pajamas and was about to start changing when I had that awful feeling again, like I was being watched.

I turned off the lights and peered out my bay window into the darkness outside. There wasn't anything out of the ordinary. I could see the neighbor's cat stalking something and Mr. Jeffrey wrestling the mail from the mailbox at the curb while clutching his briefcase and thermos precariously. There wasn't a visible menace outside. I drew in a long breath and closed the blinds as tightly as possible, dismissing the ominous feeling.

I pulled on my pajamas, then washed up in my adjoining bathroom. Our upstairs was an addition on the house that consisted of a great room, my room, and a bathroom. Besides a little television watching, I had the floor virtually to myself. I loved it, except when I got creeped out—like tonight.

I crawled into bed, leaning against my overabundance of pillows, and flipped to the synopsis of *The Tempest*. My mind drifted to the beautiful boy who had walked me to my car. Though, I was still a little miffed that he thought I needed rescuing. I was not a helpless girl, but it was a sweet gesture regardless. And the look on Robert and his friends' faces when the model-esque boy guided me out of the café was priceless. It occurred to me that Robert now probably thought I had cheated on him. Groaning, I resolved to deal with that later.

I forced myself to focus on reviewing and read through the character descriptions for *The Tempest*, and my eyelids started becoming very heavy. The last thing I read was the description of Caliban: "Caliban is portrayed as a savage, a 'demi-devil,' and 'a monster...'" My head nodded a little. "We learn that Caliban tried to rape Miranda, which is why Prospero enslaved him. Feeling no remorse, Caliban tells Prospero he would have violated Miranda..." My head nodded again. "He is incapable of moral improvements..." My eyes closed for a moment. I struggled to finish the paragraph. "Caliban is a devil, a born devil, on whose nature/Nurture can never stick; on whom my pains/Humanely taken—all, all lost is quite lost!"

Unable to keep my head up any longer, I reached over and turned off the lamp. I slumped under the covers, rolling onto my side, and drew my ragged teddy bear to my chest.

A strange thought occurred to me. *What if Caliban hadn't looked like a monster? What if he had been attractive?* And then, I drifted off to sleep...

3

TORTURES & A TOUCH OF JOY

W hen I woke, my room was darker than normal. I usually didn't sleep with all the blinds shut, so I wasn't sure what time it was. I rolled onto my back, breathing evenly while I recollected in bits and pieces my dreams from last night.

Strange, intensely colorful images. I dreamt I was living on an island with a few others, and that the island was being ravaged by a terrible storm. The storm washed up a group of men thought to be lost at sea. The air in the morning was heavy, and the jungle atmosphere thick with water from the rains. Two of the men caught my attention, one with dark hair and one with light, both of them beautiful and quite different from the others.

I watched them as I was concealed in the foliage; they moved gracefully as they helped the others. After a short time, I lost track of one of them, and at that moment of my realization, I was discovered. When I looked up, I saw the beautiful dark-haired man. I recognized him, but at the same time, I didn't. And oddly, I loved him instantly and completely. His beautiful face seemed to be filled with love, too. I looked away, towards the survivors, embarrassed. The other beautiful man stood like stone, staring at us, and as his attractive façade dissolved, he became horrific—a monster.

I shuddered at the thought and sat up. *Note to self: no more evil Shakespearean characters before bedtime.* I looked at the alarm, and it was only 8:00 A.M., so I flopped back down. But then I could smell bacon and coffee and waffles. I rolled out of bed, a little less reluctant than before. I remembered the locket I'd found in my car last night and slid it over my head, finding it strangely comforting after my dreams.

Staggering towards the smell of food, I wearily clomped down the stairs, my hair poking up in all directions, but I didn't care. My brother was happily munching on some bacon at the kitchen table with my dad. They were deeply steeped in some comic book card game, and they barely noticed my entrance.

"Good morning, sunshine," my mom brightly greeted me.

"Mmmmm," I responded, not quite ready to talk. I slumped onto a stool and put my head down on the granite counter. It felt cool on my cheek. She walked over to me and gently ran her hand through my tangled locks. It felt good, so I didn't move and let out a coo.

"You sleep okay?" she said with a little concern.

"I guess. Weird dreams though…" My voice trailed off as I recovered more of the disturbing visions from my dream.

"What about?" she asked, her curiosity a little peaked.

"I think, it's that play, *The Tempest*. The one we saw at the

Oregon Shakespeare Festival last summer. I was reviewing it when I fell asleep. I think I was dreaming that I was Miranda or something, but things were different." I sighed. "It was just a dream, but so vivid though."

"Oh, sorry, sweetheart, I wish you'd slept better. You want some breakfast?"

"Mmmm, yes, please."

"What would you like?"

"A little of everything," I said sheepishly.

"No problem. There's coffee in the French press."

Sliding off the stool, I doctored my morning brew. Once I was back on my perch, I ate my breakfast while chatting with my mom. My dad and brother continued eating and playing cards. Then my mom got a funny look on her face like she wanted to ask me something.

"What, Mom?" I leveled my eyes at her.

She looked concerned and like I might be upset with her. My mind started to race. She finally began, "Well, you know your brother has summer camp next week in Twain Harte, right?"

"Yeah." Okay, not the direction I had thought she was going to go, so I relaxed.

She continued, "We were thinking about heading up a little early and visiting your grandma while Cameron's at camp, since Sonora is right there." I was still waiting for the catch. "He finishes school on Wednesday, and you aren't finished with school until Friday, and your birthday is Saturday." I still wasn't following.

"You want me to miss my party on Saturday?" It was the only conclusion I could draw.

Her brow furrowed. "Well, Grams was hoping we could come up on Thursday or Friday, because Aunt Lisa will be up there for the weekend, and then we were thinking of staying the week while your brother is at camp."

"Oh." My shoulders slumped. They wanted me to leave before my party AND go away for more than a week? I had already made plans for my birthday with the girls, as well as trips to Santa Cruz to hang out at the beach. I supposed it wouldn't be the end of the world, but being around my grandma and her less-than-helpful comments for nine days was not exactly my idea of a great beginning to the summer. I loved my grandma dearly, but small doses of her were a little more manageable. Then my mom shocked me out of my reverie.

"We were actually thinking about going without you, but it makes me feel really bad not being here for your birthday." She looked at me, weighing the reaction on my face.

I tried not to jump up and do a happy dance. Did she actually think leaving me here would upset me? I took in a breath, deliberately concealing my excitement. "Oh, I guess that would be okay. Are you all right with me being alone? You guys have never left me here for more than a weekend before."

"Sweetie, we trust you. You have never given us any reason not to. But I feel really bad about not being here for your party."

"Mom, no. Really, it's no problem. We can have a family party when you get back. I don't mind."

She seemed okay with my reaction. Of course, now that I was minus a boyfriend, they were probably more okay with leaving me here. Not that I would have taken advantage of that anyway. Even when Robert saw me drifting away from him at the end and had tried to push me to get more physical, I had always kept my hormones in check, even if I didn't *want* to in the moment. *Evidence of my parents' brainwashing, no doubt.*

"I already called Marie's mom to see if she can stay with you for a few of the days," Mom informed me.

"That would be great. Too many days here by myself would get a little creepy. I could probably get Kaela or Breanna to stay over some, too."

"You're sure you're fine with this?" She was still evaluating.

"Mom, trust me; I would tell you if I wasn't." I gave her a sideways hug and cleared my plate, rinsing it in the sink and placing it in the dishwasher.

Since I was getting together with the girls for the study session later, I decided to get a jump on my chores instead of dragging my feet. I was also a little excited about having the place to myself very soon. I could go into complete night owl mode with no one to wake me with loud cartoons at the crack of dawn.

After finishing my chores, I felt very accomplished, and sat at my desk. I turned on my laptop and fiddled with my locket. Closing my eyes while I waited for the computer to boot up, my thoughts were on Joshua.

It was then that I felt myself slipping into a daydream. In the last few weeks, my daydreams had become so intense that I would momentarily forget where I was; I didn't fight it.

I was in the past, standing with an umbrella on my front porch, holding a plate of food in my left hand. The fat droplets of rain were soaking my shoes despite being under the overhang. Taking in a deep breath, I pushed away the sadness that was choking me and jogged across the street.

When I reached the front door of the Copeland's house, I noticed it was ajar. I slowly pushed it open. "Joshua? It's me." Dropping my umbrella on the stoop, I entered.

The house was dark and full of boxes, taped and ready to be moved out. Yesterday had been his parents' funeral. I crept through the entryway and down the hall to the living room. The back sliding door was open, and the room smelled of rain and wet cardboard.

"Josh?" I called again.

When I circled around a tower of boxes, I found him sitting on the floor, staring into the backyard. He turned his eyes towards me. His lips parted as if he was going to speak, but he only looked at me with such loss that I was afraid my already breaking heart would stop beating.

I placed the plate of food on the coffee table and eased down next to him. There were so many things I wanted to say, but the words fell away. Nothing but time could help.

After several minutes of silence, I finally took his hand in mine, kissed it, and held it to my cheek. "I love you," I murmured. It was the only comfort I could offer my friend— more than a friend—he was part of my family.

He looked over at me, and his bottom lip trembled ever so slightly. His green eyes were rimmed with red, making them even more vibrant. A breath hitched in his chest as he gathered me to his side. We sat huddled on the floor, locked together by overwhelming grief until my parents eventually called me home. Leaving Joshua alone in that empty house had been impossibly hard, but he wouldn't come with me.

I sucked in a breath as the daydream receded. It had seemed so real that I had a hard time coming back to the present. I could smell the rain and damp cardboard. My chest ached with the loss of the Copelands all over again.

Unable to shake the feeling, I decided to write Josh, even though I had not heard from him in almost two years. I twisted a lock of my hair until it spiraled into an eight, while I contemplated. Then I started to type:

JOSHUA,

HEY, ME AGAIN. I KNOW THIS IS AN EXERCISE IN FUTILITY SINCE I HAVEN'T HEARD FROM YOU IN SO LONG, BUT I THINK I SIMPLY NEED THE ACT OF WRITING TO HELP ME SOMETIMES. PART OF ME IS GLAD YOU ARE NOT READING THIS, BUT THE OTHER PART WISHES YOU WERE. THERE IS DEFINITELY AN ABSENCE OF BIG BROTHER TYPES IN MY LIFE.

SO ANYWAY, I BROKE UP WITH ROBERT A FEW WEEKS BACK. I KNOW YOU WOULD BE THRILLED. I BELIEVE YOU CALLED HIM "DULL AND UNWORTHY," NOT THAT HE LIKED YOU EITHER. BUT THAT IS BESIDE THE POINT. HE IS STILL A NICE BOY, JUST NOT RIGHT FOR ME IN THE LONG RUN. I KNOW I MADE THE RIGHT DECISION, BUT EVERYONE IS TREATING ME LIKE BROKEN GLASS RIGHT NOW, AND IT IS RATHER ANNOYING. I'M NOT THAT BREAKABLE, AND I'M THE ONE THAT DID THE BREAKING, NOT THE OTHER WAY AROUND. OKAY, SO NEVER MIND. WELL, I GUESS THAT'S IT. I MISS YOU, AND I WOULD LOVE TO HEAR FROM YOU.

LOVE, A

. . .

Exhaling, I clicked send and pushed away from the desk, not feeling any better. I'd sent an inarticulate e-mail that didn't say much. *Bravo.*

Then I remembered that I had turned my cell phone on silent and checked it. There were sixteen text messages. My forehead wrinkled. I never got that many messages this early on a Saturday. Then I noticed that most of them were from last night. I opened the group thread.

"U have some explaining to do," from Marie.

All the other texts were some variation of that sentiment from all the girls. I put my cell back on the nightstand without reading all of them and crawled back in the bed. Apparently, my leaving the coffee shop with the beautiful boy had caused more of a ripple than I had thought. I sighed, knowing that the incident wasn't going to go unnoticed; I was going to have to deal with it.

I decided to take a long, hot shower to calm my nerves, but instead of relaxing under the water, my stomach only got tighter. And unfortunately, the rest of the anxiety-ridden afternoon passed slowly. I finished prepping for the study session, then I joined my brother on the couch, watching a *Spiderman* marathon on one of the cartoon channels. That burned the remaining time before the now dreaded study session.

When I arrived at Breanna's house in Los Gatos, everyone else's cars already lined the street. Even Marie and Kaela's cars were there, and they were always late. *Not a good sign.* I sat in my car a moment, preparing for the inquisition, since I hadn't answered a single text. I was sure that had worked them up into a frenzy.

I knocked on the oversized front door to Breanna's upscale home, and it opened before I could land the third knock. April had a sheepish grin on her face before she turned to lead me into the kitchen. I sat down at the huge out-of-date kitchen table. The inside of the house was still stuck in the 1980s, complete with pale blue linoleum floors and roller chairs at the Formica kitchen table.

My nerves rose again as I organized my notes and got settled. The room grew quiet. I wondered how long it would take before they started hurling questions at me. Of course, I could've volunteered the information, but something stubborn in me wanted to make them squirm with expectation. The anticipation was palpable.

"Soooo," I began. They leaned forward. "Who has the first section?" I tried to suppress a grin and look earnest.

"Uhhh. I do," Marie replied, looking at me suspiciously.

"Great, let's get started," I suggested, my voice a little too high-pitched.

Kaela looked at me and rolled her eyes. "Cough it up, chick."

I sighed. "Hmmm. How about we start with what you heard?"

Breanna burst with information, as she filled me in about the aftermath; they had walked in just a few minutes after I'd left Campbell Perk. The girls overhead enough of Robert and company's conversation to put together a fairly accurate outline of what had happened. Apparently, Mark and Tyler were fervently trying to convince Robert that I had been cheating on him the whole time. Peter didn't think so, but Mark and Tyler were bitter and argumentative.

Robert took everything in, not saying much and not knowing what to think. Their conversation was loud enough that when my friends inserted themselves in the discussion, it turned into an argument, and everyone was asked to leave. The girls felt blindsided, but were sure that I would've said something if I'd been dating someone else, so they'd defended me with zeal.

I, in return, filled in the gaps, weaving my short tale of Bowen Reynard, my "rescue," and our short stroll to the parking garage. Of course, they would've paid good money to have seen it for themselves. Kaela implied that I was exaggerating about Bowen's beauty. I assured her I wasn't.

Marie was disappointed we hadn't exchange numbers or at least e-mail addresses. I informed her that he had said he would see me again, but that I was not getting my hopes up. They finally eased up on all the questions, and we had a productive work time.

Sunday seemed to be a mirage that passed before I could really take notice. Then on Monday, I woke to the alarm blaring in my ear. I sped through my morning routine and was out the door in less than twenty minutes.

My thirteen-mile drive to campus was filled with anticipation. I worried about my two unit exams *and* the possible fallout from Friday night. I wasn't sure what to expect the first time I saw Robert after leaving with Bowen.

As I pulled into the parking garage on campus, I tried to ignore the sidelong looks from some of my peers. I hadn't even made it into the buildings yet, and conversations were halting when I got too close.

This is not good, was all I could think.

Not. Good.

4

NOT GOOD

Mark Twain once said, "A lie can travel half way around the world while the truth is putting on its shoes." I had a strange feeling that this quote was going to be very meaningful after today.

The school was built on a hilltop, and the two main buildings were gigantic beige monuments. The structures ran parallel to one another.

Building A was four stories, two above ground and two built into the side of the hill, and it housed most of the academic classes. Building B was five stories tall, two above ground, including the gym and English classrooms, and three stories of parking garages that were built into the other side of the hill. The garage was for faculty, seniors, and a few random juniors. Somehow I had been given a garage spot. It was nice, but sometimes creepy if I left after dark.

I couldn't walk anywhere on campus without heads

turning and whispers hissing. I was the object of unwanted attention.

And today, since I had to go back and forth between both of the buildings over and over, it made me feel like I was running through a gauntlet of rumors.

After lunch, I reluctantly headed to AP English to take the *Gatsby* Unit Exam. The irony that it was a novel about affairs and betrayal wasn't lost on me. I had managed to avoid Robert and his cronies all day, but there was no avoiding him next period, where our seats were conveniently located next to one another in the back.

Class started, and I saw him look at me several times, but I kept my attention at the front of the class or on my test, without wavering. He even cleared his throat once, trying to break my gaze at the teacher. I flared my nostrils and gritted my teeth. He didn't try to get my attention again.

The moment the agonizing class was over, I rushed from the classroom and hid in the girls' restroom, waiting for the swell of students to dwindle. I felt like an idiot hiding. But I didn't know if I could keep my emotions in check, so I paced back and forth agitatedly. I was angry. Angry about the rumors. Angry Robert seemed to believe them. Angry that he might have started all the rumors. Angry that I still felt guilty *all the time*. I wanted to scream just to let out my frustration.

At that moment, I heard a group of girls open the bathroom door, and I ducked into a stall. *Hiding, of all things!* They were wildly wrapped up in their own little world of gossip.

"Did you hear that Ali was cheating on Robert the *whole*

time?" one of the girls squealed in excitement. "Some college guy."

"Yeah, she didn't even deny it to anyone today," another eager voice chimed in.

"I always knew she was a slut. Too good for everyone else," the first one said.

"How could anyone do that to Robert? He's sooooo cute," crooned a third.

Then the fourth girl softly said, "I always thought she was nice."

"Really, what—"

That was all I could take. I steadied my breath and flushed the toilet, though I hadn't used it. It seemed less pathetic. The voices halted when they realized they weren't alone. I opened the blue door and let it slap the stall wall with a metallic clang and calmly walked to the sink, taking my time to wash my hands. It was a group of sophomore girls that I'd frequently caught stealing looks at Robert over the last two years. *Figures*.

As I dried my hands, I kept my cool façade as I looked each one of them in the eyes. Not one of them moved an inch. I flung my bag over my shoulder and walked out. Once the restroom door closed behind me, I could hear a cacophony of shrieks behind the closed door.

I exhaled and started to make the trek to my locker in the other building.

Most of the students were gone at that point, and not many noted my passing. I thought maybe that was the end of it for today. But that thought was too good to be true.

As I rounded the corner, I could see Mark's hulking body

fiddling with items in his locker. I proceeded to my locker anyway. No more hiding, as it obviously wasn't helping the situation. I opened my locker, dumped the stuff I didn't need, and grabbed what I did.

It was oddly silent next to me. I was glad the locker door was blocking Mark from my view. Then I heard him take a step back, and he placed his left hand on the locker to my left. I backed up half a step and bumped into his chest—trapped. I calmly zipped my bag and twisted so I could get my locker door shut.

Instantly, his right hand crashed into the locker to my right. He had me walled in. I fought to keep my anger in control. I turned around to see his red face was way too close to mine.

I took a deep breath, waiting for him to start. He had this smug expression. "Soooo. If I knew you were going to give it out so easy, I would have gotten in line," he spat.

My mouth dropped open with a pop. All I could think was, *WHAT??*

"So how long were you shacking up with him?"

His accusation burned into me. I didn't want to dignify him with a response, but I couldn't help it. My rage started spilling out.

"I have never given out *anything* to *anyone*," I said, through gritted teeth.

"Suuure." His eyes mocked me, his face still too close to mine.

"Mark, let me go." He didn't move, so I added in a steely tone, "Or I will hurt you." He laughed in my face, knowing that he had a hundred pounds on me.

I looped my left hand more securely onto my bag and looked him square in the eyes, hoping he would catch fire from my gaze. Then with one swift movement, I poked his Adam's apple with my right index finger. He shot back, clutching his throat and gasping for air as he fell to his knees.

I sprinted down the hallway and up the stairs before he could recover and tried not to think about the inevitable consequences for that move. I was also a little pleased about using what I had learned in those self-defense classes. He would probably be too embarrassed to tell anyone that a girl had taken him down with one finger.

The plaza was almost empty as I passed through to the other building. I raced down the three flights of stairs and only slowed when I entered the garage to catch my breath.

I fumbled for my keys as I walked, stopping short about a car length away from my parking spot. Robert was leaning against the driver's door of my car. I exhaled violently. *Okay, so it's a really bad day.*

He looked up at me with his large brown eyes, immediately disarming me. There was nothing aggressive in his stance, just hurt. I stood there awkwardly waiting. I could tell he was mulling over what he was going to say, and then he finally opened his mouth.

"Is it true?"

Sighing, I took a few steps to close the gap between us, and looked him in the eyes. "No, Robert. I would never do that to you."

He nodded his head slowly, his eyes still searching my face. "I didn't think so. You are too…"

I raised one eyebrow.

"Ethical."

This was true. I should've been angry knowing that he didn't exactly stop the rumor. I was sure I knew where it originated, namely Mark and Tyler. *And what was up with Mark and that "get in line" comment?* But before I could get too distracted, I looked back at Robert. He was still nodding. I suppose he was accepting the truth.

I didn't want to talk about any of this anymore, but added, "I didn't know him. He saw your friends giving me a hard time while you were away, and he helped me out is all."

He looked down for a moment, and when he raised his head, he was choked up, his eyes red. "Okay," he whispered. Without thinking, I stepped forward and put my hand on his elbow. He started to reach for my hand, but I quickly pulled mine away before he could touch me.

"Sorry," I said, my voice a little shaky.

He shrugged.

"I…" I hesitated. "I was wondering if I could ask you a small favor? Look, I know you hate me right now, but could you please ask your friends to lay off a little? I am seriously running out of patience."

"I don't hate you, Ali. Yeah, I'll talk to them. And see if I can stop the rumor. I should've known better. You always do what you think is right—even when I don't like it."

"Thanks." And with that, I took a risk and hugged him. He held me tightly for a long time, both of us just breathing in and out in silence.

As he pulled away, he kissed my forehead and murmured, "I'll always love you." I could hear finality and acceptance in his voice.

I was afraid to say anything, so I just nodded. He looked at me one last time, then slipped away towards the stairs. I unlocked my car door, collapsed into the seat, and held my face between my hands.

The drive home seemed very, very long.

After dinner, I decided to return to my favorite haunt to finish my homework, still too distracted to work at home. My dad insisted on driving me and picking me up. I started to kick up a fuss, but caved. A girl from the university just a few miles away had gone missing on Friday—that was two girls in two days. It probably had nothing to do with all the disappearances in the North Bay, but it would be better not to go out on my own at night.

I entered the café, and out of the corner of my eye, I noticed my favorite leather chair was taken. I grumbled to myself about my bad day, but then took a double take. The person in my chair was Bowen. I blinked in recognition.

He was reclining with a book in his lap, and his all-too-beautiful face displayed a grin. I felt my cheeks flush, and my heart skipped a few beats as his shockingly blue eyes watched me. I quickly looked away.

I never really considered the possibility of seeing him again. Maybe this wasn't the worst day ever, after all.

5

INESCAPABLE

I realized he had said he would "most definitely" see me again, but I hadn't wanted to dwell on whether he had really meant it or not. Now, seeing Bowen here, part of me wanted to turn around and run out of the café, not ready to even contemplate liking someone right now—not this soon.

The other part of me felt impossibly drawn to him. It almost seemed unnatural. Maybe I just wanted to be comforted after all the high school melodrama unfolding around me. I despised drama.

I glanced at him again. He was smiling directly at me with such confidence. I froze; my feet felt cemented in place. It took me several seconds to finally break free and approach him, dumping my bag down on the table next to him.

"So, here you are again," he greeted as he opened the conversation.

"Yeah, you too." I was feeling a little stupid about my inability to think of anything witty. I tried to calm my heart.

There was amusement in his eyes. Hopefully, he couldn't see exactly how much he was affecting me.

"You seem surprised to see me," he said, almost playfully.

"Uh, yeah, I guess I am," I admitted.

"I told you I would see you again."

"Yes, yes, you did. I just didn't expect it," I confessed as I slid into a seat.

He motioned towards my bag. "More homework?"

"Yeah," I sighed. "Finals next week."

"I'm just finishing mine this week," he replied.

"Oh, where are you going to school?" I asked, trying not to sound overly curious.

"San Jose State," he answered.

So he *was* in college. I tried not to look disappointed and show how deflated I felt. "What year are you?"

"Just finishing my freshman year."

Still a possibility, I thought. I was old for my grade level, so I realized that our ages might not be that far apart. Then I caught myself. I still wasn't ready. Why was I getting my hopes up? I just couldn't help myself. He was almost magnetic.

It took a few seconds to pull myself out of my head and formulate an appropriate answer. "Oh, that's nice. Do you like State?"

"It's okay, for the most part. But..." he paused and looked at me flirtatiously. "I'm liking the area more and more."

"That's right, you said you had just moved here a few months ago." He seemed pleased that I remembered.

"Yes, there was a change of plans, and I decided to come out here."

"Where were you before?"

"I was attending Penn State."

"Oh, I used to know someone who went there," I said, thinking of Joshua. "Didn't you like it?" I added and tried not to think about my absentee friend.

"It was fine, but I felt…drawn to California. And now, I'm really happy I came," he admitted as he leaned closer.

I had to look away—it was too intense. I couldn't form any sentences, and the ones I could were completely stupid. I stood up abruptly, and he seemed to tense up.

"Gotta get my coffee. I'll be right back," I assured him, and he relaxed. I needed a moment to get this silly crush under control. Did I really have to react like this?

When I returned, he'd moved to the table where I'd set my bag, so he was sitting across from me. Then something changed; my nerves died down, and the conversation flowed.

It was as if I had known him for a long time. I realized that I really liked talking to him, and not just because I found him attractive. We had a real connection, and I was pretty sure he felt it too.

We continued to talk for the next hour until it came to my attention that I hadn't gotten any of my homework done. I called my dad to pick me up.

Bowen seemed genuinely disappointed, but I wasn't about to blow my chance to get my grades back up. A boy was the reason I'd gotten myself into this situation. Bowen walked me outside and dismissed himself seconds before my dad rounded the corner.

Over the next couple of days, the gossip at school died down. It seemed that Robert had curbed the rumors, as promised. I still got a few furtive glances from those all too eager to believe the worst about someone, but overall, the week kept getting better.

Each evening, I went to the café, dropped off by my dad, of course, and Bowen was always there to greet me.

I felt giddy. Part of me had a hard time believing that such an amazingly gorgeous college guy was so interested in me. So many college guys would have a serious hang up going out with someone still in high school, even though Bowen was just fifteen months older than I.

He seemed interested in everything about me. He offered to give me a ride home each night, but I was still trying to keep him at an arm's length, not quite ready to embrace a relationship yet, or whatever this was.

On Thursday, the girls joined me. Bowen wasn't at Campbell Perk. I was more disappointed than I should have been.

Marie, Kaela, April, Breanna, and I all got out our review sheets and started our study session. We sat discussing all of the sample questions, filling in extra notes as we added our insights to the conversation. And then I was startled.

"Hey," April said, interrupting my train of thought and looking straight at me. Her wide brown eyes danced. She was twisting her almost waist-length, brown hair around her fingers.

My eyes focused on her, but my face was blank. I hadn't realized I was staring off into space.

An impish grin lit her face. "You really like him, don't you?" The others looked up.

"Um, I don't know what you're talking about," I said, staring back.

"Well, you are obviously looking for *someone*. You keep scanning the café every five minutes, and then you zone out," she accused.

A few giggles erupted from around the table. I took a sip of my coffee, not sure how to reply, but my silence was enough.

"I don't know what you're talking about." I stuck my nose in the air, knowing that they could see right through me. To admit it to them would make my little dream seem real, and right then, I wasn't too sure how real it was.

Kaela made some kissy sounds in the air, and more giggles ensued.

"Okay," Breanna said. "But we are on to you," she added, with a super awkward wink.

"Sure," I chuckled, rolling my eyes. "I need to use the little girl's room." And I removed myself from the table before they could question me anymore.

As I walked away, Kaela whispered something, and then I heard someone say, "Saturday," probably talking about my party next week.

When I returned from the restroom, I made it about five steps, then froze in place.

Bowen.

He was leaning against the counter, his deep blue, button-down shirt fitted to his slender, yet obviously well-muscled frame. My face flushed again. I managed to walk a couple of steps towards him, and he met me in the middle, with a stupid grin on my face.

I felt like an idiot again.

He raised his hand and traced under my jaw with his fingers. He hadn't touched me since that first night that he'd caressed the almost invisible injury on my cheek. His hands were still cool, and it sent a chill down my spine, followed by a warmth that seemed to radiate throughout my body.

He smiled as I was still standing there, staring into his eyes, not saying anything. His eyes held me there, always so hypnotic. "I just wanted to stop by for a minute. I have...late dinner plans," he grinned.

"Oh," I managed, then pinned my eyebrows together, "real late," realizing the time.

"Yeah, I know. I just didn't want to go without seeing you today."

"Oh," was all I could get out. No *nice to see you too.* Nothing. I cringed.

"I'll drop by here tomorrow," he said in almost a whisper before he turned and walked to the door. But right before stepping out, he eyed my table of friends who were staring with shocked faces as he released the most devastating smile.

I kept standing there for a moment, remembering the warmth of his cool fingers. As I turned to return to my friends, I realized that all eyes were now fastened on me.

Still dazed, I drifted back to the table. The warm feeling from his touch melted away in a few seconds, and I came back to reality. There were four pairs of expectant eyes staring at me in silence. I plopped down in my seat. They were still staring.

Finally, Kaela erupted with, "Holy crap!"

I shrugged. "Yeah, that was Bowen." My blush reappeared.

"No wonder Robert almost had a coronary when you walked out with him," April said, dramatically fanning herself as her long, brown locks flittered from her waving hand.

"He's," I cleared my throat, "moderately attractive." My understatement was obvious.

Breanna threw her folder at me, and it hit me with a *thwap*.

"Sure, moderately and that makes Brad Pitt—what, passable?" Marie quipped.

"Ewww, he's old," Breanna said.

Marie threw up her hand. "Still hot." Then, everyone turned to me again.

"Look, I don't know how I feel." More of my fears than I intended started spilling out. "I'm not sure I'm ready for any of this." I shook my head, obviously uncomfortable. "He doesn't seem real, or maybe too good to be true. So I'm just not going to think about it," I declared with finality.

They obviously wanted to continue talking about him—and us. But Marie and Kaela, sensing my distress, glared at the others, so they let it drop. There was an occasional giggle, but we got back to studying.

Kaela drove me home so my dad wouldn't have to pick me up. She didn't say much while she drove, but when we pulled into the drive, she simply stated, "It's okay to have a rebound relationship. Just have some fun. You don't have to walk around, feeling guilty all the time." And that was it. She smiled, her pale green eyes reassuring me. Kaela could always see through me more than others.

"Thanks, Kaela. And thanks for the ride. See you

tomorrow." Closing the door, I jogged to the front of the house. I flashed the porch light when I got in and waved from the window.

I went to sleep holding my locket, wondering what I should do about Bowen.

The way I was drawn to him felt…

…it felt both natural and unnatural.

Inescapable.

6

TOO FAR

The next week flew by. I only had five finals since my two AP teachers didn't make their classes take one. My chemistry final was the only one to be apprehensive about, and of course, it was the last one. I had the pleasure of worrying about it all week.

Bowen met me at Campbell Perk every night, and since he was finished with his finals, he graciously quizzed me until my brain was numb. We alternated between studying and talking, but I felt like he was getting to know me better than I him. He seemed to answer my questions honestly, but there was always a sense of mystery in his words, almost like I wasn't in on some dark secret.

Again, each night he offered to give me a ride home or even go somewhere else more date-ish, but I was determined to focus on my studies. I was in trouble because of a boy, and I wasn't going to ruin my chances for grade recovery due to a new one. Additionally, I was trying to reign in my feelings for him. It was still at the crush, butterflies-in-the-stomach level, but it was growing—too fast. It terrified me a little.

On Thursday, I walked to Campbell Perk in the afternoon to study for my last exam. My parents wanted to have family time together before leaving for Sonora, so I needed to get an early start on reviewing.

I was a little disappointed because I would probably miss seeing Bowen. He never seemed to show up until after sunset. Then I realized that it was starting to get dark, so I gathered my review sheets and books together and started out the door for my walk home. Just as I got to the door, Bowen was there opening it for me. His face lit up, and my heart skipped a couple beats.

"I was hoping I would catch you," he said pleasantly.

"Oh, I was about to walk home before it got too dark," I answered, a little disappointed that I had to go.

"Well, since I would still like to spend a little time with you, would you mind if I walked you home?" he offered.

I wasn't sure if I wanted him to know where I lived yet. But I didn't know where my reluctance was rooted. I had spent almost every evening the last two weeks talking with him. He reached out and twisted a lock of my hair around his finger flirtatiously before he pulled his hand back. I blushed. His eyes said *please*, and my reservations melted.

"Uh, sure," I replied, a little embarrassed by my flushed face, again.

We strolled down the quieting streets, our conversation always so easy; his vocabulary surprised and pleased me. There was something old-fashioned about it; he must have had strict parents. He quizzed me about my likes and dislikes.

Favorite places to visit. Places to which I dreamed of traveling. His answers to the same questions always seemed incomplete, like he was telling the truth, but only part of it.

We arrived at my home. "This is it."

"Aren't you the poster girl for middle-class America?"

"No picket fence."

"Is there a mini-van in the garage?"

"Guilty."

His reply was a rather satisfied smirk. He walked me to the door, and there was an awkward silence. I felt like I wanted to invite him in and that he wanted in, but I wasn't ready to do the whole introduction-to-the-parent-thing.

"So, I should probably get in there; my mom will be serving dinner soon."

"May I come in?" He hesitated and quickly added, "And meet your family?" He smiled and ran his finger over my cheek. I closed my eyes; he smelled really good, and it made me lose focus for a moment.

"I'm sorry. Maybe later."

"I'll hold you to that." He winked and disappeared into the now dark street.

Immediately after dinner, my family started bustling around the house, finishing the last minute packing. Retreating to my room, I went through my flash cards, listened to music, and e-mailed Joshua again. He was heavy on my mind. I drew in a deep breath and flopped onto my bed. I felt like I should get everything in order. I had that unsettled feeling that things were about to change. All indicators for the future were positive, but I couldn't shake the feeling. I went to bed with a knot in my stomach.

Pushing the sweat drenched hair from my face, I woke from a nightmare and leaned to see the clock—3:00 A.M. With a groan, I tried to remember the dream, but the harder I tried to remember it, the more it eluded me. I trudged down into the dark kitchen to get some water. The foreboding feeling from my dream seemed tangible. I returned to my room, stretched out between the cool covers, and inhaled the comforting smell of the fabric softener on the sheets. There was a pressure on my ribcage, making it difficult to take a deep breath. Despite the feeling, I drifted off to sleep.

My family left first thing, and even though I slept horribly last night, my last final went well. The stress and anxiety over it was all for naught. The exam was much easier than I had anticipated, and I felt as though I could breathe again —liberated!

This marked the official arrival of summer, senior year— and two days until my eighteenth birthday. Marie and Kaela had kept me in the dark about most of the birthday plans; all I knew was that at 7:30 P.M. sharp, I was supposed to meet everyone at the Italian restaurant at THE Lane tomorrow. Nothing bad could come from an evening starting out with good Italian food.

I had promised Bowen that I'd drop by the café. I took a nap and then walked down. I stopped for a little while in the used bookstore, and picked up a few novels I wanted to read over the summer.

There was an oddly familiar man in the bookstore. I could've sworn that he kept glaring at me...*weird*. I made my purchase and headed out to do a little reading before Bowen arrived.

The delicious smell of coffee hit me two stores down, and I started to salivate. After getting the usual, I settled into my chair with my libation and my books. I glanced out the window, and the angry-looking man from the bookstore stalked by, making eye contact with me for a split-second. I shivered, though I was not cold. Something about him was unsettling.

He had jet-black hair, so dark it had a blue cast like a raven's feathers, but his skin, in stark contrast, was so pale. His eyes, deep in their sockets, appeared as black as his hair, the edges of his lids red. His thin frame hunched over a little, as though he didn't want to be seen. He was wearing dark jeans, a black t-shirt, and a slim-cut cargo jacket with a '70s collar in deep green and a messenger bag slung over his shoulder.

He disappeared around the corner. I still couldn't place where I had seen him before the awkward experience at the bookstore. I shook it off and opened my book.

Bowen arrived a few minutes after sunset, and I lost myself in conversation with him, although he seemed different tonight, his eyes colder. It started getting late, so he offered to walk me home. I accepted.

We ambled down the street towards my home, conversing about anything and everything that came to mind...pop culture, books, movies, and our hatred of people who insisted on talking and texting while watching the aforementioned movies.

Bowen gently interrupted the flow of conversation. "Would you mind if we make a quick stop?" he asked, his voice soft as silk. We stopped walking; he ran his fingers over my cheek and that familiar, warm sensation coursed through me.

"Not a problem," I answered.

He put his hand on the small of my back and led me around the corner. "I left something at my place." He pointed down the street. "It'll just take a moment." We walked about a half a block and stopped in front of some apartments. I had cut down this street in the past and seen the buildings before. They were painted a deep coffee brown, and with the surrounding pine and redwood trees, the buildings looked like they belonged in the mountains.

He motioned towards the cement staircase at the center of one of the buildings. "I'm on the second floor."

I hesitated in front of the building.

He grinned. "Come on up."

"Uh, that's okay, I can wait here," I said. *Awkward.*

"It's okay," he said, eyes beckoning while his hand slid down my arm and took my hand. His cool skin gave me goose bumps. My reluctance melted away with the warmth that followed his cool touch. I trailed behind him as we climbed the stairs. He unlocked the door and stepped through.

I hesitated at the door, hovering, but he took my hand again and ushered me in. I left the door open behind me and leaned against the wall just inside the opening.

"I'll be right back," he said and disappeared around the corner.

The living room was large with mossy green walls and light carpet. There was a very large sectional sofa that encompassed the entire corner of the room, fronted by a huge ottoman with an intricately woven blanket decoratively draped over the edge. The colors coordinated with the tasteful, oversized art displayed on the wall. The room was so stylish you would think he had had it professionally decorated. The apartment had a clean smell, with a hint of cinnamon and pine.

He appeared again with a small velvet box. "It's for your birthday," he said as he handed me the box with a crooked smile. My heart raced when he flashed his smile.

In surprise, I stuttered. "I don't remember telling you about my birthday."

"You didn't. I overheard your friends at the café. I just wanted to get you a little something."

"Oh, well, thank you," I said, feeling a little embarrassed. I took the small box hesitantly and opened it. A simple pendant with a single pearl set in a flourish with what looked to be a small diamond gleamed at me. It was beautiful. When I didn't say anything, the smile melted from his face.

"I didn't know what you would like, so I thought your birthstone would be nice. The pearl—"

I interrupted him. "No, uh, no. I love it. I don't know what to say. I…I…" and my words failed me.

He smiled, and pressed closer to me.

My breath became uneven.

He pulled the necklace from the box. "May I?" he said, opening the chain.

I nodded, afraid my voice would falter. I was still leaning against the wall, feeling unsteady. I lifted my hair, and he reached around behind my neck, clasping the necklace without breaking eye contact with me. His face was only inches away, and his sweet breath caressed my face. He slowly pulled his hands back, moving them up my neck and across my jaw line as he murmured, "Beautiful," still not breaking eye contact. I had the feeling he wasn't commenting on the necklace.

He tilted my head up and leisurely bent down and kissed my cheekbone, tracing my jaw with his lips. My heart started pounding, and I couldn't keep my breath steady, no matter how much I tried. He leaned back for a moment and smiled his most disarming smile again, and then closed the gap between our bodies, pressing me against the wall, and kissed my lips while still holding my face. I stopped breathing and grabbed onto the doorframe. I felt him smile without pulling away. "You might want to breathe."

I felt light-headed; he put one of his hands around my waist and held me up as he turned my body and guided me to the couch, prying my hand from the doorframe.

He flicked the front door shut with his foot and said, "Maybe you should sit down for a moment."

I wanted to go.

I wanted to stay.

Or go.

I was afraid I couldn't control myself, but I literally

couldn't stand. I sagged into his arms, and he took on much of my weight, holding me tight.

I didn't want him to stop kissing me, but I did.

His touch made me feel the opposite of what my instincts were telling me. As he backed me across the room, he continued to kiss me as he lowered me to the couch.

The longer he touched me, the less control I felt. My limbs felt heavier, the odd warmth I always felt from his touch flowing through my body all the way to my toes. He was mesmerizing. His breathing was also ragged.

He kissed my collarbone and then worked his way up my neck and kissed under my chin. Almost involuntarily, I arched my head back as my head grew fuzzier.

I was completely under his power.

He laid me back even more, his weight moving on top of me, his hand unbuttoning the top buttons of my blouse. I couldn't control my breath; I started breathing too quickly.

Hyperventilating.

Too far.

Too far.

No. Too far.

I couldn't get my body to move or my mouth to work. I struggled to breathe; my senses seemed to dampen. I could hear my uneven breath and feel him kissing me, like I was outside myself. I started to panic. I managed to move my head back a little and saw his eyes had changed—they were glowing and intense.

Something was wrong.

I fought for control, my mind tearing through the thick feeling that trapped my thoughts and my body.

It took all my might, but breathlessly I said, "Please no, please."

He seemed amused and my heart froze.

Tears started stinging my eyes. I tried to push him back, but he was too strong, like iron.

Suddenly, his head snapped up like he'd heard something, he craned his neck to listen, and then his breath came out in a hiss.

He kissed next to my ear and softly whispered, "I think breaking you will be much more fun. I'll see you soon."

Breaking me?

And then he added, as if an afterthought, "Tell him hello for me."

Then, his mouth locked onto the base of my neck and something pierced my flesh...*his teeth?*

It hurt. Despite my panic, after a few moments, my heart slowed and everything became distorted as the blackness came for me.

I clawed in the darkness, angry and terrified. My eyelids felt sealed shut, but everything was different now, like I was physically drained. His presence was gone, but I wasn't alone.

A new voice—gruff and husky. I wanted to look and willed my eyes to open. But my body was being stupid and unresponsive.

Someone touched me and I wanted to shrink away, but my limbs didn't react. A man. He touched my shoulder, and then placed his warm, firm hand to my neck, assessing me.

He answered someone else, but I couldn't hear the question. "She's alive. No, stay back. *Now*, I mean it." He growled the command and paused. "She lost a lot of blood...I don't think so...No, he didn't."

At that moment, I felt pressure on my throbbing neck. My mind flooded with questions, but I couldn't focus. I could hear two, maybe three people—one of them breathing hard and sounding pained near the door. But I couldn't hear voices other than the one over me.

The pressure on my neck stopped for a moment and then returned. I felt something stretching over it...tape...maybe. Then something sharp in my arm. I felt more relaxed, and the ache dulled. I was still fighting with my eyelids. *Why can't I open them?*

"We can move her," the man said.

A moment later, someone picked me up. Maybe the third person? Not the one by the door. *Why can't I open my eyes?* I started to feel angry. The night air hit me, and I could hear a van door open and close.

The gruff man barked, "Are you sure?"

I didn't hear a response, but I was quickly cradled onto someone's lap, and my hair was being pushed back from my face. Then all the pain was gone, but this time, I didn't feel scared or angry. I pulled in a deep breath and let the darkness take me.

7

ESCAPE

I woke up in my room from a dreamless night of sleep and felt rested. Stretching and taking a deep breath, I snapped out of my sleepy state when I felt tape pulling at the base of my neck. Flipping back the covers, I realized that I was still in my clothes from yesterday. Memories from the night before came in a flood, almost drowning me.

Sickness hit the pit of my stomach, so I sprinted for the bathroom, my body spilling onto the floor. I thrust my head above the toilet bowl and heaved and heaved, but nothing came up. My nose was running, and I was blinded with tears. I slumped onto the cool tile floor just as an ugly sob rocked my entire body. All of the stress and agony from the night before was crushing me—pinning me.

The odor of my stale clothes mingling with the sweat and salt on my skin made me even queasier. Then, I realized that I could smell *him* on me, and I wretched into the toilet all over again. Wild, reckless thoughts pulsed through my brain. I felt so alone.

So violated.

I cried until I'd cycled through shock, disbelief, anger, violation, fear, and shame over and over again, to the point where I no longer felt anything.

When my hurricane of my emotions ceased, so did my tears. I lay in silence, unmoving for what must have been a half hour. Finally, I pulled myself together enough to rise, albeit shakily, and gazed into the mirror, leaning heavily on my hands.

I was pale and had dark circles under my eyes. My hair was in a snarl, but my clothes looked exactly the way I remembered from last night...the two buttons Bowen had unfastened. But no more. I felt foolish for allowing myself to get into that situation. All I felt was self-loathing and stupidity. Somewhere deep inside, I'd known he was dangerous; that was why I had fought so hard to keep him at arm's length.

I stared at myself in the mirror. Silently processing. My eyes went to my neck. I pulled my shirt back slightly to reveal a tightly taped bandage. The tape lined the entire area, sealing the gauze completely to my skin. I slowly pulled the bandage off, my skin rising and turning red. I folded the tape onto itself and tossed away the spent bandage.

There were two perfect half-moons beginning to bruise, accented by a pair of puncture marks. I forced away the ludicrous conclusions I wanted to draw, thoughts that could get a person locked in a loony bin. Flashes of memory surfaced again—his teeth and his glowing eyes. I had to be mistaken. I was in shock.

I turned on the shower and undressed, letting the bathroom get steamy. I wanted to disappear in the fog. The heat from the water burned me, but I didn't turn it down. I wanted to burn, just to feel something.

After my shower, I toweled off my hot, pinked skin while the bathroom walls dripped with moisture. I opened the door to my bedroom, steam spewing into the room with my entrance. I sat on the corner of the bed, not caring that the dampness from my towel was soaking into the comforter. Feeling numb. Wondering how I had gotten home. There was something I wasn't remembering.

After I'd cooled off a little, I went back into the bathroom and re-covered the wound with an oversized Band-Aid.

When I returned to my room, I realized it was already mid-afternoon. I was supposed to meet the girls at THE Lane in a few hours to kick off my birthday celebration. I'd weaseled more information out of April and found out that after dinner, we were returning here for a slumber party.

My stomach grumbled, and I realized that I hadn't eaten yet. I didn't think I could handle much, so I forced down some yogurt without taking pleasure in it.

I headed back upstairs and put on a little makeup. I still looked pale, now just more presentable. My body temperature felt a little off, like I was fighting a mild illness. But if I could manage a smile, no one would be the wiser.

Standing in front of my closet, I decided on my sheer, red shirt with the attached matching tank top underneath. My mom had trained me to dress up when feeling bad. This shirt always made me feel confident.

For a few minutes, I contemplated calling someone to carpool, but it was taking every bit of my energy to work up a desire to see people tonight. I selfishly wanted every moment I could without talking to or seeing another human being.

I decided to kill my remaining two hours watching TV. After flipping through channels, I finally settled on some black and white film and stared at it without really watching, although I did notice that the character who had originally appeared to be the good guy turned out to be evil. I winced again at my own stupidity.

When it was time to go, I stuck my money, license, and cell into my pockets. I didn't feel like hauling a purse around, no matter how small.

I drove down Winchester Boulevard in no hurry—still numb. Time seemed disjointed. I took a right on Owens and headed for the back parking lot, avoiding the closer parking garage; the walk in the fresh air might clear my head.

Nabbing a spot in the far corner, I could hear live music and the clamor of a crowd in the distance. The sun had just set, and the golden light reflected off of the buildings, creating a warm and inviting glow.

As I ambled onto the main drag, I looked at all the happy faces. Every snippet of conversation I heard seemed petty. Just a week ago, I had been distancing myself from a break up and worrying about finals. Now, after a single night, everything seemed insignificant. Sickness hit my stomach again. The memory of *him* caressing my skin made me ill; I pushed down the thought.

Compartmentalize and deal with it later.

Shaking my hands, trying to shake off the way I was feeling, I started working up my energy again. I smiled, hoping the physical action would help me to be happy for my friends.

The last bits of golden light disappeared, and the haze of blue evening took over, the cool tones warmed by the thousands of little lights woven through the trees. THE Lane was three blocks deep and five blocks wide of the most trendy restaurants, spas, clubs, and clothing stores in the area. Built to resemble an Italian getaway, it was always crowded with people. Warm-colored buildings, each one with its own unique façade, lined the streets, the sidewalks littered with various café tables.

If it wasn't always so busy, it would be a beautiful place to hang out, but as it was, I only came down here when pressed by my friends. Since I usually did the planning in our group, I usually spared myself the exasperation of this place. I would never let my friends know how much I disliked it, though.

I crossed another street and made a left. I was just over one block away from the Grand Piazza, and the music that I had been hearing was obviously a live band playing in the open air. The restaurant was on the far side of the piazza. I got trapped behind a large, slow-moving couple. No matter how many times I tried to get past them, I couldn't. I started getting frustrated, but instead, I took a deep breath, then strolled behind them. I had plenty of time.

They finally peeled off and crossed the street. I glanced towards the parking garage I would normally have parked in and froze mid-step. Almost concealed in the shadow of the walk-in entrance to the garage was Bowen, his presence menacing as he scanned the crowd. All the sweetness and kindness I had seen in him before had evaporated his beauty tainted by what I now knew to be his true self.

I realized that I was standing completely within his line of sight. I broke from my stationary position and backed up into a doorway. I looked through the glass in the entryway towards the garage. His stance remained the same; he hadn't seen me, but he had his nose in the air like a wolf catching a scent.

My mind raced. *Should I return to my car?* This required walking almost two blocks within his visual range, with no guarantee that someone would shield my retreat. Then his words came back to me: *"We'll meet again soon."*

There was no doubt in my mind that he was looking for me. I decided to see if I could go through the back of the building into the alley and circle around the other side of the piazza. If I could get to the restaurant using another route, I could ask one of my friends to drive her car next to the entrance of restaurant. We could leave and go as far away as we needed. We could pick up my car another day.

I ducked through the door and was greeted by an overly cheery salesgirl. Her dark blonde waves resting on her shoulders as she danced towards me. "May I help you with something?" She grinned. I glanced at her name tag.

"Um, Danielle, may I use your back door?"

Her face darkened with the loss of her imaginary sale. "I'm sorry, but it's employees only in the back," she stated dutifully.

I nodded and felt the blood drain from my face. I walked towards the entrance and tried to see if I could view Bowen. I couldn't see anything. I turned to the salesgirl who was staring at me oddly.

"I'm sorry, but could you do me a favor? Could you see if there is a tall, blond guy, standing in front of the parking garage?" My eyes pleaded for help.

She started to shake her head no, but then agreed, probably from seeing the look of desperation on my face.

She took one step out the door, spied down the street, then turned to me with a look of concern, and asked, "The hot one?"

"Yes," I replied, and sank down onto the ledge of a display. I felt weak.

She stepped back in the store and looked me up and down. "I guess no one has to know. Come with me." She led me through the back and opened the heavy metal security door with a loud clank. She exhaled and said, "I hope whatever it is works out."

I tried to smile and replied, "Thank you," while slipping down the alley. I was able to get almost a block behind the stores completely concealed from the public. I reached a T-shaped intersection and started heading back towards the piazza. With any luck, the throng of people would be enough to keep me hidden. I kept as far away as I could from Bowen's last known position.

I started to weave through the crowd while I tried to hold some vague pleasantry on my face to mask the sheer terror I felt. I slumped down and slid through group after group of people, in an attempt to vanish into the night. Then I caught a glimpse of Bowen. He had moved from the garage to the corner near the shop I had cut through. He was scanning the crowd again.

This was working. A small amount of relief washed over me as I continued edging my way towards the restaurant. I glanced down at my red shirt, dismayed that I had worn something so conspicuous. A couple of guys attempted to flirt with me, but I decided to ignore them. For a moment, I considered flirting back simply for the muscle, but trust was not at the top of my list. My friends' joke, *boys are bad,* was all I could think.

I edged closer to the dance floor in the middle of the piazza. Silky, all-encompassing music enveloped the air. People were dancing in the subdued lights of the evening, pressing close to one another.

I could see Bowen moving methodically in my direction, still scanning the crowd. And then a hand gently wrapped around my waist and pulled me onto the dance floor. A wave of panic gripped me for a split second, but it wasn't Bowen—I could still see him several yards away.

"Still have the boys chasing you, Als." And in what seemed like one movement, my dance partner had pulled my arms to his waist and pulled me further onto the dance floor, turning and blocking me from Bowen's view. I didn't fight the embrace. My mind searched frantically, and then in an explosive moment of recognition, I felt safe.

"Josh?" It had taken me a moment to process the annoying nickname he had for me. He was the only person who could call me that and not be sentenced to immediate death.

He smiled calmly and pulled me closer. I leaned my head

back to see his face and felt wobbly. I hadn't realized how long I had been holding my breath.

"How?" I stammered. "I haven't seen you in…but—" I was too shocked to articulate my jumble of thoughts.

"Just got back into town. I didn't expect to have to save you from admirers the second I saw you," he chided, diverting me teasingly.

"I can take care of myself, thank you very much," I replied, feeling a little indignant.

"Yes, I can see that; you are by yourself—at night—running from stalkers. You have things totally under control." I could hear the smile in his voice, underpinned with exasperation.

I grumbled, knowing that I should have picked up a friend on the way so I wouldn't be alone, especially with my family out of town. I could feel my face flush, both from frustration and knowing that I had been stupid. *Again.* Then my stomach turned as I thought about last night. Evading the remembrance, I turned my attention back to Joshua and examined his face.

He was three and a half years older than me, but he didn't look like he was in his twenties. He looked almost my age. He still had the dark, wavy hair I remembered, but he was so pale now. His green eyes, with a few tiny flecks of gold had always carried so much knowledge, even when we were kids. They seemed greener now, more intense. Even in my idealized memory, I couldn't imagine him looking more perfect—anyone looking more perfect now.

He pulled my head to his chest, and I let out a huge sigh. He plucked the jacket from his waist and wrapped it around my shoulders while surrounding me with his arms.

"This should make you a little less visible. We'll just stay here for a tiny bit." My head was pulsing with questions. He seemed to know way more than me. As we danced, he kept turning me little by little. I didn't want to think about Bowen circling the crowd.

I let the questions fade for a moment and buried my face in his chest; he always made me feel safe. Taking a steadying breath, I couldn't help but notice how good he smelled. Then I noticed that his breathing was very uneven.

He pulled back from me and gently looked into my face with an odd mix of emotions. He brushed the hair back from my face, without touching my skin, his expression unreadable. "Keep your back to the restaurant. It's time to go," he instructed softly. "We'll need to move quickly. Are you okay with that?"

"Yeah, I can keep up."

An odd smile played at the corner of his mouth. "Would you mind putting the jacket all the way on?"

"Okay," I mouthed and shrugged into his jacket.

He put his hand on the small of my back and guided me through the crowd, placing his left shoulder just ahead of me. We sped down the streets, weaving through all the people who were out enjoying the cool summer evening. I could see the parking lot at the end of the street. It was brimming with cars, but there were no people in sight.

Josh glanced back and said, "And this is when we run." Trusting him completely, I broke into long strides next to him. I reached into my pocket as well as I could while running and pulled out my keys. I pressed the alarm button twice, unlocking both sides of the car. We hit the car, flung open the doors simultaneously, and lurched into the vehicle. I didn't bother with the seatbelt, but instead jammed the key into the ignition; my hands shook from adrenaline.

I stomped on the clutch, kicked it into gear, screeched into reverse, then jammed it into first, tires chirping as we flew forward. I got through the exit of the lot and went out the back way to avoid the light. I felt something hit the back of the car, specifically the top of the trunk, but I didn't see anything through the rearview mirror. My heart was pounding as I fought to control my breath.

Josh looked over at me. "It's okay. Use the freeway, and we'll put a little distance between us."

I shot a wary look at him, not knowing what to ask. We roared onto the freeway, and I pulled off two exits down. A few minutes later, we pulled into the drive, flew out of the car, and ran up to my house.

I started to open the front door and go in when Josh paused and lightly grabbed my elbow. "Promise me something," he pleaded.

"Let's just go in, *please.*"

He tightened his grip on my arm. "Just promise me you won't invite anyone in that you haven't known for years. *Anyone.*" His voice cracked, and he grabbed my other arm to look me square in the face.

I didn't understand his reasoning, but I nodded mutely.

"Don't invite anyone in, and stay inside. It's going to be fine. I'm sorry. I have to go," he said abruptly as he shoved me through the door. "Close it," he ordered, so I did.

I was dumbfounded as I stared at the closed door. I

wanted to open it and go after him, but the fierceness and urgency in his eyes convinced me otherwise.

The house felt so empty. Then I realized that Marie and the others were going to kill me. *Crap! I had stood them up again! And on my birthday of all things!* In just a few short days, I had gone from being the most reliable friend to the least reliable. How was I ever going to explain *this*?

I pulled out my phone and texted everyone: "There's a prob. Can u get my food 2 go? Meet @ my place? Please, Xoxo." I wasn't sure what I was going to say when everyone arrived.

Breanna replied: "Since it's YOUR bday. No prob see you soon ;P."

That had bought me some time. Now, for the reason.

Option A: Tell the truth.

Option B: Lie. Lie. Lie.

I debated for a few minutes, or more like, agonized. I despised dishonesty—being truthful was part of who I was. But, I wasn't sure if I was ready, or even able, to explain last night. And I wasn't completely sure I knew what had happened. There were alarm bells going off in my head, saying it was safer for my friends if they didn't know. I felt angry with Joshua for leaving and not explaining anything.

About thirty minutes later, I heard a couple of cars pull up and park. I ran to the window and composed myself. Marie and Kaela were walking up with the food, as well as sleeping bags and everything needed for a girls' night. Breanna and April followed close behind.

I felt intense relief, but also fear. Part of me didn't want to be alone, yet I wondered if I was putting them in danger. I tried to get my thoughts organized as I tromped to the door to open it.

Hating myself, I went for the lie. I explained that my car wouldn't start and we might as well take advantage of my parents being out of town. No one seemed to be suspicious of my explanation. They made fun of the huge Band Aid I had on my neck. They assumed it was some sort of acne break out, and I let them believe it. The Italian food they had brought was fantastic, followed by the obligatory singing with cake and ice cream. It was my favorite chocolate cake, too. Heavenly.

We parked ourselves in front of the television for a nice evening and rolled out our sleeping bags. The whole room seemed to be covered in blankets and pillows, which was very calming.

We watched *Emma,* one of our favorites, because what's a girls' night without some Austen? We popped in another chick flick, but it was getting late, and everyone was still really exhausted from the late nights studying for finals. Around 1:00 A.M., I noticed everyone was asleep, so I turned off the TV.

I lay there amongst my friends for at least two hours, listening to the sounds of their breathing. Everyone seemed so peaceful. Breanna murmured something about feeding her cat, Marie mumbled something about Mr. Knightly, and Kaela muttered something about making toast, then started speaking in Spanish. My friends even chattered in their sleep.

I was wide awake, with no sign of blissful slumber in my near future. I sighed softly and got up. I carefully tiptoed downstairs into the kitchen. The moon was full outside, and the moonlight flooded into the house. There was no need to turn on any lights to see.

I walked to the back door and stared into the silvery backyard. Everything was still, but I caught a small amount of movement near the gazebo in the corner of the yard. Once my eyes fully focused, I was shocked to see the figure of a man sitting on the bench. My blood ran cold. I glanced at the phone, wondering if I should call 911. But at that moment, I realized it was Joshua.

He looked white in the moonlight, almost ghostlike. I grabbed my sweater off the back of the chair at the kitchen table and crept out the back door.

I took a deep breath, knowing that things were about to change…

with Joshua…

with everything.

8

JOSHUA

He saw me standing on the step next to the sliding door and sighed. He obviously hadn't expected me to find him out there. I made my way to the gazebo and approached him with caution. His face was conflicted. He glanced at the gate several times, and I half-expected him to bolt as his body tensed.

"Hey." I kept my voice even, but my mind was racing.

He bowed his head in greeting.

I sat down on the padded bench, a foot away from him, aware that I was getting my pajama bottoms dusty. It was cooler outside than I thought, so I tugged my sweater closed and hugged my legs in front of me for warmth. I glanced up at the sky for a fleeting moment. The light of the city obscured most of the stars, save the Little Dipper and the North Star. I drew in a long, slow breath of night air—the silence awkward. Returning my gaze to Joshua, I noticed he was watching me pensively.

Despite wanting to barrage him with questions, I decided to wait him out. The breeze twisted strands of my hair gently across my face, loosened from my messy ponytail. The birch trees softly rustled. Jasmine and orange blossoms overpowered the scent of pine from the neighbor's tree. Everything in the yard was in shades of grey, silver, and blue.

I drew my eyes back to Joshua and was surprised to find that he was still staring at me. The intensity of his gaze made me feel self-conscious. I smiled, and the corner of his mouth twitched.

"Joshua, how long have you been out here?" I whispered, not wanting to alert the girls upstairs.

He motioned towards the upstairs window. "Since Mr. Knightly realized he was in love with Emma," he replied.

I crinkled my forehead. "That was hours ago."

He shrugged.

I didn't know which question to ask first; my head was spinning with them. I decided to start with something easy. "How long have you been back in town?"

"I got in yesterday," he said with an odd emotion.

The timing was too perfect. Was he there last night? Was that how I'd gotten home? Was that why I had somehow felt safe after...my stomach twisted into knots just thinking *his* name. Joshua glanced at the gate again, and my heart sank—it seemed that he was straining to stay with me.

"How?" I didn't know how to finish my question.

He looked at me, puzzled.

I rephrased my question as my voice choked. "Can you tell me what is going on?" I asked in almost a whisper, and then I added, "Please," in a fairly pathetic tone.

He pursed his lips. I hated to see him look so…tortured. I had known him my whole life, and he had always been my respite, my place of peace. The one person who would always tell me the truth, even if it wasn't pleasant. Our communication had always been natural, seamless, as was our reading each other.

But now, he was so altered. I hated whatever had happened to him. I wanted to destroy whatever could have made him so hard and so sad. My breathing became labored, and I tried to get my anger under control. I glanced up at his face, and he seemed startled by my emotion. He was examining every reaction and movement I was making.

Finally, he responded, "I am in a delicate situation here. I don't know what I should tell you. And…" He paused for a long moment.

"And?"

"And I don't know what I *want* to tell you." He rubbed his forehead.

"I don't understand," I said, shaking my head, yet trying to be patient.

"You're going to be angry with me. You're going to hate me," he said, his eyes blazing and pleading at the same time.

"I won't be angry with you, and I could never hate you. Please tell me what this is all about, please."

"You are angry at me now."

I exhaled, exasperated. "I'm not angry at you. I…I'm angry at whatever has done *this* to you…" I explained, waving my hands up and down in his direction. I closed my eyes and took a few small breaths, relaxed my shoulders, and unclenched my fists.

I fixed my eyes on his face again; he still seemed conflicted.

"You *will* hate me, Als," he assured, his tone absolute and broken.

"Joshua, you are the last person on earth I would hate," I assured, as I reached to take his hand, but he flinched and crossed his arms across his chest.

He coughed, "Person," under his breath, almost too low for me to hear, confusing me further.

"Please don't leave me in the dark. You know how I hate that. I can handle whatever it is. I'm strong."

"I know you are. I know I can trust you, but…"

"Josh, you are family to me. I won't hate you, and if you don't want me to tell anyone, I won't. You're killing me here."

"I don't even know where to start," he replied, sounding overwhelmed.

"How about the beginning?" I wanted to cringe. I totally sounded like my mom.

He exhaled and seemed to be searching through memories, probably figuring out how much he should edit. He relaxed a little and put his hands on his knees.

"Fall, almost two years ago, I went downtown with some friends after midterms were over. They knew a pub they could get me into, so I tagged along. And they were right. They were all twenty-one, and after they checked the first few IDs, the rest of us were waved through. I felt so cool being nineteen in a bar," he chuckled, but there was no amusement in his laugh.

"We ate and drank until late into the evening. I was getting tired, so my buddy tossed me his apartment keys and told me to crash at his place. So, I set out to walk the two blocks. It was humid, and people were milling around the streets, enjoying the evening. I could hear the muffled music of the live bands through the walls of the clubs I passed." His voice trailed off for a moment; I could tell from his tone of voice that this was a story he had gone over in his head many, many times. I could visualize everything so clearly.

"I glanced down an alley, and I could see a couple in the shadows. The guy had one of his arms around the girl's waist, and the other against the brick wall behind her. I did a double take because he was lifting her up and her feet weren't on the ground. I felt like yelling, 'Get a room!' in my drunken state, but when I took one more step beyond the alley, I heard her say something.

"She said, 'Please, no,' and then let out the most pathetic sob I had ever heard. I stopped and leaned against the wall just around the corner of the mouth of the alley and debated with myself. I could have called the cops, but this would have probably been all over before they even got here. I could have pretended I hadn't noticed, but you know me." He shrugged. "Or, I could choose to go down the alley and try to help the woman, hoping it wasn't a ploy to get me down there to mug me."

I moved closer to hold Joshua's hand, but he jumped when he saw me reaching and crossed his arms tightly across his chest again.

Josh closed his eyes as he continued, "I felt a little shaky, and my head wasn't quite clear from the beer, but I drummed up the courage to go down the alley. The man was completely in the shadows, but I could see her from the light of a nearby window. He was still holding her around the waist, pressing her body to his, but she was completely limp. He was kissing her neck, and she wasn't resisting anymore.

"I cleared my throat to announce my presence. His body tensed almost imperceptibly, but his face never left her throat. She looked weak, and I almost wondered if she had passed out. Then she opened her eyes, and I could see tears streaming from them. Everything in my body told me to run, but I couldn't just leave her there.

"I was a few feet from the guy when I reached out to tap him on the shoulder. His arm swatted back as if to shoo away a fly, and I hurled backwards, through the air, until I hit the opposite side of the alley, dropping to the ground. The back of my head felt wet, and something punctured my leg. I looked down to see I had landed on a wooden chair that had buckled and snapped when I fell on it. I pulled the shrapnel from my leg and started pushing myself up against the wall. I grabbed another piece of the chair to use as a weapon.

"My head was swimming, and I felt like I might lose consciousness, but I willed myself to stay awake. I glanced over, and the man was just a few yards from me. He straightened up, and I watched the girl's body crumble to the ground like a spent wrapper. He turned and looked at me, and I saw his face for the first time.

"He grinned and wiped something dark from the edge of his mouth with his thumb. He shook his head in disapproval, which surprisingly turned to amusement, then irritation.

"Without warning, he came at me, so quickly he seemed a blur. I did the only thing I could do because I knew my legs would give out if I tried to run. I held up the broken chair leg, anchoring the back of it against the wall at the last second.

"And then he was on me, and I could feel coursing pain in my neck.

"He stopped, and I realized that the wood was planted firmly in his chest. He pulled back a little bit and looked me square in the face. The amusement in his eyes came back. He laughed, and when he did, a spray of blood escaped from his mouth and covered me; I had obviously punctured his lung. He fell backwards and collapsed on the ground, his body motionless.

"At that moment, my legs gave out and the sounds in the alley became muffled. I seemed to hear several things at once or close together. I'm not sure. There was a light thud next to me, like something had landed next to me. The man moving in front of me. The clank of wood on the ground. And I also heard a set of heavy-booted footsteps in the alley, followed by someone hoisting me over his shoulder, and then everything went black."

He opened his eyes and looked at me with some incomprehensible emotion on his face before continuing, "When I woke, I was in agony. I looked around, and I could hear birds outside, a lot of them, like I was out in the countryside. Then I realized that I was in some sort of holding cell. My arm was in a heavy shackle bolted to the wall, and I was lying on a thin, foam mattress on the floor.

"My wounds had been patched up. There were bandages on my head, leg, and shoulder. But my shoulder was searing with pain, while my other wounds didn't seem to be bothering me. I remember worrying about a fractured skull after hitting the wall with such force, but I didn't even have a headache. Just this immeasurable amount of pain in my shoulder that seemed to be inching its way down my arm and across my chest.

"And then I heard a voice that I didn't recognize. I turned to see an unknown man as he said, 'I'm sorry, son. I'm afraid there isn't anything I can do for you.' His eyes were full of regret.

"I didn't know what to ask first. Who are you? Why am I here? Why in the hell am I chained to the wall? What do you mean you can't help me? What happened to me last night? What was with that guy who attacked me?"

Josh continued his story, but I realized that my breathing had become jagged, so I tried to calm myself. My curiosity and concern were close to whirling out of control.

He looked at me warily. "He told me that I was going to die." He paused as if he was waiting for the information to sink in. My mind raced. Did his attacker have AIDS? Did his blood get in his wounds? This didn't make sense.

Somehow seeing my train of thought, he smiled. "No, it's not what you think. Als, this is going to be the hard part. The world isn't as it seems. There is more darkness out there than you have ever imagined. There are unseen wars being fought." He hesitated, then with a tremendous weight added, almost ashamed, "Monsters exist."

I couldn't follow. I didn't want to. My forehead scrunched up as I tried to force myself to understand. "Okay, monsters exist. Are we talking 'Creature from the Black Lagoon?' The Boogeyman?" I added with a sharp, humorless laugh.

He changed the subject. "Tell me everything you know about the man chasing you earlier tonight."

"Bowen," I rasped. Saying his name made me feel ill.

"Yes, Bowen. Everything, especially the things that don't sit well. The things you don't want to admit to yourself." His face looked probing and somehow, hopeful.

I could feel myself pale and was sure Josh noticed my reaction.

"Okay, start with the physical description," he prodded.

"Ummm." I took in a deep breath. "He is tall, probably around 6'2," blond, pale skin," I paused, "abnormally pale skin. He has blue eyes..." a chill went down my spine, "impossible blue eyes. I could swear they gl—" I cut myself short, feeling stupid at the thought, not trusting what I saw. I continued, "His skin is always cool and firmer than normal, like his skin is thicker, but still soft. He is amazingly strong..." And then I hesitated.

He prompted me, "What about the non-physical description? You have always been discerning. Use that gift."

I didn't want to sound stupid, like I was making things up, but I continued, "He is hypnotic. Like if he touches me, he can convince me to do anything, even if I am saying no. I just can't fight him...unless I really concentrate, but it's almost impossible."

And then I thought about that strange warm feeling that coursed through my body from his touch. I broke from that thought and continued hesitantly, "Sometimes, it seems like he moves faster than he should."

I was connecting the dots, but still not wanting to admit

what I was thinking. Click, click, click—each piece was snapping into place.

"I have never seen him eat anything, even though we spent most of our time at the café. I only see him at night or at least, after the sun has set, but it's almost dark." I could feel myself growing colder as my epiphany drew closer.

"He kept asking for me to let him into the house. And he knows too much. His senses, they almost aren't..." I choked out the last word, "human..." My voice trailed off.

I looked at Josh, trying to read his expression. To see if he was going to laugh at me, but he didn't. He was absolutely still, staring directly back at me. The night air was cool and heavy with a floral scent that seemed almost overwhelming.

We sat looking at each other for a while.

"Josh?"

"Yes?"

"What did the guy who attacked you look like?" I asked quietly.

"About 6'2", blond, pale..." and he almost chuckled, "impossible blue eyes."

Feeling sick, I nodded in response, accepting the truth.

I reached out for his hand again. He started to pull it back, but then allowed me to touch him. His hand was cool. Too cool. His skin was pale. Too pale. It felt thicker, yet appeared thinner because it was more translucent, and the veining was more visible. And he had barely aged since I had seen him years ago; we looked about the same age now. I kept holding his hand, and he looked at me like he was waiting for me to be revolted—for me to hate him.

"Soooo, he isn't just a stalker, is he?"

"No, I'm afraid not." His eyes looked miserable again. I was rubbing small circles on the back of his hand with my thumb.

The word *vampire* was hanging in the air, but I was deathly afraid to say it out loud. The thought had occurred to me when I'd examined the punctures on my neck, but I was still afraid to consider it. Still thinking that it was something they gave you hug-me-jackets and padded walls for believing.

"Monsters exist," I whispered, almost unable to say anything, and certainly unable to say *vampire*. I could see Bowen's glowing eyes and feel his teeth plunge into my flesh. The fear and pain I felt was tangible. I'd had to battle the strange power that dulled my senses every time he had touched me in order to retain my wits.

Joshua looked at me cautiously and stated my fear out loud in the softest voice, "Vampires exist."

I shrugged. "So, I not only get a stalker, I get a vampire stalker." A slight tremble in my voice betrayed me. "I'm the luckiest girl in the world."

He rolled his eyes at my humor. "Als, this is where you freak out a little. You get scared. You hate me. You get angry. You don't make a joke."

"Josh, why would I hate you?"

"I'm a monster."

I shook my head. "I don't believe that."

He paused and looked utterly guilty. "This is my fault. Bowen is here to hurt you because of me."

I furrowed my brow. "Why me? I haven't seen you in years. Why not attack you directly?"

He searched for the right words. "I not only interrupted the joy of a kill for him, but I wounded him. I bruised his ego

—being a mere mortal and stopping him. Once a vampire sets on a course, there is no changing it. And *he* is particularly vindictive. He is known to take years to seek revenge on someone. It's not like he is going to run out of time. He researches and then exploits whatever he thinks will be most painful. If he just kills me, it'll be over, and he wants me to suffer."

"Oh," was all I could manage.

"You are the only connection I have left that matters. I don't have any family left. I had some superficial friendships, but nothing deep. I didn't even date anyone after my parents died. I didn't want to be close to anyone. So..." He didn't finish.

"How did he find out about me? Wait. Who was that guy who 'couldn't do anything to help you' and had you chained up?" I asked, remembering that he had halted his story for my epiphany.

"His name is Sebastian. He was tracking Bowen and had witnessed my attempt at heroics. Long story short, he took me from the alley that night, not sure if I had been turned. He tended my wounds and waited. He realized that I'd been infected right as I woke up. He was supposed to destroy me, but he couldn't bring himself to do it.

"He's a *Watcher*, a member of a secret organization that monitors immortals, and when necessary, eliminates them." He sighed. "I was in that cell for a very long time. New vampires aren't exactly under control. I'm an experiment, of sorts. After he could trust that I was under control, he and someone named Gabriel started training me. And I have been working with them ever since." Then, he added thoughtfully, "I suppose Sebastian is a surrogate father, of sorts."

"Where is he now?"

"Close. When I figured out that Bowen was going to come after you, he sent someone to keep an eye on you. He didn't want me to come. He was afraid that I wasn't ready. But when Bowen showed up, I finally convinced him I was."

"Not ready?" I asked, coaxing more information out of him.

"Not ready for a lot of things. One, Bowen is very old, at least 300 years. But with his identity changes and such, he could be older. I don't really have the skills to go up against him in a fair fight.

"We get stronger the older we get. I could best any human on the planet in seconds and many of my kind, but going up against someone his age would be like...a college athlete going up against a professional kick-boxer. He might get in a shot or two, but it would be over quickly. I am not to approach Bowen on my own." And then Josh stopped again.

I looked at him expectantly. "And two..."

"I have good control, but it could be dangerous to be this close to you. If there's blood...I...When I saw you again, I..." He wasn't able finish.

I changed the subject. "How did you know Bowen was coming here?"

Joshua shook his head in disgust. "He broke into the place where I was living. As I'm a member of the undead, he didn't have to be invited in. I could sense that he had been there, but it was several days before I had realized that something was missing. I assumed he was going to attack me directly, but he is very underhanded.

"He took a postcard and a picture that I had shoved in the back of my journal. It was a picture of us at Campbell Perk. We were standing in front with my parents, and I had my arm on top of your head like you were furniture. So, even though I had destroyed everything with information about my past, I had selfishly saved that photo and a postcard you had sent. He had the name of the café, a picture and a partial name. I didn't know if you still went there or not. But if you did, he would be able to find you. He is patient enough to wait."

"And find me there he did." The breeze picked up, making me shiver.

"Yes, I'm sorry," he apologized, agony back on his face.

"I can't be mad at you for keeping a picture. Josh…" I hesitated. "Were you there last night?"

He looked at me hesitantly. "Yes."

Another piece, *click*. Today wasn't the first time he had saved me. Joshua had been there at *his* apartment. That's why I had felt safe.

"Thank you; that's two I owe you."

"You don't owe me anything. My fault, remember?" He pulled his hands away.

"Still."

He shook his head in disgust.

"So, what's it like? Being, um, a vampire?" I practically stumbled over the word.

He exhaled loudly. "It's my own personal hell, Aleria."

My heart was breaking, at seeing the despair in his eyes.

His nobility was still there. All I could think was it was wrong for him to feel this way.

I was afraid to ask, but I did anyway. "Have you," I paused, "killed people? Is that why—"

"No, I haven't. Not people, anyway. I've killed other vampires. Sebastian believes that I still have a soul. Until I kill an innocent. He believes the first kill is what takes your soul and condemns you. Most sires make sure that happens right away so they can control their new creation."

"Sire?" I questioned.

"When you spawn or bring another vampire into existence, the 'parent' is called a sire."

I thought about it for a moment. "You won't kill anyone…a human, anyway," I said with a surprising amount of confidence. "Is it hard to be around people?"

"No, not really. I only have trouble if I actually smell blood from an open wound. Like last night, when we found you. When I smelled your blood—" He stopped abruptly from the memory. "But I'm still young, and I haven't had a sire to train me. Sebastian and Gabriel, the guy doing my physical training, have done a great job, but there is only so much they can know.

"It is also supposed to get easier with time. After a while, most are able to use a familiar, a human that willingly lets a vampire feed on them, or other methods to feed. Vampires have enough control to stop once they start. I have never fed on a human, so I don't know if I would be able to stop like that.

"Not killing your food keeps a much lower profile. It's best to keep the murder statistics within reason. Of course, not all covens believe that is necessary. Maybe someday, if I live that long..."

"If you live that long? Don't you live forever?"

"Like I said, I'm an experiment. Look, I can't talk about it right now."

I could tell from his tone that it was the end of that topic, for now anyway. I changed the subject to some items of curiosity. "So, can you turn into a bat?" I asked playfully. He seemed relieved that I didn't pursue the other subject.

He chuckled. "Nope. That would be cool, though. But I can jump a long ways—it's about as close as I get to flying."

"Really?"

"You wanna see?"

"Uh, yeah."

He stood and strode through the yard towards the house. He glanced at me and winked. He turned back to the house and bent his knees slightly, and in a flash faster than I could follow, he was standing on top of the second story. He bowed theatrically, then stepped off the roof as if stepping off a curb, gently landing on the ground without a sound. By the time I blinked, he was already at my side again.

"Wow, just wow," I exclaimed, my eyes wide.

He shrugged. Then my questions overflowed.

"Garlic? Holy water? Crosses? Sunlight? Coffins? Stake to the heart?" I blurted.

He rolled his eyes. "No, partially, no, yes, no, sort of."

I rolled my eyes this time. "I don't even remember what order I just asked everything."

"No on garlic; holy water won't kill, but it's a deterrent; and no on crosses. There's a lot of fiction to distort the truth. Direct sunlight kills us, though once the sun sets, there isn't enough UV to kill us. It is uncomfortable, but the older we get, the more we can tolerate. So, the second the sun sets, Bo—*he* is out and about, whereas I have to wait a little while. But we can never handle direct sunlight during the day. We prefer beds to coffins, so a windowless room or thick curtains do just fine. But we don't need much sleep. Half of what you need, so three or four hours are fine. Many of us sleep longer to pass the time. It's still pleasurable to sleep."

"And the stake to the heart?"

"Paralyzes, but doesn't kill. That's what saved me in the alley."

"How do you, I mean, *he* bit me, so why am I not like you?"

"The bite infects you with a virus of sorts, but you need a catalyst to accelerate it."

I looked at him, waiting for the catalyst.

Then he added, "His blood or any vampire's blood. The saliva carries a virus that quickly preps the body. You may have noticed flu-like symptoms within minutes. It preps the body from the outside to the inside, saving the digestive system for last. If any of the sire's blood is present..."

This made sense. "So when you stabbed him, it punctured his lung too."

"Yes. And you will always have the virus. If you are infected by blood..."

I took a deep breath to steady myself. "How long does it take?"

"It depends on the amount of blood you ingest. I was merely sprayed with his blood, so it took days before it worked through my system. But if you were to actually drink from the sire, it would only take a matter of hours."

"I still feel like I have a touch of the flu," I confessed.

"Als, in truth, you are becoming a vampire, but without the blood, your conversion would take two lifetimes. A catalyst is simply an accelerant; all the properties for the recoding of DNA are present, but it isn't strong enough to do it with any speed. You will die a happy old woman long before there is any life-altering change."

"Oh…" I let that sink in for a moment. "Any other special abilities?"

"Als, we can talk about all that later. I think you should get some sleep. It's almost four in the morning."

I was so wrapped up in our conversation that I didn't realize how exhausted I had become. My lids were feeling dry and scratchy like sandpaper. I apparently had forgotten to blink very much, too. I yawned uncontrollably once he had brought it to my attention and agreed.

"Later then, you aren't going to disappear on me?" I asked, examining his expression.

"Not until this is over and I know you're safe," he confirmed.

I didn't completely like that answer. "And if I am safe, you will say goodbye. You won't disappear without a word," I said, knowing that he would disappear unless I could get a commitment.

He sighed. "I give you my word." He smiled reassuringly. That made me feel better.

"Okay. I would hate to have to track you down and kick some vampire butt."

He rolled his eyes this time and stood to walk with me. I staggered to the door as he held my elbow for support. I stepped through the doorway and turned to say good night, but he was already gone. He had vanished without even a whisper of noise.

I locked the door and trudged my way upstairs, sliding past the slumbering bodies. I returned to my perch on the couch and snuggled into a blanket. Despite the overwhelming amount of information, much of it disturbing, I felt at peace.

Within moments, I drifted off to sleep where unsettling dreams awaited my return.

9

INVITATIONS

Everyone was still asleep. I had kept all the blackout blinds closed after the movie last night so we could sleep in. I fumbled for my phone to see the time—9:00 A.M. Almost five hours of sleep was not too bad.

Most of my friends could be professional sleepers, especially Marie. I was so jealous that they could handle sleeping in all the time. My mind and my dreams never seemed to allow me to sleep that much.

I carefully crept through the maze of bodies, traversed the stairs into the kitchen, and started cooking a makeshift frittata. I spun around to the freezer and grabbed a can of frozen orange juice and dislodged the frozen glob with a wooden spoon. I stirred in the filtered water while staring out the back window, reviewing recent events.

Nightmares had plagued me since…well, since I had met Bowen. I'd had streaks of them in the past, but this was different. Almost every night, I woke soaked in sweat, and last night was no exception.

I dreamt that I was standing in a pool of sunlight, facing a wall of darkness. I was being beckoned into the darkness. I didn't want to move, but I had to...to protect someone or something, even though I knew I would fail. I stepped towards the darkness and woke up quietly gasping, smothering the sound with a pillow so I wouldn't wake anyone.

I glanced down and realized that I had been stirring the orange juice for several minutes. I dropped the spoon into the sink, closed my eyes, and leaned against the counter.

The events of the last two days had altered my take on everything. But somehow, I wasn't worried about the sadistic vampire that might be trying to steal my soul. All I kept picturing was Joshua's perfect face and his sadness.

I heard some murmuring upstairs and quickly tried to focus my mind, but was struck by misery knowing that as soon as this was over, I would lose Joshua forever.

Breanna interrupted my musings. "Wow! It smells amazing in here," she exclaimed. She shuffled into the kitchen, her hair sticking up in different directions like a long headdress of curvy straw.

I smiled as well as I could. "It's almost ready. Another ten minutes max. Is everyone awake? Well, let me rephrase, everyone but Marie?"

"Yup."

I smiled. "Should I wake her?"

"Your funeral."

I wagged my brows and took two steps at a time going upstairs.

Besides taking my life into my own hands by waking Marie up for breakfast, the day went well, with no real life-threatening situations. Breanna and April left around 11:00 A.M. Kaela and Marie lingered into the early afternoon and returned home to catch up on everything they had put off during finals. They offered to come back and stay the night again, but I told them maybe tomorrow. I needed a quiet night of non-socializing. They both understood and didn't argue too much, although Kaela looked at me with an odd expression for a brief moment.

I wondered how transparent I was. I really did want to be alone, but more importantly, I didn't want to put either of them in danger. If death was coming for me, I wasn't going to have my friends close enough to be collateral damage. I would face it alone.

The afternoon was spent doing anything I could to distract myself. The hours dragged on. I cleaned out my binders from the school year, filing anything I thought might be useful in the future and dumping the rest into the recycling bin. I started some laundry and finished up the dishes from breakfast. I put away the movies we had pulled out for our evening. My room was still cluttered, as usual, but I wasn't up to dealing with the nitty-gritty, just the easy stuff. So I shoved everything else under my bed.

I looked down and became conscious of the fact that I had spent the entire day in my pajamas. That wasn't a bad thing, but I was kind of a mess. The phone rang and startled me. I realized I was much more on edge than I thought, and I felt especially silly since it was still daylight, and the sun wasn't going to set until 8:30 P.M. or so.

Kaela called and asked if she could drop by; she had forgotten her toiletry bag in the downstairs bathroom. I told her it was not a problem, figuring she wouldn't be here past sunset.

She arrived at 7:30 P.M., grabbed her missing items, and then joined me in the kitchen. Afterwards, she casually pulled herself onto one of the barstools. I had expected her to leave right away, but she obviously had something on her mind.

I kept glancing at the clock as slyly as I could. She was chatting about her two brothers, but not getting to the point. It occurred to me that I wasn't going to be able to get her out of the house before dark without tipping her off that something was really wrong. I decided I might as well ask her to stay while I took a shower. I felt a little vulnerable and didn't want to shower with no one home. I prayed that Joshua was close so that Kaela wouldn't be in any danger and dashed upstairs. I glanced at the clock, and it was already 8:15.

I showered as quickly as possible. Once dressed, I scampered downstairs to the kitchen. I looked at Kaela still perched on a stool, munching on some crackers, but my eyes were drawn to some flowers on the kitchen table.

I looked at her confused. She shrugged. "Bowen dropped them off for you."

Paling, I leaned on the doorframe for support. He was here...next to my friend. He could have—I stopped that thought. He didn't hurt her. I tried to control my reaction, but her eyes narrowed at me a split second after my initial response. My weak smile and "Oh, that's nice," didn't fool her.

"He left a note," she said, examining my every move.

I moved towards the table, my legs sluggish. I reached to pluck the note from the flowers. Just a few simple words written in script that befitted the Declaration of Independence:

"Looking forward to seeing you soon. ~B."

I tried to smile while reading it, but the implied menace made me falter.

She stared at me, then finally demanded, "Dish it, chick. I know something is weighing on you. I wanted to talk with you last night, but we were never alone. And then..." She shook her head and looked at the flowers, then me expectantly.

"I decided I'm not interested," I said, before quickly tagging on, "or ready," hoping that might appease her.

"Ali, can I ask you something?" she inquired, contemplating something. It worried me a little. This was the tone of voice she used when she had some type of revelation about me. When she saw too much. Somehow she could always see right through me. I cringed.

"You can always ask." I tried to sound playful as I arched a brow.

The corners of her mouth pulled down as she concentrated. "I know something happened to you the other night. I didn't say anything in front of everyone last night.

But..." I looked over at her, a little worried. *Was I that transparent?* She continued taking in my reaction and changed what she was going to say. "Don't worry; you put on a good show."

I smiled weakly.

"I know it was Bowen."

I froze. I was sure my lack of reaction was confirmation enough.

"You don't have to tell me."

I swallowed.

"And...who were you talking to outside last night?"

I took some air a little sharply.

"It was Joshua, wasn't it?"

Apparently, I need to add eagle eyes to her list of attributes. "Yes," I answered succinctly.

"I didn't realize he was back in town. Don't worry, I wasn't listening, I just wondered where you were."

I tried not to make my relief visible.

"So, is not being interested in Bowen because of Joshua?"

"No...and Joshua is just my friend."

"I figured it was something else with Bowen." Then she rolled her eyes. "But you have always been in love with Joshua."

My eyes bulged. "He's like family, nothing else."

She looked at me piercingly. "Uh, no. You have always been *in love* with him."

"No, I haven't, too much of a big brother type, and he is totally older than me."

"That age gap is closing, and you are a legal adult now. It doesn't matter."

"You are so annoying sometimes."

"I'm only annoying because I am right. Admit it. I'm right."

"Gah! There's nothing there, okay? He's just visiting for a few days, and then he will go back East again. I will probably never see him after that."

My heart sank with the realization that I *wouldn't* see him again after I was safe. How was I going to live with that? How did Kaela always figure things out before me? *Damn it! Love him? Do I…love him?*

I stood there at the precipice of my epiphany, not wanting to accept it. I lingered there for a moment before I acquiesced. My knees weakened, and my head felt light. How did everything change so quickly? How was it that Joshua seemed as necessary to me as breathing? I forced myself to pay attention to Kaela. I had to keep the spinning-out-of-control compartment locked until she left. I looked at her with my mouth open.

"If that's what you say." She shrugged. "I just wanted you to hear it out loud." She looked smug.

I sighed.

"Well, I should probably go. My family wants to have a game night," she said as she slid off the stool and gathered her belongings. She probably left them here on purpose so she could talk to me, the rotten sneak.

At that moment, there was a knock at the door. My stomach tensed. I walked to the door with Kaela on my heels and cautiously looked through the peephole. *Of course, what timing.* I closed my eyes and leaned my forehead against the door for a second, and then opened it.

Josh was standing on the stoop, eyes alert, but when he saw I wasn't alone, his expression instantly smoothed.

Kaela crooned, "Well, *hello, Joshua.* See you later, Ali," as she stepped past me onto the porch and threw a self-satisfied look over her shoulder before she darted to her car. I controlled my sigh, *love him* echoing in my head.

He smiled. "Kaela."

"Please come in," I stepped aside to allow him entry. The second the door was closed, a look of panic replaced the pleasant mask previously plastered on his face.

"He was here," he gasped and put his hand on my elbow.

"Yes, how did you know?"

But he wasn't paying attention to me. He already had a phone on his ear. "Gabriel, *he* was here...No, *it is possible.* Don't tell me that it isn't," he barked, his anger barely reigned in. He twisted the bottom of the phone away from his mouth and addressed me, "How long ago?"

I glanced at the clock. "Fifteen minutes?"

"Fifteen minutes ago. Well, obviously he wasn't where you thought he was." Then he hit the end button, making an exasperated sound at the back of his throat. He turned to look at me, and his face softened. "Are you okay?"

"Yeah, I didn't actually see him." I cringed. "He spoke with Kaela while I was in the shower. He could have," I paused, to even out my voice. "He just dropped something off."

Josh's hand was still on my elbow. I slid my arm through his grip, gently latched onto his hand, and pulled him towards the kitchen. My hand tingled and felt hot, even though his hand was so cool. I could hear Kaela's voice again saying, "*You love him.*"

I dropped his hand as soon as we were in the kitchen, feeling awkward about touching him, though holding his hand was nothing new. I waved towards the flowers like a game show hostess.

He pursed his lips and snatched the note. He looked up at me again, calmer, but his words spilled out in a rush. "I am so sorry. I got here the second it was dark enough. Gabriel and Sebastian were tracking him across town. He shouldn't have been able—"

"It's okay. I'm fine. Kaela's fine. Nothing to worry about." I seized the flowers, tossed them in the trash and shut the lid. "There, all better," I said with a satisfied gleam in my eye. It was sort of sacrilegious to dispose of perfectly good flowers, but *he* was the last thing I wanted to think about.

Joshua took my hand once more. The tingling came back, and this time I had butterflies in my stomach, too. It took every bit of my strength to keep my breathing from stuttering like my heart. He had touched me a thousand times, and I had never thought twice about it. Now, after one conversation with Kaela, I didn't know what to do with myself.

I peered up at him. His mind seemed to be a hundred miles away as he toyed with my silver Claddagh ring on my right hand. He drew in a shallow breath and asked, "This means something, doesn't it?" indicating the ring.

"Um, yeah." I had to refocus my thoughts for a moment. "It's an Irish ring; the hands mean friendship, the heart love, and the crown loyalty. And depending on how you wear it, you can know someone's romantic availability. The heart outward like this, on my right hand, means my heart has not been captured." I looked down at the ring to avoid eye contact; it felt weird saying I was romantically available to him.

He seemed to absorb the information for a second and then changed the subject back. "We will get *him*, and you will be safe," he reassured.

"I know." I tried to smile convincingly.

His phone buzzed, and it was instantly at his ear. "Yes... yes. I'll meet you outside." He ended the call abruptly. "I need to speak with Gabriel and Sebastian. They are out front in the van. I'll be right back." He gave my shoulder a gentle squeeze.

"Sure." I tried to sound nonchalant, even though I was suddenly petrified of being alone.

Next thing I knew, he was gone. I heard the front door click, but he moved so fast, I missed his passage. I walked to the front window. There was a large, industrial-looking black van, with tinted windows and grey lettering on the side, parked out in front of the house. Due to the darkness outside, I couldn't quite make out what was written on the van, but I did notice that on the left-hand-side there was some sort of odd-looking symbol with elegant script.

I stared at the vehicle, waiting for Joshua to emerge, but I eventually gave up and went into the kitchen. Kaela had left the cheese and crackers out, so I put them away and grabbed the ingredients to make my mom's enchilada casserole, layered them in the pan, and popped it in the oven. I returned to the front window and peered out at the van again. It had been over a half hour since Joshua had gone out there.

Debating, I stood there working up the nerve to head out to the vehicle. After a full minute, I took a deep breath and walked out into the night. When I was halfway across the lawn, I was startled by someone slipping out the back of the van. I stared after him for a moment and realized that I had seen him before. It was the raven-haired guy I had seen in the bookstore and outside the café. He glanced back over his shoulder at me and shook his head as he disappeared around the corner.

I refocused and knocked on the sliding door of the van. It opened, and the tension in the air was thick. Joshua was rigid with his hands on his temples. There were two others with him.

The first was a distinguished, older-looking gentleman I assumed was Sebastian. He looked to be in his fifties and faintly stout, yet strong. He had medium brown hair that was grey at the temples, as well as a highly manicured beard with a striking grey streak at the chin. Small wire-rimmed glasses gave him the look of someone who had squinted over too many books in his lifetime. His presence was commanding and intimidating, but there was kindness in his eyes. Somehow, I knew I could trust him, like how you feel safe with your grandfather—but he wasn't that old.

The other, I imagined, was the Gabriel who Josh had told me about. He was in the back corner of the van, barely in view. For some reason, I was afraid to really look at him. There was something menacing about him, but I couldn't quite figure him out. I realized I had been standing there for about four seconds, not saying anything. I swallowed, my mouth suddenly pasty, and said, "I would like to invite all of you in for supper."

"Thank you kindly, my dear, but we have some business to which we need to attend," Sebastian replied in his deep, resonating voice. His accent was very crisp. I couldn't tell if he was American and had spent a significant amount of time in England or vice-versa.

I shook my head. "I know, and your business most likely involves me. So, please come in and sit down at a real table and have some home-cooked food. If you don't come in, I will simply bring it out to you." I widened my eyes and added, "And who knows what could happen to me between here and the house." I was fully aware there could be some truth to that.

They glanced at Joshua, and he half-smiled. "She won't give up; she is more stubborn than I am."

Sebastian let out a sharp chuckle. "We'll be along straight away. Thank you."

I smiled and headed back to the house, feeling a little nervous.

There was a knock at the door a few minutes later. I opened the door wide, and all three of them filed in. At that moment, the timer went off on the oven. "Please, come on into the kitchen. I'll have everything ready in a moment." They trailed behind me. "Please take a seat." I motioned towards the table.

There was an awkward shuffling behind me as I removed the contents of the oven and placed them on the trivet in the center of the table next to the salad I had made. I quietly bowed my head for a two-second prayer, and I noticed that everyone else had done the same.

Joshua looked distant while the rest of us ate. I could tell he was trying to keep a pleasant look on his face, but I knew him too well to be fooled. I had so many things I wanted to ask them, but the bravado I had in inviting them in had completely gone away. I actually felt shy.

I couldn't tell if Sebastian and Gabriel were quiet because they liked the food or if they didn't want to speak in front of me. I was guessing from the sheer quantity of casserole Gabriel consumed that it was the food.

A little while later, Sebastian wiped his mouth with his napkin and pushed back from the table slightly. "Well, that was delightful. It *was* nice to have a home-cooked meal. I thank you."

"Yes, thank you," Gabriel added.

"Any time. All of you are protecting me. The least I can do is some cooking."

Sebastian looked over at Joshua with concern. "Joshua, may I speak with you outside?"

Josh tightened his lips and followed him silently out the back door.

I felt awkward being left in the room with Gabriel. Honestly, I was afraid to even look at him. His whole presence was unapproachable—and dangerous. He abruptly stood up and helped me clear the dishes, a gesture I wasn't expecting. He removed the leather cuff over his wrist before he plunged a plate under the stream of water, revealing a circular tattoo. I glanced at his face, and he was grinning down at me. For the first time, I allowed myself to actually look at him.

He appeared to be in his late-twenties, or maybe early-thirties. He was tall, broad-shouldered, and had an olive complexion paired with deep chocolate-brown hair. Part of his dangerous presence was because of the wicked looking scar hugging the entire length of his left cheekbone in the shape of a jagged fishhook.

Once you could get past the disfigurement, he was very attractive. He had a wide forehead, with perfectly arched eyebrows, and a delicately shaped Roman nose with full lips. His eyes were shiny and dark-rimmed with long, graceful lashes that any woman would kill for. But there was something more about his eyes. They sparkled with wisdom from a hard life, and maybe intuition. His strong jawline completed his perfectly angular face. His presence was confident, maybe even a little cocky, but more endearing than annoying.

"You have been quieter than I expected," he mused, his expression kind.

"Uh, I don't find the need to fill silence unless I actually have something to say, I guess. And well..." I felt sheepish.

He raised his left eyebrow.

"All of you are a little intimidating." I felt oddly vulnerable and a little embarrassed about my admission.

He smiled again. "I guess I cannot disagree."

I sucked in a sharp breath and blurted out, "Where do vampires come from?" He looked at me, surprised. I was sure he was expecting me to ask about something having to do with the current situation. He exhaled, strolled back to the table, and sank into a chair. I cut a piece of leftover birthday cake and slid it in front of him. He accepted it readily.

"How well do you know your Old Testament?" he asked.

"Some of it well. Other parts a little rusty."

"You remember King Solomon and the twelve tribes of Israel?" he questioned.

"Of course," I replied.

"Towards the end of King Solomon's reign, God became displeased with him. He was a good king, but he had a weakness when it came to women. God warned Solomon not to fall for pagan women and especially not to marry them. But Solomon allowed himself to be distracted, and he did not heed God's warning.

"He married women from far-reaching places—the more exotic, the better. Queen Agrona traveled from Northern Europe to meet the legendary king. She was unlike anything he had ever seen. Her small kingdom, now in modern day France, consisted of Celts and Germanic peoples. The parade of fair-skinned, blond, blue-eyed warriors must have seemed magical. He married her, and she brought her gods with her and added some of the local ones too. She used her influence to sway people towards her beliefs."

I could picture it in my head, dust rising from the feet of the caravan of Northern warriors entering the city, their fair skin a stark contrast to the olive-toned people native to the area. I imagined them clad in leather and painted with strange markings in blue like the Celts I had seen in books. Much of their skin would have been bare and pinked from the harsh sunlight over the beige, dusty city.

Gabriel cleared his throat, and I realized that I had drifted off in thought. He continued, "Her entrance into the city was only bested by the Queen of Sheba a few years later. Anyway, as punishment for Solomon not obeying, God told him that He would strip him of the tribes, but since he had been a good king, it would not happen until after his death. His son,

Rehoboam, would pay the price, and he would lose all but one of the tribes.

"If you look carefully, you may notice a discrepancy. It says that one tribe was left with Rehoboam, and ten tribes were given to Jeroboam. Did you ever wonder where the other tribe went?"

I remembered the story, but it had never occurred to me. "No, I had never noticed. Where does it say this?" I asked as I stood up.

"I believe it is in I Kings 11."

I went into my dad's office, grabbed a Bible off the shelf and flipped to Kings. I read as I returned to the table. "[10] Although he had forbidden Solomon to follow other gods, Solomon did not keep the Lord's command. [11] So the Lord said to Solomon, 'Since this is your attitude and you have not kept my covenant and my decrees, which I commanded you, I will most certainly tear the kingdom away from you'... [35] I will take the kingdom from his son, Rehoboam's, hands and give [Jeroboam] ten tribes. [36] I will give one tribe to his son..." I scanned the rest of the chapter, but Gabriel was right; there was no mention of the other tribe. I looked at him, bewildered, as I slouched into a seat.

"So what happened to them?"

"Long story short...they were cursed by God, as was Solomon's wife, Queen Agrona. They formed their own council of twelve and eventually scattered all over Northern Africa and Europe. There are still twelve major tribes, or covens, all originating from the cursed tribe, and a newer American coven—thirteen total; the oldest members, the Ancients, are almost three thousand years old and immensely powerful. We are not sure how many of the original tribe still exist because they are closely guarded."

"Why don't people know about this? I mean, a whole tribe cursed? Wasn't that a really big thing?"

"It was, but many assumed that the tribe was absorbed into the other tribes. From what we can gather, many left because of the pagan blood worship that took place once Queen Agrona took power. Only about a third of the original tribe remained; the rest of it consisted of followers from many kingdoms, both Jew and Gentile. There was even a group of the Queen of Sheba's followers who joined the cult. God sent a prophet to warn them. Instead of listening to the prophet, they sacrificed him to their blood god. In turn, God, in His wrath, cursed them to an eternity of darkness, bound by that which they worshipped. The sun and food were part of their gluttonous rituals."

I sat still for a long while, processing all he had shared, until I timidly asked, "Do you think they still have their souls?"

He drew in a long breath. "I did not." He glanced out the backdoor at Joshua and Sebastian discussing something intently. His face softened, and his tone of voice sounded thoughtful. "I have been hunting them for a long time and have never thought twice about it. I did not allow for there to be the possibility of good vampires. But...

"Joshua *is* good. And admittedly, most vampires do not kill their food. Most covens frown on the practice, but that may simply be for self-preservation." He paused. "Maybe Sebastian is right, and they lose it when they take an innocent. I am simply not sure anymore." He looked tired.

"What did Joshua mean about being an experiment?"

His mouth flattened into a thin line. I was sure he was thinking about what he should and shouldn't say. Gabriel, though an elegant speaker, didn't seem accustomed to talking so much. "Let us just say he is the first one of his kind to work with us, and it is causing some...conflict within the Council."

"Conflict?"

There was sorrow in his eyes for a brief moment. "Some of them want Joshua dead. They do not trust any of his kind and do not want him to know any of our secrets." He looked at me with wary eyes, judging my reaction.

I remained calm. "Thank you for telling me."

"Joshua told me that you like truth, even if it is something you do not want to hear."

"Yeah, I'm stupid that way." I shrugged my shoulders and tried to think of some humorous way to joke about it, but I could come up with nothing. I just kept thinking about Josh.

The vampires want him dead because he's working with the Watchers. The Watchers want him dead because he knows their secrets. He is torturing himself with guilt because I was pulled into the situation. And, to top things off, he may or may not have a soul.

Gabriel got up to look out the back window. He turned back towards me and asked, "What was Joshua like before all of this?"

I thought for a moment. "He was the popular guy in high school who was so nice, you couldn't actually hate him." I smiled a little. "I was a freshman when he was a senior, and he never ditched me or was embarrassed by me. He was," I searched for the word, "unflappable. He didn't care what other people thought, but in a good way. He always looked out for me, probably more than I realized."

"So you were always close?"

"I don't remember life without him. Even when I lost contact with him, I never stopped thinking about him. But as he was older, I'm sure the bond I thought we had was more on my part. I doubt I was on his mind much with all that has happened." I tried to brush it off as no big deal, but my voice wobbled a tiny bit.

Gabriel had a faint smile on his face. "He did not forget you." He didn't elaborate more than that, but turned and looked out the window again. I could see a shift in him. His thoughts appeared to be far off. He became the warrior again, the softness I had seen in his face gone.

I decided to risk one more question. "Who was the man with the black hair who walked away from the van when I came out?"

"He is a Watcher, but stay away from him. He is not like us," he almost hissed.

I fell silent from the strength of his reaction. I grabbed the last plate off the table for something to do. Gabriel went into the front room and looked out at the street. Conversation over.

I heard my phone chime with a new text. It gave me an excuse to go upstairs. It was Marie: "Need company tonight?" *Sure why not come join the party. I already have two Watchers and a vampire over. Maybe we could find a werewolf and a zombie or two.*

"No thanx going 2 bed early, xo. Still going 2 beach tomorrow?"

"Pick u up at 8. Want 2 beat traffic."

"K. Good night." *Miracles happen*, I thought. Marie was going to get up early.

I hung around my room for a little while, and then decided to assemble my supplies for the beach trip. Afterwards, I paced around, looking for something else to do. I fed the animals, and then considered going to sleep. I felt too agitated to go to bed, though. And there was too much tension downstairs. I retrieved the book from my beach bag and retired to the couch in the great room.

As I read, I could hear the muffled voices of Josh and Sebastian outside, the whisper quiet steps of Gabriel as he paced in the front room, and the dog's whimpers in the side yard. I noticed that I had read the same paragraph three times before I gave up on the book.

I felt small. I had been plunged into a world so immense that it was not just huge, but literally of *biblical proportions*. It was hard to wrap my brain around three-thousand-year-old beings, curses, and myths. I wondered if Solomon's wife, Queen Agrona, was still alive. And why had that black-haired Watcher looked like he hated me? What had Gabriel meant by "he is not like us?" Was there some type of division within the Watchers? My brain hurt.

I heard the backdoor slide open and then close again. I went downstairs, hoping to see Josh, but only found Sebastian looking intently out the front window. I listened, but it didn't sound like anyone else was in the house. He glanced over his shoulder. "He isn't here, child."

Normally, someone calling me 'child' would have perturbed me, but somehow, the word seemed endearing coming from Sebastian. "Is everything okay? Josh didn't seem very happy."

He paused for a moment, choosing his words. "The boy you saw outside, Phineas, has increased some tensions. It's nothing for you to worry about." *So that was the dark-haired boy's name.*

"So he doesn't like vampires, and therefore Josh, and is having a hissy fit about it."

He chuckled. "I guess you could put it that way."

"Gabriel told me to stay away from him, that he isn't like you. Does that mean he is dangerous, or does that mean he resents your involvement with me?"

"I would say you are right on both counts."

"Sorry, but the phrase he used *'not like us'* made me curious. If I am prying, I'm sorry, but…" I struggled to phrase my question correctly. "Are there different kinds of Watchers?"

He contemplated my question, his dark eyes benevolent. I couldn't help but like him. Years of hard experience had creased his face like a roadmap.

"There was a schism a few decades ago, dividing the Watchers in half; the two sides have vastly different ideologies. Phineas belongs to the other sect, the Conclave, and doesn't agree with some of our choices. But it will get worked out." He patted my shoulder reassuringly.

I frowned, not entirely convinced. "Thanks."

He started to open his mouth to say something else, but stopped.

I motioned towards the stairs. "I think I am going to head to bed. There is a guest room with clean sheets down the hall, first door on the left. Any of you are welcome to use it."

"Thank you for the offer."

"Good night."

"Pleasant dreams, Aleria."

Pressing my way upstairs, it felt like every step was steeper than normal. I half-heartedly washed my face. My body felt so sluggish that it was hard to pull on my pajamas. I crawled into bed, barely able to cover myself before I plummeted into oblivion.

I slept hard…until the nightmare. I woke screaming with such ferocity that the sound reverberated in my room. Soaked in sweat once again, I desperately tried to catch my breath. My panting was bordering on hyperventilating.

The dreams were getting worse and much more realistic. Josh appeared in my doorway. He paused, and then was at my side. He pulled me into his arms, and I went limp and started to sob. I was so exhausted, I was beyond feeling embarrassed.

He gently rocked me and murmured in my ear, "I'm here, you're safe," over and over again.

When the storm passed, I sat up again, and he handed me a tissue from the nightstand. He held my free hand as I tried to compose myself. My breathing still stuttered a little. "I'm sorry."

He stroked my face, wiping fresh tears from my cheek. "What do you have to be sorry for? Nothing. Everything is going to be fine."

I tried to nod, but my head felt heavy, and I started to droop. I eased back under the covers and took a couple of deep breaths. "You don't know if it will be fine," I mumbled.

"It will; have faith." He pushed a stray curl off my face. "You should get some sleep." He started to get up, but I panicked.

"Please don't leave." My voice broke on *leave*. He exhaled, and an expression I couldn't read raced across his face.

"Okay, I'll be right here." He straightened the blankets and lay on top of them on his side, facing me. There was a foot between us. He was close, but not too close, always the gentleman.

I rolled on my side to face him. The room was dim, but I could still see his eyes. We stared at one another in comfortable silence until I couldn't keep my eyes open, and my lids drifted closed. He stroked my hair and murmured reassurances as I drifted to sleep.

With each breath I silently said, *I love you*. And it terrified me. I thought for a moment that he traced my lips with his finger, but I may have been dreaming.

I did not have another nightmare that night.

10

LIGHT AND DARK

When I woke, my room was flooded with light, and Joshua was gone. It made me wonder how long he had stayed with me and to where he had vanished. I contemplated whether his thirst had made it hard for him to be close to me like that. I had felt more at peace during those quiet moments last night than I had in weeks.

I rolled over and felt paper. I looked at the pillow next to me; there was a manila envelope with something that felt like a book inside. I started to open it, then caught a glimpse of my alarm clock. It read 7:51 A.M. At that moment, my phone chimed. I glanced at the screen.

It was Marie: "Running early be there in 5."

I stashed the package under my pillow, rolled out of bed, and sprinted to the bathroom to get ready.

I decided to wear my bathing suit under my clothes. It was still too cold for shorts, so I slid into my favorite pair of jeans and a turquoise t-shirt that perfectly matched my two-piece.

Grabbing my bag, I skipped downstairs just as I heard the distinctive squeak of Marie's car brakes as she pulled into the driveway.

I hurried outside and locked the door behind me. I thought about the envelope upstairs and wondered if I should go up and fetch it, but I heard excited chatter and turned towards the car. Kaela and Breanna were already crammed into the back seat of the silver Civic, bubbling with laughter. Marie tossed me her keys. "You drive. I hate driving over the hill."

"We can take my car," I offered.

"I get better gas mileage," she chirped as she climbed into the passenger seat. I couldn't disagree. My old car's V8 wasn't exactly environmentally friendly. And I wasn't going to argue about driving. I loved driving over the hill to Santa Cruz. It's not so much of a hill though, as a fairly sizable mountain with a formidable road snaking over it, known to be one of the most dangerous roads in California. Despite the dangers of the sharp turns and blind corners, I loved the challenge and beauty of the drive.

I stuck my head through the driver's door. "Ready?" I was met with giddy laughter.

"Get in, already. Let's go!" Marie tossed her beach towel at me, hitting me in the face, and burst with laughter.

We pulled onto Highway 17, and Marie turned up the music. Happy rhythms befitting summer wafted out of the open windows as we traveled. I pulled my hair into a messy ponytail to keep it from whipping my face. Everyone was wrapped up in some conversation, but I lost track of what they were saying and retreated into my own thoughts.

I kept thinking about the concept of light and dark, both on a figurative and literal level. My days were normal, bathed in sunlight and filled with the trivial. And then when night fell, I was surrounded by myth and fear—everything so epic.

The nightmares had made me almost afraid to sleep. I had dark circles under my eyes all the time, and I still felt like I was fighting a cold. At night, everything seemed louder, smelled more acute, and my senses surged.

My thoughts drifted to Joshua, and I couldn't help but smile as the butterflies returned to my stomach. I remembered the peaceful look on his face as he had run his fingers through my hair last night. And I remembered the feel of his cool fingers brushing my cheek.

I was snapped out of my reverie when Kaela yanked on my seatbelt from behind. "Hey! Aren't you even going to defend yourself?" she shot at me.

Defend myself? "All I know is that I'm *awesome.* I don't need defending," I retorted sarcastically, hoping that fit. There was a roar of laughter.

"Whatever!" Kaela responded, kicking the back of my seat.

I had no idea what was going on, but I relaxed my shoulders and laughed with them, for no other reason than not to be caught zoning out.

I suddenly realized we were missing a person, and no one had mentioned her. "Hey, where's April?"

"Oh, she had to work with her dad on the apartment building for a few hours. She'll meet up with us at the beach. She said she might pick up some of the boys."

"Mmm," I murmured as we pulled onto Ocean Street. "Hey, are we going to the Boardwalk or Natural Bridges?"

"Boardwalk," they chimed in unison.

"I want clam chowder from Rita's for lunch," Kaela added.

I picked up a parking pass from the tollbooth and parked on the wharf. We decided to walk through some of the stores, and then get an early lunch first, so we left our beach bags in the trunk. Since it was already heating up, I traded my jeans for shorts. We shopped and bought chowder in bread bowls to go, then strolled down to the end of the wharf to watch the sea lions. I leaned against the railing, savoring my soup, and a pelican landed a couple of feet from me. I was startled and froze in place. I had never been so close to one. It looked me in the eye for a long moment, and then made a guttural hissing sound and flew off.

"That was weird," Breanna mused.

"Yeah." I felt a little unnerved for some reason. Then something occurred to me. My cat hadn't slept on my bed since my family had left. He was normally a little lover-kitty, seeking out the nearest lap. Odd.

We headed back towards the car. April called Marie on her cell and told her that she was pulling onto the wharf to park. I could see her car in the distance turning into the slot next to mine. It looked like she had at least two others with her.

When we got closer, I could see Wyatt and Daniel. Wyatt was the boy who wanted to go out with Breanna; she always seemed to have some boy waiting around for her. Then, Peter got out of the car with a red mark on his face where he had been leaning against the window, and he looked rather sleepy. He had on a red "Lifeguard California" t-shirt and khaki shorts.

I let out a little-too-loud squeal and ran to him. I

embraced him with such force that I almost knocked him over. I thought I had lost him to Robert completely, that I would never get to see him again as a friend of mine. He laughed and hugged me back hard.

My face stretched from my huge smile. I realized how seldom I had smiled in the last few days. The only joy I had was Joshua, and he had not exactly been smiling about the circumstances of his return. I finally released Peter and said, "I am so happy to see you!"

"I'm happy to see you too, and with that reception, I'll tell you I can't hang out with you more often."

I punched him.

"Okay, okay. Sorry." I continued to glare. "I missed you, Ali, and Robert is doing okay now. I think I can sneak over enemy lines once in a while." He winked.

I frowned. "How is he?"

"Improving, slowly."

"Good. You don't need to say anything else. I wouldn't want you to feel like a double agent."

"Thanks."

"So we are just Ali and Peter. There is no Robert, *and* things can be normal," I said happily.

Peter smirked. "I don't know how normal you can be, but—"

I opened my water bottle and flung the contents on him and ran towards the beach. I got a good head start as he stood there shocked, a sizable amount of water dripping down his face and shirt.

I heard April yell, "You had better move faster than that, Hayes!"

I jumped down the staircase leading to the beach in four bounds, lucky that I didn't fall on my face. The sand slowed me, but it would slow him, too. I could hear his footsteps growing closer, the sand grinding under his feet. I was going to pay for soaking him. I risked a glance over my shoulder the second I hit the wet sand and picked up speed. Just then, I felt his hand on my elbow. I let out an involuntary screech. He threw me over his shoulder and paused. "According to your tenfold rules, I have to get you ten times as wet."

"Don't you dare!" Then, despite my weight, he took five long strides straight into the surf and tossed me in. The water was icy as I plunged beneath the surface. When I came up for air, I jumped on his back and took him under. The water appeared beige with all of the sand churning up from the bottom.

"Okay, truce, truce!" I squeaked.

We trudged out of the ocean, salt water splattering and making dark, fat circles on the dry sand. The others arrived on the beach, carrying all of our stuff. We walked down a little further and set up for the afternoon. It was in the mid-80s with a perfect breeze.

April, Breanna, and Wyatt went for a walk down the beach and everyone else settled onto the king-sized blanket Kaela had brought. I shucked off my wet clothes and draped my clothes over the cooler, casting a glare at Peter.

Kaela was already stretched out next to me, working on her tan. Peter and Daniel were sitting behind me discussing baseball while Marie had her nose in a gossip magazine with the headline, "Stars with the Best Beach Bods."

I extended my legs out in front of me and started applying

SPF 50. Then, I heard Peter ask in a very shocked voice, "Ali, did you get a tattoo?"

I swiveled around to look at him confused. I followed his eyes to my lower back where my swimsuit had dipped down in the back. "Oh," I mumbled, "uh, no," and tugged the back of my swimsuit up a little in an attempt to cover it.

Marie and Kaela giggled.

Peter looked at them wondering why they were laughing. "What?"

"She has a natural tramp stamp," Marie teased.

I grabbed my wet t-shirt and flung it at her.

"Thanks, I was getting hot," she replied, fanning herself.

"It's a birthmark," I answered Peter.

"Wow, it's like an artsy little star," he said with a grin that quickly drained off his face when he saw my expression.

"Yeah, I will never need to get a tattoo," I grumbled and flopped on my back so no one could look at it anymore.

"Don't worry about it, Peter. She gets all weird about it for some reason," Kaela added to ease some of the awkwardness.

I actually wondered why I always felt so weird about it. For a birthmark, it was kind of cool, but I always tried to keep it covered, like it was instinct.

After an hour or so, most everyone walked up the Boardwalk to go on a few rides. I opted to stay behind and watch our stuff. I stretched out the rest of the way on the blanket and closed my eyes, my eyelids red from the inside and warm from the afternoon sun.

My lips tasted salty from my dip, and my skin tight. The smell of the ocean helped clear my head, and I realized how much I missed Josh. I wished he could be here with me, enjoying the sun and sound of the waves crashing on the beach, hearing the giggles of children building sandcastles and the squawk of seagulls soaring overhead. It grieved me knowing that he could never feel the warmth of a sunny day at the beach again.

I sighed and sat up to reapply sunscreen. I poked at my skin and realized I needed to put on my cover-up or be lobster girl for the next few days.

Everyone returned from the rides and started a game of Frisbee. As afternoon faded, we decided to go back home. Wyatt attentively carried all of Breanna's things. She seemed oblivious to his intentions. Peter and Marie were talking in hushed voices; they had obviously grown closer throughout the day. Even Daniel and April seemed to be flirting a little. I linked arms with Kaela as we walked back to the vehicles.

I looked down at her. "You are so sexy with your nose all pink like that," I teased.

"I know you want me, but I like boys. When will you learn that?" she countered. Then she got quiet for a moment. "Speaking of boys…" and her voice trailed off.

I rolled my eyes. "You have been waiting all day to ask me about boys, haven't you?"

"A specific boy, yes."

"Thanks for not saying anything to anyone else," I said quietly.

"Yeah, I'm cool like that."

"I don't really have any news for you."

"Are you going to admit you love him?" she pressed.

I drew in a long breath. "I won't deny it."

Her eyes sparkled with triumph. "Are you going to see him soon?"

"I would say there's a high probability of that happening."

"Is that why you won't let anyone stay over?"

"No. Really. No." I exhaled in a gust. "He is not the reason, and there is nothing illicit going on." *The real reason is that I am trying to keep you out of the path of a homicidal vampire, but no biggie.*

"Just checking in," she replied, her light green eyes looking almost silver as they glittered in the light reflected from the water.

As we walked those last few yards, I realized this was exactly what I had needed—close friends and no worries. I took in a deep breath, fully expanding my ribcage, and smiled.

We shuffled passengers in the cars. There was the going-to-coffee-car and the not-going-to-coffee-car. Breanna, Daniel, and Wyatt went over to April's vehicle so they could go straight home. Peter joined Kaela, Marie, and me so we could hang out at Campbell Perk for a little while before going home. We laughed most of the way back.

We ordered coffee and sandwiches for an early supper. The food tasted especially good after all the activity. I hadn't realized how hungry I was. I tried really hard not to shove all the food into my mouth at once. We finished up around 7:00 P.M. There was still another hour and a half until sunset. It felt like I hadn't seen Joshua in days.

I went around the corner to use the restroom before going back to my place. After washing up, I headed out the door and was so wrapped in my own world, that I didn't notice where I was walking and ran directly into someone exiting the men's room. My face burned with embarrassment as I struggled to focus my eyes on who I had just plowed into.

As I opened my mouth to apologize, the man seized me by the throat and pinned my head against the wall with a thump. I was so taken off guard that I didn't resist for a moment. His left hand immobilized my right arm, and he dug his fingers in throat and my arm intentionally to inflict pain. Then I realized it was the raven-haired Watcher, Phineas.

He hissed at me, barely containing his contempt, "You and your abomination need to stay away from me."

My eyes wide, I couldn't respond as he was cutting off most of my air. I gasped and tried to nod, feeling the blood pulsing in my temples and hearing a rushing sound in my ears. It made my head swim and my vision darken.

He leaned in next to my ear, his hot breath flooding over the side of my face, smelling of stale coffee. "As far as I am concerned, you are expendable."

I was dumbfounded, no other words to express my utter astonishment. He shoved away from me and disappeared back into the café. I gasped for air and stood there for a moment, clutching my neck as I steadied my breathing. Gabriel wasn't joking when he had said to stay away from him. After I composed myself, I walked back around the corner.

Peter looked at me warily. "You okay?"

I grinned, concealing my shock. "Just a little too much sun today. Nothing a good shower and some sleep won't take care of."

He returned my smile, but I wasn't sure he believed me.

Then he reached over and gave me a sideways hug. Kaela gave me a furtive look, not missing anything.

I tossed Marie her keys, and she drove to my place to drop me off first. I crawled woodenly out of the car. I was still shocked from my bizarre confrontation with Phineas.

I grabbed my bag and walked to the door, waving farewell to everyone in the car. I stuck my key in the door, and heard someone running up behind me. I whirled around wildly, brandishing my keys like a weapon.

"Whoa there, killer. You forgot your sunglasses." Peter folded them into my hand. He looked at me with a worried expression like I had confirmed some type of suspicion.

"Sorry. You startled me," I laughed, but it sounded uncomfortable and forced.

"You sure you're okay?"

"Yeah, totally fine, just jittery for some reason. No worries."

He nodded and gave me a huge hug and a peck on the cheek before he loped back to the car. I was startled by the kiss on my cheek but dismissed it, although I could feel Marie's eyes burning into my back. I knew she liked him, but it wasn't like I was acting any differently around him. *He was just encouraging me, right?* I put my key back in the door, my hands shaking, and let myself in. I waved as they pulled away.

The beautiful, golden pre-sunset light spilled through the back windows as I climbed upstairs to get cleaned up. Showering off all of the sand was number one on my list. Afterwards, I stalked downstairs and looked out the front window for the van, but it was absent. I wanted to see Joshua, but I could hardly hold my eyes open. My muscles ached dully from all the goings-on at the beach.

The house felt oddly silent, and I was too exhausted to fight sleep. I decided to set my alarm and see Joshua in a few hours.

I made one last sweep through the house, flipping off the last few lights, and made my way back upstairs. I froze the instant I shut the door to my bedroom—there was no need to turn around because every part of my being knew what waited for me. I wanted to open the door and run as fast as I could, but it wouldn't do any good. Ice ran through my veins, and it was difficult to will myself to turn around.

Bowen was casually sitting in the wingback chair in the corner of my room with a satisfied grin on his face.

11

ANGELS ARE TERRIBLE

I controlled my breathing, trying not to reveal my paralyzing fear. Bowen's piercing gaze was so smug. I finally broke the silence, "How did you—"

"Your friend was kind enough to invite me in yesterday when I dropped off the flowers."

"Well, I un-invite you," I retorted.

He chuckled. "Sorry, honey, it doesn't work that way."

"It was worth a try," I muttered.

"I was happy to finally see that you were unaccompanied. I wouldn't want anyone to interrupt our *quality* time."

The blood drained from my face. "I'm expecting company momentarily."

He wagged his finger at me. "I'm afraid they won't be here anytime soon."

My heart broke into a sprint. Had something happened to them? Had he done something? Was Joshua okay? Gabriel? Sebastian? I took in a deep breath, trying to calm myself. A lazy grin spread across his face, and I was sure he could hear my heart all too well.

"Well, a girl can hope," I said, feigning some sort of confidence.

"You know, this is working out much better than I initially planned," he said almost playfully.

"Oh?" I replied coolly.

"The initial plan was to kill you the night you were located. For you to disappear like all the other girls in the area," he mused.

My stomach tightened. I hadn't made the connection. All of the other missing girls—they would never return to their worried families, never finish school, and never have a family of their own. They were casualties because he was looking for *me*.

"But after we were interrupted..." his voice trailed off, and he was suddenly across the room, inches from me. My heart stopped.

He seemed pleased again. He gently stroked my trembling lower lip with his index finger as his warm breath washed over my face, sweet and inviting. I pressed myself up against the door, straining to get as far from him as I could. He reached his arm around my lower back and pulled me to him. I remained rigid and leaned my upper body as far away from him as I could. His embrace was like iron; he could snap me in half if he desired. I was helpless—mortal. My eyes started stinging, but I forced myself to still.

He continued, "I don't think breaking you is the best choice either, so for the third time, the plan has changed. I admit I am normally much more decisive." His eyes narrowed.

"Don't worry, killing you is too final. If I finish turning you, it would be a constant reminder for him." He leaned down and kissed my neck, continuing to whisper into my ear.

I couldn't move. I could feel the warmth moving through my system again, breaking my will. My mind was racing, trying to think of any way to escape. Different scenarios sped through my head, but they were all ridiculous. How could I stand up to a vampire?

"If I take your precious soul. If you were bound to me," he crooned. "Well, that could be much more gratifying. If I turn you into the monster he fears to be." He ran his nose up my neck. "Losing his true love and having to hunt you himself."

"Um, I think you are confused. I am not his true love." My voice trembled slightly, my thoughts slow.

"So you say. Of course, you could choose to come with me," he paused. "I would like that very much. You would be beautiful forever," he purred as he ran his tongue along the edge of my ear and pulled me closer. I suppressed my cringe.

He sickened me, but at the same time, part of me wanted to go with him. Was it his hypnotic ability? Was it the virus which he'd infected me with? Did some part of me want to be a vampire? My legs felt weak. There was no way to escape. I was doomed.

I resorted to the unimaginable. I turned my face slightly and ran my lips over his jaw towards his ear. I relaxed my body and sank into his embrace. "Immortality is an appealing offer," I whispered.

He pulled back, surprised. I took advantage of the space between us and calmly stepped out of his encircling arms and moved across the room. I sat on my desk, pushing my books to the side. I kept my eyes locked on his, trying to seem confident in my statement. I wondered if a pencil was a large enough "stake" to paralyze him temporarily. Not that I would be fast enough or strong enough to actually drive it into his chest. His hypnotic impact started to wear off. I just needed to stall.

He prowled towards me. I strained to hear anything outside. My mind was screaming for Joshua. All I seemed to be doing was delaying the inevitable. I couldn't hear anyone outside, and my heart sank. He finished his slow approach and put his hands on my knees. His touch made me want to recoil. I forced a smile and clutched a pencil behind my back, firmly in my right hand. My heart started beating harder, and my breath became more uneven. His eyes were intent on mine.

"You could be a princess in my world." He bent down, kissed the left side of my neck, and whispered into the hollow under my ear, trying to woo me. "I could take you to the places you dream of visiting and more. You would have centuries to explore the world."

I took in a small breath as he started kissing the other side of my throat. "All you need to do is choose me willingly," he cooed. And then I realized why. He wanted me to break Joshua's heart by my willingly leaving with him. He wanted Joshua to lose me and watch Bowen take my soul. Everything was a calculated maneuver—a seduction.

I concentrated to fight his mind-controlling ability, unable to stand one more moment of his touching me. I plunged the pencil towards his chest with all my might, but it didn't even pierce his skin. It snapped in two with a pathetic crack.

He hissed at me, his eyes fierce, and with one small movement, he brushed me to the side, launching me into the adjacent wall. My head smacked against the sheetrock, jarring me. There was a piercing pain in my side where his hand had connected with my ribcage. My breath was knocked out of me, and I made a horrific sucking sound as I finally pulled air into my lungs. I sat up, still disoriented, hoping he would quickly finish me. To be turned by him, I would slaughter people, and that would be worse than death.

He crossed the room, shaking his head as he brushed the splinters of pencil off his shirt. I clutched my ribcage. I expected his face to be filled with rage, but it wasn't. Was it regret I saw? He was almost to me when I heard something land lightly outside the window. At that moment, Joshua stepped through the window. Bowen whirled around and growled, "Hello, child," through his teeth as he launched himself towards Joshua.

There was a loud sound as Bowen hit his intended target and spun around. I focused my eyes just as Joshua heaved Bowen into the opposite wall. Bowen flashed back at him, grabbing Joshua by the throat, pinning him to the wall. I pushed myself up using the wall behind me and desperately looked around for something I could use to help. They tumbled to the floor, their movements too fast for me to see everything. I felt like the stupid girl in horror movies who stands there doing nothing, only without the screaming and the mini-skirt.

I couldn't tell who was winning. I felt helpless. *Think! Think!* I chastised myself. Bowen tossed Josh onto my desk, and the stack of books I had pushed to one side crashed loudly to the floor. Pain seized Josh's features. He grappled with Bowen and was launched across the room again.

Bowen was about to spring at him, but he stopped short and a guttural sound emanated from deep inside his chest. His eyes locked on my bedroom door. In the next moment, he escaped out the window, and Gabriel burst into the room.

I slid back down the wall, sat on the floor, and started to hyperventilate. I put my head between my knees, trying to gain control of myself. My eyes welled up with tears. Joshua was immediately at my side.

"Are you hurt?" he asked, his voice urgent while taking inventory of my wounds.

I just looked at him, unable to gather words together.

"Are you hurt?" he repeated, then wrapped his arms around me to help me up. I tensed and moaned in pain. He jerked back as I clutched my right side.

"I think he broke a rib," I gasped, the roar of pain turning to a throb when I sat still.

"I am so sorry. We shouldn't have left you unguarded. We were tracking him. The moment we lost him, I rushed back." He shook his head. "We thought we had him. I don't understand how he got here so quickly. I'll never forgive myself."

"I'll be fine. You don't need to be dramatic about it." I paused. "But don't go too far away again, okay?"

He let out a single hard laugh. "Deal."

Gabriel was looking out the window from which Bowen had escaped, scowling out into the night. Gabriel looked at us. "No sign of him."

I looked at Gabriel. "I don't understand why he ran like that. I thought Bowen was powerful."

Gabriel smiled ominously.

Josh interjected, "Bowen doesn't like it when the odds are against him. Yes, he can easily best me alone, but not with Gabriel here."

I was confused. "I thought you were human?" I looked at Gabriel inquisitively.

"I am...mostly."

"Ali, he's not a Watcher; he works with them. He's a Slayer —still human but vastly more powerful."

I laughed. "I thought Slayers were supposed to be helpless-looking girls to lure in the vamps."

He shrugged. "Some are."

"So you aren't the only one?"

"No, there are quite a few of us." He grinned.

I was about to respond, but winced when I took in a deep breath.

"We should get you downstairs and have Sebastian look at you."

Josh started to pick me up, but I refused his help. "I can walk; it's a rib, not my legs."

"Stubborn as always," he breathed as he helped me up.

As we descended the stairs, I kept hold of his arm to keep my torso steady. I sat on the kitchen table and rolled up the bottom of my tank top. There was a red welt over the offending rib, and I could smell the sweat and fragrance of my soap on my skin. I flinched as Sebastian probed the area with his fingers.

"It isn't too bad," he assessed. He looked at my arm and

under my chin. Bruises were starting to show a little color where Phineas had dug his fingers into me. My fair skin had always marked up at record speed. "These happened hours ago," he observed, indicating the oncoming finger bruises.

"Oh, umm, we were goofing around at the beach," I replied, but my voice came out a little shaky. I didn't want to cover for Phineas; frankly, he scared me. But I didn't want to make tensions any higher between Josh and the other Watchers. I hoped that Josh would be objective, but I let the thought go. It was Gabriel who seemed to notice my hesitance. I could see that Josh was too distracted to notice, probably beating himself up about Bowen getting into the house.

So yet again, I was in Bowen's clutches, and the three of them rushed in to save me. I realized this and chuckled. They all looked at me.

"What?" Gabriel asked.

I shook my head and replied, "Nothing."

Josh raised his right eyebrow at me.

"It's stupid." I sighed and felt even more embarrassed. "*Gabriel* and Joshua *Michael* Copeland…my guardian angels."

Gabriel smirked, and Joshua's face became even paler.

Almost under his breath, he murmured, "I am not an angel," as he closed his eyes in lament. "I—"

Sebastian interrupted, "You are an angel in this situation."

Josh scoffed, "I am cursed—in no way can I be an angel."

Sebastian turned pensive for a moment. His voice changed, as if quoting something:

"*Every Angel is terrifying*

Regardless, beware for I will serenade these
almost dead birds of the soul
and knowing all around you...

Where the brightest one stood in the plainest
door,
somewhat disguised in travel clothes and now
less terrible...

Would the most dangerous archangel himself
now,
step out from behind the stars and walk
towards us our own heart would slay us!"

He paused for a long moment. The room was silent, save my labored breath. "Angels are many things. They are wonderful, beautiful creatures, but they are also terrifying and terrible. Remember that God sent them to destroy as well as protect. How frightening to meet one." He paused again, Josh still as stone, not breathing. "Joshua, you are an angel. I know you are angry about many things, but have faith."

The room remained quiet as Sebastian taped up my ribcage and gave me some painkillers.

I finally whispered to Sebastian, "What were you quoting a little while ago?"

"It's from 'Second Elegy,' a poem by Rilke."

"Mmmm. I like him. I've never read that one."

"Aleria," he said, his look stern. "Do you know how Bowen infiltrated your home?"

Both Gabriel and Joshua looked at me, waiting for my

answer. I relayed all the information about my friend inviting him in, as well as his plans to finish turning me. All three of them winced. The painkillers started making me fuzzy as they eased the throbbing and chased away the last vestiges of the adrenaline rush. I felt overcome with the tiredness I had felt earlier, my limbs heavy.

They continued to talk and strategize, but I couldn't focus. Joshua, lost in thought, staring out the back door, seemed oblivious to the conversation.

I started to head upstairs, but paused, debating. "I don't think this means anything. I mean, this is probably stupid, but the way he said it…" I got embarrassed. "Never mind." I closed my eyes and climbed the bottom steps.

Sebastian said, "Aleria, nothing is inconsequential when it comes to Bowen. What did he say, child?"

I shivered. I thought about his pulling my body against his, kissing my neck and whispering in my ear. I felt violated again.

"He said he would make me a princess if I asked. If I came willingly."

Sebastian and Gabriel locked eyes, and the Slayer's nostrils flared. Instantaneously it seemed, as if by an act of will, both of them smoothed their features. I pretended not to notice, partly because I was too tired to care, and continued up the flight of too-steep stairs without another word. I entered the great room, but couldn't shake the feeling of being watched, so I shut the blinds and eased onto the couch, holding my ribs. I clicked on the television; it hummed and projected cool colors in the dark room.

I kept drifting off to sleep for brief moments, but my body

would convulse. I would start awake again and again, like when you fall asleep, sitting up in a public venue, and your head bobs and jars you awake, only to do it again and again. It made me unsettled.

Each time I dozed, I would go to the same place. I dreamt that I was standing before a panel of men. The light was behind them, so their figures were shrouded silhouettes. They were important somehow. I needed them to like me, but I couldn't remember why. Whatever was decided was going to change everything.

REFLECTIONS

Giving up on sleep, I rubbed my eyes and suddenly remembered the package Joshua had left me. I stood, clasping my torso, and walked to my room. I pulled the package from beneath my pillow and opened the manila envelope as I returned to the couch and eased down. Slowly, I pulled out the contents. The enclosed note was in Joshua's handwriting, and tied with twine to a worn leather journal.

Als—

I never want you to think that you were not on my mind during the last two years. I was struggling, and Gabriel feared the worst, that I would lose my humanity. One time, he caught me checking my e-mail in the middle of the night. He was angry with me for violating the rules, but then he reconsidered. He thought that keeping some connection with my past might help keep me grounded.

The abbreviated version is that he printed your e-mails for me (don't worry, he never read them), but I was not allowed to contact you. It wouldn't have been safe—or fair. It tore me apart not being able to answer you, especially when you were hurting. I wrote the responses I was never able to send in here. These were written to you, so it seemed appropriate that you should have them. I realize you were probably more candid since you thought I wasn't reading them, but then again, I never thought you would read my responses either.

Yours—Joshua

I opened the cover, and there were my e-mails neatly taped inside with a reply written in his hand. I flipped through the pages and came to one dated two months after he had stopped returning my emails.

JOSH,

HEY, I HAVEN'T HEARD FROM YOU IN A WHILE. IT MAKES ME WORRY THAT SOMETHING HAPPENED. OR MAYBE YOU'RE JUST TOO BUSY WITH YOUR EXCITING COLLEGE LIFE. IF YOU HAVE AS MANY FRIENDS OUT THERE AS YOU HAD HERE, THEN YOU MUST BE BUSY ALL THE TIME.

THIS MORNING I GOT TO SCHOOL LATE AND HAD TO PARK IN THE LOT A MILLION MILES AWAY. ON MY WAY TO THE CAR AFTER CLASSES, I WALKED BY THE SOCCER FIELD. IT MADE ME MISS YOU —ALL THOSE HOURS I SAT DOING HOMEWORK IN THE STANDS WHILE YOU PRACTICED, AND I WAITED FOR YOU TO GIVE ME A

RIDE. I MISS OUR TALKS IN THE CAR AND THE STOPS FOR FROZEN YOGURT ON THE WAY HOME.

I DON'T TALK TO OTHER PEOPLE LIKE I TALKED WITH YOU. MAYBE I SHOULD BE EMBARRASSED THAT I TOLD YOU EVERYTHING. NO FILTER. DON'T WORRY; I'VE DEVELOPED ONE SINCE. ;0) PLEASE, PLEASE WRITE.

XOXO, ALI

Als—

You are worried something happened to me. I guess that would be an understatement. If you knew what I've become, I doubt you would continue to write. Part of me wishes I could tell you, and the other part thinks that would be the worst thing in the world.

The guys used to tease me that you were out there during practice every day. I personally liked it. Somehow you managed to catch everything that happened in practice and keep your head in a book. But you've always been better at multi-tasking than me. I'd forgotten about the frozen yogurt—you would always make those gross combinations that you called "culinary adventures." Not sure culinary and frozen yogurt should actually go in the same sentence.

With all my heart, I wish we could sit in the car in front of my house and talk. I liked that you told me everything. Of course, you would be mortified if you knew I actually acted on some of it. I will now admit that the junior boy (what was his name?) that harassed you didn't exactly stop on his own. I may have cornered him in the locker room, grabbed him by the collar, and told him that if he ever acted inappropriately towards you again, he would have to answer to me. I know you are tough and can handle yourself, but I had to look out for the people I care about.

And, I knew your filter would kick in at some point.
I wish I could send this. I miss you too.
JMC

I skipped over what must've been a hundred pages and came to an entry from the following summer. It had been a few months shy of a year since I'd heard from him.

AUGUST 11

JOSHUA,

NANA DIED TODAY. I FEEL HER LOSS MORE THAN I THOUGHT I WOULD. I KNEW IT WAS INEVITABLE. SHE DID JUST HAVE HER 100TH BIRTHDAY, BUT WE HAD SUCH A UNIQUE CONNECTION. I THINK SHE FELT THAT WAY TOO—SHE ALWAYS SPENT MORE TIME WITH ME THAN THE REST OF HER GREAT-GRANDCHILDREN. OR MAYBE THAT WAS BECAUSE I WAS THE ONLY GIRL.

I REMEMBER THAT SHE LIKED YOU. I'VE BEEN THINKING ABOUT THE ROAD TRIP BOTH OUR FAMILIES TOOK TOGETHER UP TO OREGON. DO YOU REMEMBER STAYING AT THAT HUGE HOUSE SHE HAD? IT SEEMED SO FAR AWAY FROM CIVILIZATION. I DON'T KNOW WHAT BROUGHT THIS TO MIND, BUT I WAS THINKING ABOUT THE WALKS SHE MADE YOU GO ON. OR MAYBE SHE DIDN'T *MAKE* YOU; YOU ARE PRETTY AWESOME THAT WAY. DID YOU KNOW THAT I WATCHED BOTH OF YOU FROM THE UPSTAIRS WINDOW? I ALWAYS WONDERED WHAT YOU TALKED ABOUT AS YOU STROLLED, ARMS LINKED, THROUGH HER EXTENSIVE GARDENS. WAS SHE FLIRTING WITH YOU? HA HA, I KNOW I AM HILARIOUS. THOUGH, I WOULD LOVE TO KNOW WHAT SHE SAID

TO YOU THE LAST DAY WE WERE THERE. YOU SEEMED A LITTLE SHAKEN.

WE WILL BE HEADING UP NEXT WEEK. SHE ASKED THAT WE SPREAD HER ASHES ON THE RIVER AT SUNSET AND SEND THEM OFF WITH FLOWERS CUT FROM HER GARDEN. IT SEEMS SORT OF POETIC.

I MISS YOU AND I WISH WE COULD TAKE ONE OF THOSE LONG WALKS IN THE GARDEN TOGETHER.

HUGS,

A

Als—

I am truly, truly sorry for your loss. Your great-grandma was probably one of the most interesting people I have ever met. No, she never made me go on those walks with her. She asked me the first day to "take a turn in the garden," and it became our habit. I felt a little like I was in one of those Victorian novels you love to read.

No, I never did tell you what she said. I always felt like she was seeing into my soul when she looked at me. She had those same eyes you do. She told me many things, but on that last day, there was a strange kind of urgency. She told me that I would experience great loss, but not to lose heart. That death can be seen as a new beginning. That great good could come from darkness.

She said that I needed to look out for you—that you were special. That sometimes family is chosen and it doesn't make them any less your family. She continued on the subject for a little while. Everything she said felt so real. But it couldn't be true. I will never be able to see you again and with that knowledge comes great sorrow. I know logically it is for the best (but my head and heart war with one another sometimes). I wish I could be there for you.

JMC

I flipped through more pages and stopped at one particular entry, the content of which made me feel a little queasy. I felt embarrassed knowing he had read it.

APRIL 28

JOSH,

GUYS. I DON'T UNDERSTAND SOMETIMES. THINGS ARE CHANGING WITH ROBERT, AND I DON'T KNOW WHAT TO DO. I WISH I COULD TALK TO YOU. YOU HAVE ALWAYS BEEN ABLE TO SEE THINGS I CAN'T. I'M GOING TO HAVE TO MAKE A DECISION SOON. I CAN'T PUT HIM OFF FOREVER.

I KNOW YOU WON'T ANSWER THIS, BUT...I DON'T KNOW. I CAN'T TALK TO MY PARENTS—OBVIOUSLY. AND MY GIRLFRIENDS WOULD HATE HIM FOR PUTTING PRESSURE ON ME.

WHY CAN'T THINGS JUST STAY THE SAME SOMETIMES?

I MISS YOU.

A

I noticed that the pen pressure in the next entry was really hard.

Ali—

If you are talking about what I think you are, I would give anything to be there and talk you out of it. You are too good for him. He doesn't respect you. He can't, if he is asking you to do something that you are not comfortable with (or is against your beliefs). He needs to back off. But honestly, guys are pigs. I am one, I know. Please wait until it is right. If I was there, I would kick his ass for even thinking about it.

JMC

MAY 3

JOSHUA,

IT SEEMS I HAVE ANOTHER DECISION TO MAKE. I HATE THIS. I'M NOT EXACTLY AFRAID OF PAIN, BUT I DON'T REALLY LIKE TO WALK HEADLONG INTO IT. I NEED ONE OF OUR TRIPS TO CAPITOLA. I HAVE THE DESIRE TO THROW HEAVY OBJECTS INTO THE OCEAN AND SCREAM. AND YOU COULD DO YOUR PART... WHICH, AS I RECALL, WAS MAKING FUN OF ME. AS I TOLD YOU LAST TIME, IT MAKES YOU FEEL BETTER. IT'S NOT INFANTILE AT ALL.

WHY IS IT THAT I CAN BE SURROUNDED BY PEOPLE...PEOPLE WHO CARE ABOUT ME AND I CAN FEEL COMPLETELY ALONE?

SO, SO ALONE.

I'LL BE FINE. I'M JUST WHINING. YOU KNOW ME, THE PUBLIC WILL NEVER KNOW THE INNER TORMENT. ;O) BUT HEARING FROM YOU WOULD BE GOOD. I DO WONDER WHY NONE OF THESE BOUNCE BACK.

LOVE AND KICKS TO THE SHIN,

A

. . .

Als—

I know how you feel. I too feel very, very alone. You have my permission to kick me in both shins—hard. I deserve it.

Man, I miss you,

JMC

And then there was a response to the e-mail I had sent just a couple of weeks ago. I realized it was actually the day I'd met Bowen. I had written it right before heading to the coffee shop.

Als—

Dull and unworthy. Yes, I do believe that is what I said—among other things. It pained me to see you with him. He wasn't a bad person—but he was NOT worthy of you. My protective instincts were definitely in overdrive. I'm glad you dumped him; I just hope you didn't do anything you regret.

You are strong and one of the most amazing people I have ever met. It kills me that I cannot be there for you. I know you well enough to know that you won't admit it to anyone if you are struggling—too busy not wanting people to worry about you. Stay strong and hold out for the right guy. There are a few out there. I just wish I could be there to give my approval—or run them off.

Love you too,

JMC

. . .

That was it...the last entry. I felt warmth run over and through me. Without being there, he had known everything of significance that had happened to me in the last two years. Then it occurred to me that when he wrote this, it must've been when he realized that the picture he had kept was missing. I had written him a few more times, but they weren't here. I felt sick to my stomach. And overwhelmed with conflicting emotion; I couldn't put a name on it.

As the television droned quietly in the background, I went back and started reading all the journals I had skipped through. After an hour or so, Josh sat on the couch next to me.

I was so sleepy, my voice was slurred with an excess of air. "Is everything okay?" I forced out as I handed him the remote and leaned onto his shoulder, keeping the journal on my lap. He felt cool and nice after all the sun from the day.

"Yes, nothing to worry about," he replied.

I didn't believe him completely, but I let it go. I was too distracted by everything I'd just read.

He looked down and tapped the journal with his index finger. "You read them?"

Swallowing to clear the lump in my throat, I answered, "Yes, most of them. Thank you." I paused. "It means a lot." I felt bombarded with emotions, but only one was clear to me. *I love you* rang out above all the others, but I couldn't say it.

I thought about how he'd signed the note he'd left with the journal: "*Yours, Joshua.*" It was a simple closing, but somehow that felt more personal than "*Love, Joshua.*" I came back to the present, and tried to speak again. *Why was I so jumbled?* "I can't believe you answered all of them," I whispered.

His brows knitted together. "If Gabriel hadn't trimmed off the IP address from the emails you sent me, *he* could've found you before I'd realized you were in danger."

"Well, it didn't. And you are stepping on my moment," I scowled.

"And *you* are exhausted. We don't need to speak about any of this now."

"Mmmmm." I wanted to talk more, to ask questions, but I could hardly move. He put a throw pillow on his lap and pulled me off his shoulder and onto the pillow. It felt good to stretch out. He gently rubbed my arm as I drifted off to sleep, my dreams awaiting me.

13

CONFESSIONS

I awoke disoriented, not knowing where I was. I wasn't in my room. I squinted and peered at the room through a sleepy fog. I realized it was still the middle of the night, and I was on the couch with Josh. I focused on the clock, the hands marking 3:00 A.M.

He was asleep, his head leaned back and his breathing even. I wondered how long he'd gone without rest. The circles under his eyes had grown more prominent the last few days. He must've been exhausted to sleep during the night.

I kept still so I could watch him sleep. He looked so... unfettered. The only light in the room was from the flickering television—blue shadows danced across his face. I wanted to run my fingers over his cheek, to memorize it with my hands, but I controlled the urge.

He stirred and furrowed his brow. I wondered if vampires dreamed. He opened his eyes and looked down at me, a faint smile stretching over his features, his eyes warm. I had another impulse to touch him, so I sat up in an effort to control myself, and then winced from a sharp pain in my side. It was definitely a little worse.

He reached towards me, helpless, let his hands fall, and gave me a concerned smile. "How's the rib?" he asked.

"I think I'll live. I'm tough; don't worry about me." I flexed my bicep.

"I know you're tough. I just wish you didn't have to be."

"Yeah, but then life would be boring."

He waved his hands in faux horror. "No, anything but boring!"

I noticed the house was eerily quiet. "Where are Sebastian and Gabriel?"

"They went to set up a safe house nearby. We are going to have some visitors. It seems…" He halted for a long moment. I held my breath, feeling anxious. "It seems that our situation here is much bigger than we initially thought. That Bowen is someone of importance in the vampire world. Council members from both sides will be convening here. And they may want to speak with you." He examined my face and studied my reaction.

"Oh," was all I said, and at that moment, I remembered my interrupted series of dreams from earlier in the evening. It seemed like weeks ago I had had them, not hours. My dreams, I mused for a moment, were different since *he* had bitten me. Not just more intense; something had changed. Josh touched my hand and snapped me back to reality.

"You're a million miles away. What is it?"

I rubbed my sleepy eyes and sighed, careful to keep my

breath shallow and not aggravate my injury. He waited with growing apprehension.

"I keep dreaming things, and some of it is true." I got frustrated with my inability to articulate my thoughts. "I have always had dreams that give me insights into things. Like, my subconscious works away at night, giving me clarity about a situation or a person. But lately, they've been more. It's like I'm seeing things coming. Not seeing the future or anything. But kind of—in a way. I don't know." I felt stupid, and I couldn't shake the fog in my brain. There were important things I couldn't remember. Dreams I had been forgetting, things I should have known.

"That makes sense…" He trailed off.

"What makes sense?" I asked when he didn't continue.

"Well, he bit you. People often experience heightened senses after being exposed to the virus, even if it isn't activated. It preps your body for the catalyst, so it makes sense that you feel different. Any talents you have could be intensified slightly without being fully realized."

I shuddered.

"You still didn't tell me what you were thinking about," he pressed.

"I dreamed I was standing before seven men last night and that whatever they decided was going to change everything."

He looked at me, his eyes wide. "Each council is sending people to meet with Sebastian. Three from the Council and three from the Conclave; it's the first time both sides of the Concilium have met peaceably in thirty years. Do you remember anything else?"

"Just that I felt it was really important that they like me.

But the harder I try to remember anything else, the more it slips away. That's how most of these dreams are. I get one bit of information, and that's all I can hang on to. There is a mountain there, and I end up grasping at pebbles. It's frustrating. And…" I paused, not sure if I should have said anything else. "What scares me is if any parts of the nightmares…" I couldn't finish. Too many dreams of being locked in Bowen's iron embrace, Joshua being pulled away by an unseen presence, and my being left in darkness. I realized I was holding my breath again.

"Not all dreams mean something," he reassured me. "The nightmares aren't necessarily going to come true."

"Geez, can you read my mind or something?"

"Nope. But I can read your face, Ali. I've known you since you were two, remember?"

"Then why do I feel like I should get my affairs in order? That impending doom is waiting to crash down on me like a helpless child sitting on the beach, making a sandcastle while a tidal wave looms above."

"Hyperbole much?"

"Ugh. You know what I mean. Everything is *now*, isn't it? There may be no future."

"I'm not going to lie to you, mostly because you know me too well to fool you. Things are not good. There are more than council members headed this way. I didn't want to scare you. They were prompted to come for two reasons: the report from Sebastian, and major movement in the French coven, vampires believed to be deceased. They have left their sanctuary and are heading to San Francisco. It's too much of a coincidence—"

"That's Bowen's coven, isn't it."

"He has managed to keep his origins a secret with his changes of identity. We thought that maybe he was a rogue, but he was too well connected. The Watchers have been tracking him for hundreds of years. They actually thought he was two different immortals, though they still aren't completely sure. He has made a few slips in the last few weeks. Sebastian ran down a couple of leads after the princess comment he made to you. It looks like he actually is a prince. The son of King Solomon's pagan queen. Sebastian has all the pieces. The vampires want him to return to France, and the Concilium is divided."

"And somehow we are caught in the middle. I suppose the other vampires won't just take him and go home, will they?"

"We don't know. We have never seen so many actually leave the country at once. They may, or—"

"Please stop. Sorry, I'm not trying to be rude. I don't want to hear anymore. Please." I stood up abruptly, ignoring the spike in pain, and walked a few steps away.

"Are you all right?" His voice softened and he rose from his seat to follow me.

"I don't know."

Josh was obviously reading my expression; he hesitated and touched my chin, tilting my face up and forcing me to look at him. His face was composed, but I knew the look; he was trying to cover up his conflict, busying himself with details so he didn't have to think about anything but the task at hand.

With sincerity, he encouraged, "You don't need to worry.

There will be a veritable army of good guys in town by tomorrow."

"Gee that's comforting. Half the 'good guys' want you dead and think I know too much." I wanted to look away, but he kept his hand on my chin.

My heart started thundering in my chest, filling my ears with each beat. I wondered if Joshua could hear its increase in tempo and see the perspiration gather on my temples. My palms were sweating. He stood with a foot between us, holding my chin and looking into my desperate eyes.

My breath hitched in my chest. I wanted to stand on my tiptoes and press my lips against his. To run my fingers through his thick hair. To feel his cool body press against my feverishly hot one. I wanted him to tell me that everything would be all right, and I wanted it to be true. I wanted him to love me like I loved him. I wanted him not to think of me as a little sister but as something else. I wanted to run from the room. I wanted to disappear completely, avoiding everything. Part of me wanted it all to end now. Then I realized everything would be different after the next two days. I would be out of time.

"There is something else you are worried about."

"No," I lied. "Tidal wave, remember?" I curled my arms above my head in a mock wave.

"That's not it." *Why is he doing this to me?*

I wanted to say, "I love you"—to scream it—but instead I blurted out, "As soon as this is over, you are going to disappear, aren't you?"

He released my chin and sucked in a sharp breath like I

had slapped him and didn't say anything. The pleasant look on his face melted into pain.

"I'll take that as a yes." I could feel moisture gathering in my eyes. I quickly blinked, keeping the tears from tumbling down my cheeks.

He sighed. "I just don't see any other way. I'm sorry. I can't help what I am. I need to do the right thing."

"But what if that isn't the right thing?"

"How could it not be?" His voice cracked, "Ali, I'm a monster. An experiment, barely clinging to my soul—if I even have one. I have spent my whole life doing the right thing. The one time I did something mildly stupid, where did it get me? I'm a freaking vampire! I can do nothing but put you in danger. Besides, I am under very strict orders from the Council." He turned his back to me.

"You are not a monster. *Never* ever say that again," I commanded as I walked around to face him.

He rolled his eyes at me.

I felt uncomfortable, exposed, and…out of time. I needed to tell him. I wrestled with the thought. The urgency of it made me feel like energy was pulsing out of my body. I decided to press forward. I took both his hands in mine, but he wouldn't make eye contact with me.

I took in a deep breath.

"I need to tell you something," I said, my voice hoarse and soft. I was working up to it. There was a dull ache in my stomach, and I couldn't feel my feet.

He looked at me expectantly and gave my hands a little squeeze. His hands were so cold and firm. "Okay," he prodded.

I paused for a long moment, and almost lost my nerve. "I love you," I said.

"I know, I love you too." He looked confused.

I shook my head, and felt more nervous now that my meaning had escaped him. Slowly emphasizing the words like I was talking to a preschooler, I repeated, "No, I... *love...*you," letting each word sink in. He sucked in another breath and held it.

"No," he whispered in a strange, strained voice, breaking eye contact.

No? I didn't know if I could survive the blow. The emotion was thick in the dimly lit room. He let out the breath he was holding, and his breathing became uneven and his face more pained.

I didn't know how to interpret the silence. I felt embarrassed. My face burned. I searched his face and started to lose hope, as he still wouldn't meet my gaze. I could feel my emotions start to spiral, and all I wanted to do was run from the room.

It took everything I had to keep my feet firmly planted and hold onto his hands. How stupid could I be? I'd not only fallen in love with someone who would always see me as a kid, but I had also fallen in love with a vampire. On the list of things not to do, this must be near the top. *Stupid, stupid, silly girl*, I berated myself. Somehow, my hopelessness turned and gave me strength.

I repeated myself with more force. "I love you."

"No," he repeated almost angrily, sucking in yet another breath.

"I love you," I said again, as he ripped his hands out of

mine and sank to his knees. I felt a stab of rejection and tears ready to plummet down my face.

"No." But his voice broke this time.

"I love you." I sank to my knees in front of him.

"No," he whispered almost inaudibly.

I sighed, "I just needed you to know…I…If you don't feel…I…" My voice cracked this time, and I couldn't finish. I gathered my strength to run from the room—unwanted.

He took my hand. My breath spilled out involuntarily. I could feel the rejection coming. This was going to be bad. *Really bad.*

My stomach twisted into knots, but he didn't pull away. He raised his other hand and delicately touched his fingertips to my temple and ran them down to my cheekbone. He paused. I could feel his eyes on my face, but I was afraid to look up.

I stared at the two perfectly round scars at the base of his neck. I wished he would get it over with and let me leave. Then he raised his other hand and gently cupped my face. His cool hands raised goose bumps on the back of my neck as I took in an uneven breath. I finally looked into his eyes, searching them. His face was full of conflict.

My heart started to beat faster. The next words out of his mouth were going to be "I'm sorry." I could feel it. *Where are the attacking vampires when you need them?*

I forced myself to take a breath. He was going to say goodbye, and I would lose him forever. It would be too awkward for him to stay. I shouldn't have said anything. He didn't feel anything more than obligation. He simply felt guilty for putting me in danger.

And then he did the last thing I expected. He nodded, not breaking my desperate stare, leaned forward and gently touched his lips to mine. After a long moment, he pulled back and tenderly ran his right hand through my hair and cradled the back of my head.

He smiled slightly and pressed his lips to mine again, this time not so tentatively. My lips parted a little, and I returned the kiss, wrapping my arms around his waist and pulling him closer. The feeling of absolute joy washed recklessly over me, each kiss giving me hope, our breath ragged.

He stopped kissing me, but didn't let go. He embraced me, pulling me so close to him, my rib started to ache, but I really didn't care. My heart was still thudding against my ribcage, shaking my entire body. I never wanted to move.

"I love you, too," he whispered in my ear and then kissed me again in the hollow under my cheekbone, his warm breath caressing my face. "I wish this was a different time...a different place...a different situation. I never intended for any of this to touch you."

"Then I can be your—unintended." I put my fingers over his lips. "No regrets, no guilt." He opened his mouth to object. "As stupid as this sounds, I am not upset that any of this has happened." We stayed there on our knees, foreheads pressed together and arms locked around one another's waists, listening to our breathing.

The moment was so perfect, I tried not to worry, but there were reasons why vampires and humans didn't have relationships. I almost chuckled to myself. *Charmed or cursed? The same place I always seem to end up.*

I finally whispered, "This just got more complicated, didn't it?"

He sighed, "Yes, I think it did."

"And we shouldn't let anyone know."

"Now, who is reading minds?" he chuckled.

"I have known you since you were six, you know."

"I think keeping it under wraps in the immediate future might be wise." He kissed my forehead and helped me to my feet.

My eyes danced with mischief as I asked, "Since we have a clandestine operation going on, maybe we should think of cool secret agent names?"

"Yeah, I'll be Romeo," he said lamely.

"Cause that's not obvious...and horrible since they both *die* because they are both stupid and impetuous."

"Petruchio?"

"So, I'm a shrew that needs to be broken?"

He raised his eyebrow, and I pushed him playfully. "Ferdinand from *Tempest?*"

"I like it. Less obvious...true love...even though it was love at first sight, there was a happily ever after."

"We could use a happily ever after. And..." he became thoughtful, "in a way, it was love at first sight for me."

"You fell in love with me when I was two, didn't you? Admit it." I laughed.

"No. I admit I was intrigued by the cretin that moved in across the street." He mussed my hair. "But I did see you as a kid. I guess I should say love at second sight, the moment I saw you last week." His face was strained, and I shivered from the memory.

"When I saw you unconscious in that apartment, everything changed that moment. For a second, I thought you were dead, that he had killed you, and then I thought he..." His voice cracked, and he changed what he was going to say. "Gabriel slammed me into the wall so hard to get me under control, a section of the wall buckled. I don't know if I can explain it..." He paused for a moment.

"Suddenly you weren't the kid I left behind. You were all grown up—transcendent. In that instant, *you were my world*. I was desperate to act normal around you."

I grinned, and he held up his finger.

"Let me qualify that: normal as I could act, being a vampire instead of the boy with whom you grew up. It was all I could do not to touch you more than I would normally. Being away from you during the day was torture." His tone turned grave. "But at the same time, I prayed you would remain uninterested, that you would only think of me as you did before. I don't know where this could possibly lead."

"Well, Ferdinand, I plan on having my happily ever after."

"Then we will make it so, my always optimistic Miranda."

He encircled me with his arms.

I held onto my happiness, though I knew it could end in two days' time.

14

NO GOOD REASON

I woke for the second time that day in my room. Joshua must have carried me in there. The last thing I remembered was sitting on the couch with his arm around me. We talked, and as we did, he would kiss the top of my head. I, in turn, would twist our laced fingers up to my mouth and kiss the back of his hand. It felt so natural, loving him. I just hoped I could conceal my adoration enough in public. I felt like something good had broken free inside me, something that I'd never experienced before.

I hugged my pillow, not wanting to think about complications or calamity. I wanted to run away with my prince and live happily ever after. I tried to stay in my happy place, a land of sunbathed daydreams where monsters and responsibilities took a vacation.

While holding my ribcage, I rolled onto my back and heard the crinkle of paper beneath my head. I freed it from under me and ran my eyes over Josh's tidy, but obviously male, handwriting:

> I pray you slept well. I will be back before
> dark with Gabriel. Be happy. Be safe.
>
> – Ferdinand

Smiling at the unspoken, "I love you," I felt almost giddy and was completely unable to stop smiling. I could've been easily convinced that it was all a dream. I decided to take care of my responsibilities. After all the necessary cleaning, I called my parents and even spoke to my grandmother.

I had an intense craving for a Monte Cristo sandwich, so I group texted the girls to see if anyone was interested in meeting me at Casper's for lunch. While waiting for replies, I found I was almost dancing through the house with what my friends called the "goofy grin," the stupid smile of newfound love, that no matter how hard you try, it continues to creep back onto your face. It worried me a little, being unable to conceal my joy, but I couldn't stop smiling. *Better to get it out of my system now.*

Marie and Breanna returned my text and promised to meet me at noon. I was grateful for the distraction. Sunset was going to be around 8:30 P.M. again, so I had a long day ahead of me, and I was already worrying about the Council meeting tomorrow night.

I needed more distractions, so I decided to find my summer reading list for AP English. There were three works: *Hamlet, Cyrano De Bergerac,* and *Walden.* I had the Shakespeare, so I scrawled the other two titles onto a scrap of paper and shoved it into the pocket of my jeans. A trip to the bookstore would burn some time.

After circling through the house a few times, thinking I'd forgotten something, I headed outside. Once out the door, the sunlight on my face felt especially good, and it stopped me in my tracks. The smell of the neighbor's mandarin orange tree wafted over in the warm breeze. I closed my eyes and raised my face towards the sun, feeling the freedom of summer. The crimson glow through my eyelids was quieting. I was glad to leave the darkness and stale air of the house behind.

I opened my eyes and strolled towards my Mustang with the familiar jingle of keys looped on my finger. Everything seemed so simple in daylight. Maybe it was the fact that I had gone an entire night without waking in terror. This fact reminded me of the nightmares, and I felt the hair on the back of my neck rise as images of blood and pain flickered across my vision.

After sliding into the car, I stuck the keys into the ignition and forced myself back to the present enough to focus on driving. A short while later, I pulled into the mall. Time seemed distorted and slow, the details magnified.

The afternoon heat was rising off the blacktop in intense waves, so I quickened my pace. Sweat was beading between my shoulder blades, the slap of each footstep heavy on the asphalt. As I passed through the hefty glass doors, a burst of clean, cool air from the bookstore revived me.

I couldn't resist the pull of the coffee shop, so I opted to start with coffee and then go shopping. Java in hand, I ran my finger over the volumes of books as I walked parallel to the shelves. *Walden* and *Cyrano* were easily found. I still had some time, so I lounged in a chair tucked in the corner by the window until I needed to go.

After reading a few pages of *Walden*, I glanced at the bookshelf next to me and noticed I was in the mythology section. My eyes drifted across the titles at eye level and halted on one: *Celtic Mythology.* Hadn't Gabriel said Solomon's cursed wife was Celtic?

I picked up the beautifully illustrated book and flipped through the pages, looking over a list of Celtic deities. I perused the female list, trying to remember the queen's name, though I wondered if I should instead be looking in a history book since she was a real person.

"Abnoba, a goddess of river and forests/ Adsulltata/ Aericura/ Agrona, a goddess of war…" *That was her name: Queen Agrona.* I swallowed hard at "the goddess of war" description/title. There wasn't much about her in the book beyond the meaning of her name, literally translated as "carnage." I pondered that for a moment. She was real, yet had somehow managed to become a myth, a deity. Was that how she had survived for so many years? I wondered how many other "gods" were real, too.

There seemed to be gods for everything. "Male—Abellio, god of apple trees." I giggled. "Arausio, god of water/ Belenus, a sun god 'shining one' of heat and healing/ Camulos, a god of war…" I checked the time and saw that I needed to go. I shelved the book since it was out of my budget, purchased what I needed, and headed out into the afternoon heat.

I arrived at the restaurant with one minute to spare, feeling a little smug about my time management skills. I glanced around the lot as I pulled into a space, searching for Marie or Breanna's cars. As expected, Breanna was here and Marie's wasn't. Marie was always late, and, of course, we always harassed her about it.

Bree was lounging on one of the stone benches in front. Pinpoints of light danced on her as it filtered through a potted tree arched above her. When she spotted me, she winked and opened her mouth to say something. I cut her off.

"Let me guess—Marie texted; she just left the house."

"You are soooo smart."

"It's a gift," I bragged, polishing my knuckles on my shoulder.

"Now, if you could just foresee the winning lottery numbers."

"You aren't old enough to buy a ticket."

"But you are," she argued.

"But that implies I would share."

"We would just guilt you into it."

"Impossible." I widened my eyes.

"Oh, I know all of your secrets, dahling. I would find your soft spot and push."

"That is low…even for you."

She shrugged. "I do what's necessary."

"You are diabolical."

Breanna laughed in a Disney character mu-ah-ha-ha sort of way just as Marie walked up.

"Sorry guys!" She made a sort of cringing smile as she bounded up to us, her wavy blonde hair bouncing behind her.

"No worries." I smiled.

"Let's go. I'm starved," Breanna said.

Breanna led the way, and I trailed into the restaurant last. It seemed dim inside after being in the bright afternoon light. It was a classy, sports-themed eatery with an abundance of addicting food. Old-fashioned plaster walls were embellished with rich woodwork, and the modern twist of flat screen televisions artfully hung amongst the sports memorabilia.

Marie spun around to face me, grabbing my elbow with a huge grin on her face. She took a breath and smoothed herself out. I was confused until I peered over her shoulder. Peter was sitting across the restaurant, having lunch with his mother. She was chatting away in a bubbly manner with her son. He was nodding his head at the appropriate intervals; however, he was surreptitiously watching the SF Giants baseball game over her shoulder. *Sneaky boy.* He was a die-hard fan of the team, even when they were the underdogs.

I hadn't realized that Marie had so much of an attachment to Peter. Maybe she had always liked him a little, but the day at the beach must have tipped the scales. I was probably right in cringing at that peck on the cheek when I was dropped off. Now that seemed like an even more awkward moment, given his relationship with my ex and Marie's getting-more-serious-all-the-time crush.

The hostess seated us several tables away from Peter and his mom. I allowed Marie to sit first so she could watch him while we ate.

I told at Marie, "I'm going to go say hi to Peter's mom."

Marie flashed a *don't-be-obvious* look at me, and I returned with a crooked grin in response. Breanna didn't seem to pick up on any of our exchange.

I ambled up to their table. "Hello, Mrs. Riordan. How are you?"

"Ali!" She greeted me with a beaming smile as she stood up to give me a hug. "Great. How nice to see you. It's been a couple of months, hasn't it?"

I paused for a split-second to formulate my response. I didn't want to discuss the breakup, even though that was the reason I hadn't been over. She must have known about it. "Yeah, the change in the social life has been…prohibitive." I paused, seeking a graceful word to use, but still felt awkward.

"I'm sorry, honey. Well, I hope we still get to see you around some."

Peter looked down at his food.

"Yeah that'd be nice. I still owe someone for my swim at the beach," I teased as I pushed Peter's shoulder. He laughed, and his mom looked at Peter accusingly.

He held up his hands in mock surrender. "I am perfectly innocent at all times, and I don't think I started it."

"Not that your son would get overzealous in his retribution."

"Oh no, he would neeevvvveeer do that," she said, raising an eyebrow at Peter.

"Okay. I had better get back to my friends. I just wanted to say hi."

"Bye, sweetie."

I wandered back to my table and said, "I love Peter's mom."

"She seems nice," Breanna commented.

"Yeah, she is. Definitely in the 'cool mom' group."

We ordered our food from a waitress with a fabulous Irish

accent. Marie and Breanna started outlining plans for the summer. They even were tossing around the idea of a trip to the Monterey Bay Aquarium and the Redwood Tree walk in Henry Cowell State Park. It felt good doing something normal, but part of it felt like an illusion.

Peter and his mother got up to leave, and as they passed by us, she waved. Peter tugged playfully at my hair as he walked by. They said goodbye to all of us, but the only name he actually *said* was Marie's. I grinned at her once they had cleared the door. This time, Breanna noticed and proceeded to analyze the encounter for her.

We talked while we munched on our food, and afterwards, the girls rushed off. I stood on the pavement in front of my car for a while. I still had hours until sunset, but I couldn't think of anything else to do in the meantime. Defeated, I got into my car to make my way home. I could always be a complete nerd and do more of my summer reading.

I glanced down at the gas gauge at the same moment the emergency gas light came on. I absently pulled into a parking lot to turn around and head back to a station. I paused and peered at the building in front of me, about to back up, and realized where I was.

Idling, I sat in front of my friend Farah's church, St. Nicholas. I wasn't Orthodox, but I felt drawn inside. I sat in the car with the engine running for a long while. I finally decided to shut off the engine and try the door. Feeling conspicuous, I placed my hand on the well-worn handle and was surprised that it was unlocked. It opened easily with a soft creak, and I peered through the doorway to see if anyone was inside. It was empty.

I eased through the door and stood in the aisle. The faint scent of incense hung in the cool, unmoving air. It was so different from the church I had attended when I was younger.

Beautiful light filtered through the stained glass windows, and the soft blue walls created a sense of calm. I had been to a wedding here a couple years ago and had loved the intricate icons that adorned the walls. I sat down on a pew and put my head in my hands, wondering why I had ended up here.

Prayers spilled out of me. I asked for clarity, for strength, for safety, for Joshua...for all the things I couldn't put into words. I needed faith. I rocked back and forth and found myself saying one word aloud over and over again: "Please, please, please..."

I looked up and was struck by a particular icon of an emaciated woman. I remembered the story behind the saint, Saint Mary of Egypt. She was a horribly wicked woman, so much so that she thought it humorous to seduce men on a holy pilgrimage just for sport. One day, she had tried to enter the church and was blocked by an unseen force. She tried three times to enter and was denied each time. She looked through the entrance and saw an icon within and was so overcome with emotion, she wept and repented of her sinful ways.

After her conversion, she fled to the desert, faced all that tempted her, and was eventually able to live a life of peace. She lived out her days free of her sins and was granted the gift of clairvoyance. It struck me as odd that I remembered the story in such detail, but the idea of clairvoyance had always been fascinating to me.

I picked up the hymnal in front of me and looked up the hymns about Mary of Egypt, some of the lines poignant:

> *You taught us to disregard the flesh,*
> *for it passes away*
> *But to care instead for the soul,*
> *since it is immortal.*
> *Therefore your spirit...*
> *rejoices with the Angels.*

And a little further down:

> *Having been a sinful woman*
> *Having attained angelic life,*
> *You defeated demons*
> *with the weapon of the Cross..."*

And then I felt complete peace come over me. I was surrounded by saints who had withstood terrible trials, and their faith had carried them through. I felt comforted by history, the fact that I wasn't alone. Gathering myself together, I headed out the door renewed.

Life may not be fair, but how we deal with it is what matters. Free will. My demons may be literal, but they can be defeated.

After getting gas, I arrived home. As I unpacked my new books, I was reminded of the Rilke poem Sebastian had quoted about angels being terrifying—and how they had to be terrible sometimes. I understood where he was coming from, but it reminded me of something else that Rilke had written. I strode upstairs and grabbed my tattered copy of *Letters to a*

Young Poet. Scanning through it, I found the passage and highlighted a section of "Letter 8."

There was a knock at the door, so I headed back down with the book in hand. After checking the peephole, I was surprised to find Gabriel on the porch since it was hours until sunset. My heart raced, thinking something was wrong, so I opened the door hesitantly, not wanting to hear bad news.

He grinned at me, and my fears were immediately alleviated.

"Hey."

"Aleria." He bowed his head slightly. "Sorry. I am early. I have some information we thought might be helpful for you tomorrow. It may make you feel more at ease."

"Great. Come on in." I opened the door wide to let him pass, but I delayed shutting the door, spying the van in the street. I looked at him awkwardly for a moment. "Umm, is Joshua out there?"

His eyes twinkled. "Yes, he is."

"Umm, I have something for him." I indicated the book in my hand. "Do you think it would be okay if I give it to him right now? And then we can get started?"

"Sure. Knock twice on the back door, and step through into the compartment. Then, once the outer door is shut, go into the main cabin. You do not want to let any light in."

"Oh, oh. Yeah. I'll just be a minute. Help yourself to some food. There's leftovers and drinks in the fridge."

"Any more Mexican food?"

"Yup. Have at it."

He strolled into the kitchen as I went out the door into the balmy afternoon. I followed his instructions and entered the van. Joshua was staring with intensity at what looked like an instructional manual. He looked up, startled.

"Oh, sorry. I can come back." I felt out of place. Maybe because it was the first time I'd seen him since we kissed. Maybe he regretted kissing me. Maybe it had been an emotional decision.

"Oh, no. No. I thought you were Gabriel. Please..." He motioned towards the chair next to him.

Relief washed over me. Stupid teenage angst had gotten the better of me for a moment. Joshua was anything but rash.

The van was much more spacious on the inside than I would have thought. Everything was dark grey and sterile-looking. There was a bank of electronic equipment, monitors, a refrigerator, and other gear on the left side topped by a bunk long enough for a very tall person. Three very comfortable looking swivel chairs were mounted in front of the monitors for long hours of observation.

The other side had a long padded bench seat that encompassed about half the wall and appeared to have storage underneath it and a bunk above it. It was backed by low profile, locking cabinets with a host of weapons strapped to the wall, some of which I had never seen. Directly next to the bench was a blank area allowing for the sliding side-door. Additionally, there was a solid door that led into the cab with a speaker next to it and flip-down chairs on either side.

"I, uhh have something for you." I paused, trying to organize my thoughts for a moment. I looked into his expectant green eyes and at the crooked grin he was wearing. I fought the urge to kiss him, though I itched to; he sat still and gave no indication of wanting to touch me.

"I was thinking about what Sebastian had said the other night, about Rilke's poem that all angels are terrible. And, I don't agree with that philosophy. I think sometimes angels have to *do things* that are terrible, but *they* aren't terrible. Rilke believes that everything happens for a reason. I wanted you to read this." I handed him the book and opened it to the passage I had highlighted. His shoulders relaxed as he read.

When he was finished, I said, "This passage gives me a lot of hope; there is so much beauty in it. I thought it might give you some, even though I don't completely agree with his viewpoint."

"What don't you agree with?"

"Well, I think you can find some peace in believing everything happens for a reason, but ultimately it is a trap. We've both learned that life isn't fair. Sometimes horrible things happen to good people for no reason. We all have free will, and the free will of some can really mess up the free will of others. I just believe that good things can come from the bad. It's the choices we make in how we deal with the bad. We can find reason in the things that happen, not that everything happens for a reason. Sorry..." I suddenly got embarrassed and could feel my face burning.

"What do you have to be sorry for?"

"I didn't mean to start a whole philosophical discussion here. I feel like I'm scolding you for questioning everything that has happened to you. I'm sorry. I don't mean to come across that way at all. I was just trying to encourage you. I..." I became more and more nervous, the words spilling out with more speed. It was compulsive; I couldn't stop myself from talking. The more I tried, the worse it got. I needed to leave. I started to get up, but he caught my wrist and pulled me back into my seat.

He interrupted my stream-of-consciousness monologue. "I didn't take it that way. I know you, remember? You don't have a mean bone in your body. You weren't scolding."

I closed my eyes and dropped my head into my hands, still feeling mortified by my speed talking. Suddenly, I felt Joshua's face close to mine; he was on his knees in front of me. He gently pulled my hands away from my face and cupped it in one of his hands. I kept my eyes closed as he ran his nose up my cheekbone towards my ear. My breathing stuttered.

He whispered, "Thank you," in my ear. I pressed my cheek to his, and felt him breathe in the scent of my hair.

I reached around him, pulling him closer, wishing this moment could last forever. But it couldn't. My shoulders slumped as I said, "I should get back inside. I don't want Gabriel to get suspicious. If he isn't already."

He kissed me, and I was unable to will myself to get up. He kissed me softly between each word. "Yes. you. should. get. back. inside."

"You aren't making this easy," I said breathlessly.

"Aren't, I?" he said, still kissing me.

"No."

"I missed you today." Josh pressed our foreheads together, stroking my face, and sighed.

"I missed you too, but I really should get inside," I said.

He agreed.

"I'll see you in a couple of hours." I touched the book in his hand. "There are a few more notes I made in there." I went back to the house, hoping the blush I felt on my face would fade.

Before opening the door, I swallowed hard. I had the feeling that whatever Gabriel was going to show me, it wasn't good.

15

COMPLICATIONS AND COMPACTS

I walked into the kitchen as Gabriel was polishing off the last of his food. He raised a brow. "You finished with your delivery so soon?"

"Yeah," I mumbled. "So, what do you have?"

"It is about your meeting with the Concilium. We decided that if you know whom you are going to speak to, it might help the proceedings. I brought a small, redacted dossier on each of the members of the council and conclave with whom you will be meeting. We are not worried about the council members so much, but the conclave has a different mandate."

"I thought everyone was on the same team?"

"Since when are things ever simple?"

"Mmmm. Never."

"Precisely. You know pieces of this, but I want to clarify. The Watchers have been around since approximately 900 BC. The first documentation we have was in Hebrew, and later,

Latin. They stuck with the Latin name *Concilium* until the schism, when the organization split in two.

"One side became the Council to which we belong. We believe that vampires are sentient beings; therefore, they have a right to live as long as they do not harm humans. If there is a rogue out there killing, or a newborn overtaken with bloodlust without a sire, that is when I come in.

"I have only dealt with the true evil. I admit that, because of this, I have had a hard time seeing any good in any of them. But those that are not causing harm we watch and document.

"The Conclave, on the other hand, believes in complete extermination. To them, vampires are the *Anathema*, or the cursed. They believe vampires do not have souls, and therefore, they have no right to life. To them, someone like Joshua should be eliminated.

"You will be meeting with members representing each of these sides."

The hair on the back of my neck pricked, and I gritted my teeth. I opened the first of the six folders to reveal a glossy 8x10 photo of a bearded man named Harold Blackthorne, a senior member of the Conclave. He was heavy-set, and his well-lined face was weighted with too many years of frowning. His hair appeared to be mostly grey, but it was hard to tell in the photo. The pores in his skin were large, and his eyebrows a little bushy, overshadowing his small eyes. He wore small, wire-rimmed glasses that pressed into the sides of his wide face.

I scanned through the pages of text. Most of the information was redacted; someone had blacked out the classified information, but it was clear he was a key member of the Conclave. In his youth, he had been partially responsible for the schism between the Council and the Conclave. His style of leadership was largely Machiavellian, in that the ends justified the means. He was a global thinker, not wanting to take into account the details, or people, for that matter.

I was a little frustrated about not being able to read more. Different names kept popping up like "Shadowforce," "Bloodkind," and "Expurgo." Of course, everything around those names had been blackened, which only made me more curious. But I had solely been given the handful of pages in the folder with the information that Sebastian had wanted me to be aware of.

I kept quiet as I looked over the next folder. This one had a color photo of a woman named Crina Rousseau. She had intensely red hair cut in a straight, severe bob that perfectly lined her sharp jaw. Her skin was almost translucent in its paleness. If there'd been faint vein lines, she would've looked like a vampire. Her eyes were such a dark brown it was hard to see where the irises started. She had vertical wrinkles crowning her upper lip, like someone who had spent years of her life smoking.

The name *"Expurgo"* appeared several times again and *"Lustro"* appeared amongst other names that were also in Blackthorne's file. She, too, was a member of the Conclave. The personality traits that stood out were cold, organized, and merciless. As a senior member of the Conclave, she did most of the mission planning because of her ability to make unemotional strategic plans.

The word *lustro* was foreign to me, and through the little

context I could read, it didn't seem good. It nagged at me. I twisted my mouth to the side, musing for a moment.

Gabriel broke into my reverie. "What is it?"

I asked, "What does *lustro* mean?"

"It is Latin, meaning 'to cleanse or purify,' but more specifically, 'to cleanse by sacrifice.'"

I nodded in response. As I chewed on the information, I pulled the next folder open.

Carl Richter, the last member representing the Conclave, had blond hair, dark blue eyes, and sharp features to match his German surname. His square jaw was wider than the rest of his face. He had small wrinkles next to the edges of his mouth and a cleft chin. His cheekbones were as pronounced as his widow's peak. I felt chills from his picture.

I didn't need to read his file, but I did. He was an expert in tactics and known to sacrifice followers for "the greater good." He'd seen combat in his younger years and even served as a driver for the French court, but had escaped before being discovered. He was obsessed with bringing down the French coven.

All three of them seemed to have an unhealthy interest in the French coven, and I wondered why they had been dispatched here. *Wouldn't it be better to have more objective members present?* Wishful thinking, maybe.

I grabbed the next folder and glanced at Gabriel. He seemed studiously disinterested, but, of course, he was reading my every breath. He appeared to be one of those people who could look at ease in any situation while simultaneously being able to analyze every aspect of the environment. I wondered if all Slayers were so perceptive, or if it was just him.

The fourth folder contained a member of the Council: a beautiful woman named Sydney Sato, who looked to be of Japanese descent. Her silky black hair was swept up in a knot with some soft wisps of hair framing her face.

Her face was square and smooth, yet her eyes were light in the black and white picture. She appeared to be young, but it was hard to guess an exact age. She was involved on missions with names such as "Ultio," "Newkind," and "Transcend," and the notations in her file boasted of her ability to accurately predict enemy movements. She was depicted as fair, controlled, and strong.

I concentrated, feeling like the information was starting to run together. I glanced at Gabriel. He was cleaning under his nails with a startlingly large knife. His eyes moved under his lashes towards me. I stuck my nose in the next file.

Rory Van Heerden was a youthful looking man with curly dark hair and olive-toned skin. He was a team leader on "*Ultio*" and had been inducted into Council leadership after he had been injured backing up a Slayer. His injury prohibited him from combat. He was well liked by his team members. Besides a willingness to sacrifice himself for someone on his team, there was no more helpful information about this guy.

I opened the last folder to reveal a kind-eyed man named Nigel Abacha with smooth dark skin. His hair was closely cropped to his scalp. He had worked with the Conclave on a few joint operations. The other information was so redacted that I couldn't glean a true character portrait from the file. The joint ops made me a little leery, but that could have simply meant he was a peacekeeper between the two estranged branches of the Concilium.

A minute ticked by as I sat quietly and digested the information.

"Gabriel, why did you show up early today?"

His eyes tightened. "We finished our research early and returned...and I wanted you to review these files."

"You wanted me to read these files when Joshua wasn't around," I stated as fact.

"We do not have much time before the Concilium meets."

"That's not it," I deliberated. "I was wondering why we keep staying at my house now that Bowen can get inside? It's been bothering me. And now..." I rummaged around for the words. "The upper-ups want to use me as bait, and you don't want Josh around because if he figures that out, he'll freak."

Gabriel pursed his lips, but didn't say anything.

"I'm right, aren't I?"

He gathered up the files, stacking one on top of the other, and held them vertically as he tapped them on the table, still not speaking. His face stoic, he finally answered, "You are insightful."

"What do you think about the situation?"

"I see both sides. However, I do not like putting you at risk. I have grown fond of you." He put his hand on my shoulder and squeezed it in a comforting way. "But I see the merits in drawing him out. He has harmed innocents; both the Council and Conclave want his existence to cease."

"Do you think it will work? Me as bait?"

He dropped his hand from my shoulder. "I do not know.

He is at least eight hundred years old. He obviously has an ability to survive." His eyes were far off.

"But?"

"You seem to have some hold on him. He is still here. Normally, he would disappear into thin air and pop up in a decade with a new name."

"Or, he just really wants to punish Joshua."

"That too. But there is something more. He has broken his usual pattern. He does not need to seek any sort of revenge now. It is nothing for a vampire to wait a decade, for what is time to them?" he asked with a shrug of his shoulders.

"I have a hard time believing it's me," I said, shaking my head.

"Aleria, you are special. Bowen sees that."

The conversation started feeling too intimate, so I stood up and walked to the other side of the counter to pour myself a glass of water. I changed the subject. "You care about Joshua, don't you?"

He bowed his head in acknowledgment. "In many ways, he is like a brother."

My throat felt choked. "But you would kill him if you needed to."

Gabriel was very still, but I could see a slight tremor from his heart thudding in his chest. His eyes were sad when he finally answered, "Only if there was no other way, and I would do anything possible to prevent that."

"Me too," I admitted softly.

"He is family to you."

"Yes."

He stared at me for a long moment. "I know he is more

than that to you." He held up his hand to keep me from objecting while my pulse raced. "It is okay, but please stay objective, and keep your protective instincts under control when you meet with the Concilium. You need to be cool and calm. Never let them know how you feel."

I knew this was an affirmation of my feelings, but would it be of any use to say anything else? "You two are a lot alike, you know."

"A few years ago, I would have torn you in two for comparing me to a vampire."

"Yeah, but you're not offended now because you know it's true. He's one of the most amazing people I've ever known."

"It will work out, Aleria."

"I *don't* know, but thanks for saying it."

He walked over to me, wrapped his arm around my back, and tucked my head against his chest. I let out a long, uninterrupted breath. At that moment, I knew we were friends. Somehow, this gigantic and intimidating, tough manly man who killed immortals for a living was my friend, and I could trust him. I could feel it in my bones.

I looked over in the corner at the oversized duffle he had carried into the house. He had left it open when he'd taken out the files, and I noticed that it was filled with weapons.

I pulled away from him and motioned at his bag. "Can you show me how to use that?"

"The crossbow?"

"Yeah. We have another hour or so before dark, right?"

The corner of his mouth twitched.

"Just for fun. I realize I have a ninety-nine percent chance of failure fighting against a vampire. I'm just curious."

"Sure. This should be entertaining." He grinned.

Gabriel followed me out the back door. In the corner of the yard, there were some bales of hay that my brother had used for his pellet gun. I went into the shed and pulled out a yellowing target with tattered edges and pinned it to the top bale. Gabriel dipped his head in approval. Then he showed me how to load the bow.

It was really heavy, but I lifted it and took aim, ignoring the pain in my rib as best as I could.

He warily asked, "Do I need to be worried about any wildlife around here?"

"Funny. I'll try to keep the body count down."

I shot the first arrow and hit the bottom of the bale beneath the target.

"Okay, take in a breath and hold it before you shoot. If you breathe while you fire, it will reduce your accuracy."

"Okay." I took in a steady breath and held it. I peered through the sight and pulled the trigger, hitting the target this time securely in the outer ring.

"Relax your shoulders, and again, take in a breath, hold it, then release."

I did and hit the target dead center. I took another breath and shot the next one, landing the arrow a half inch from the other. I smiled and looked at Gabriel. He looked utterly shocked. I shrugged my shoulders. "My dad takes me shooting sometimes."

"I guess so."

"He's a veteran." I pulled the arrows from the target and repeated the exercise, each time hitting the center ring without fail. Satisfied, I turned to Gabriel. "Is there anything else you can teach me? We still have at least a half hour."

Amused, he delved into his bag and pulled out a wicked looking dagger. It was silver with swirl-like spikes rising from the hilt, parallel to the blade. The blade itself was inlaid with a dense wood. I raised my eyebrows as I ran my fingers over the wood portion.

"You need wood for vampires," he explained, answering the question before I could ask. "It is called a Durateus blade, and it is used in our swords and knives. Wood would not endure in a lengthy battle, but encased in a blade, they last. There is no need to carry separate weapons."

"Durateus?"

"Latin for *wood*, so it is not a completely accurate description, but the original swords were mostly wood. Now we have the hybrid."

I muttered, "Oh."

He removed the blade from my hands, turned towards the target and tossed it with deadly accuracy into the hay bale. I started laughing a tired, slaphappy laugh.

"What?"

"Yeah, I can't do that."

"Humor me. Just give it a try."

He gave me a short lesson, going through the mechanics of it. After his instruction, I drew in a deep breath, aimed, then threw the dagger at the target. I hit the edge of the target with the handle instead of the blade, and it skidded into the dirt towards me. I jumped back, letting out an involuntary yelp. Gabriel bit his lip, repressing a laugh.

"Laugh all you want."

He chuckled more openly. "You might be able to give someone a dreadful bump on the head with that throw."

"Cute. I told you I could never do throw it like you did."

"*Never* is an appalling word. You know that."

"Yeah, I think God has a sense of humor—whenever I say *never*, it seems to bite me in the behind."

"Try again?" he teased with a crooked grin.

As a diversion, I asked about something that genuinely interested me. "What does your tattoo mean?" I gestured to the one I'd seen earlier on his wrist.

He took off his leather cuff and let me see his arm. The tattoo was circular with a wide border, and there were symbols on the four sides, like those of a compass, that I recognized were for earth, fire, water, and air. There were Latin words on the border inscribed between each of the elements: *vitae, veritas, aeternitatis,* and *dignatio*. In the center was a pair of wings and a dagger that looked similar to the Durateus dagger in my hand. There was a Latin phrase beneath the wings: *Custodite proxima et futura*.

"It is the sign of a Slayer that belongs to the Watchers." He pointed at the phrase beneath the wings: "'Take care of or guard the past things and future things.' Or 'preserve the past and future.' The Watchers have a similar tattoo, but theirs has an eye in the center." He grinned at me. "And nice try, by the way. Again?" He pointed at the dagger.

"Fine," I grumbled.

He was amused by my attitude, at least.

I listened to his instruction again and again. No matter what I did, the dagger seemed to glance off and skitter towards me. Each time, I jumped as if the thing was a venomous snake, intending to bite me.

Finally, he raised his hands in defeat. "All right, all right. I give up—for now. Maybe we will have time tomorrow," he said as he plucked the now-filthy dagger from the ground.

"Sure. I'm confident I will magically get better as I sleep."

I pulled the hair off my neck, trying to cool down a little. I dropped it quickly when I saw the grim look on Gabriel's face. He approached me, pushing my locks aside. I started to pull away, and he shook his head. He examined my neck, the bruises from Phineas' fingers already purple in one day's time. *I guess I need to add speedy bruising to my super abilities.*

"I do not think those were from goofing around at the beach."

"Oh, I mark up easy."

"Those are from Bowen?"

"Mmmm." I pursed my lips and didn't look him in the eye.

"Aleria?" He didn't accept my vague non-answer.

"It's nothing."

"It does not look like nothing."

"I bumped into someone at the coffee shop, and he got upset. It's fine."

"Who?"

"What is it with men? Does the testosterone make all of you overprotective? It doesn't matter. I'm fine."

"Who?" he pressed.

I squirmed for a moment, then exhaled, exasperated. "Phineas."

"He—" He stopped short, and the muscles in his jaw flexed as he fought to control himself.

I changed the subject before he could say anything else. "Okay, I need food," I decreed.

"What is for dinner?"

"You just ate," I reminded him playfully.

"I am always ready for more food."

"I was thinking about curry chicken." I moved towards the house.

"Perfect," he said as he slid the weapons back into his duffle, then trotted behind me into the house. "And this is not over."

I slumped my shoulders and continued into the house. *Not over.* I frowned. At least he was letting it go for now.

16

RESPITE

I dropped the last of the dishes into the dishwasher with a clank and wiped the splattered water off the counter. Then I heard Josh's familiar knock at the door. Scampering to the entry, I swung the door open, an ear-to-ear-smile plastered on my face.

Joshua greeted me with a crooked grin. "Good evening."

He stepped over the threshold and gave me a sideways hug as he looked past me into the kitchen. Gabriel was seated at the dining area, within view of the front door, writing on a yellow notepad; his large hands were moving fluidly over the page. The notes were in some type of code, or maybe an ancient language. I wondered how many languages he spoke.

Joshua proceeded the rest of the way into the kitchen while I hung back in the doorway. He slid a chair away from the table, the wood squeaking on the tile as he parked himself across from Gabriel, his back to me. "You finish your briefing?"

"Yes, I did. She seems to have picked up on all the important details."

"Will it help?"

"I believe so," Gabriel replied, nodding in my direction.

Josh twisted in his seat to look at me standing in the doorway. "You going to be okay meeting with the Concilium?"

"Aren't I always okay?" I said, hoping my voice or my answering his question with a question didn't betray my nervousness.

"Yes, you always seem to handle everything well." His eyes were warm as he looked at me. He seemed to catch his look of adoration, as if his feelings for me were too obvious. His face cooled, and he returned his gaze to Gabriel. I crossed to the counter and leaned forward on my elbows, cradling my chin in my hands.

Gabriel chuckled. "Well, not everything." He looked up from his paper and winked at me.

I put my hands in front of my face in embarrassment and cringed, remembering my performance with the dagger. I parted my fingers and narrowed my eyes at Gabriel. I pulled my hands away to make my retort. "Careful—I seem to recall something I was good at," I threatened mockingly.

He let out a single laugh. "Yes, I promise not to irritate you when you have a crossbow."

I curtsied. "Thank you."

Josh looked confused. "Did I miss something?"

"Your girl seems to be apt with a bow."

Josh stiffened infinitesimally. I was not sure if it was the *"your girl"* comment, or the fact that I'd been handling weapons.

"Just a little target practice while we waited for sunset," I explained.

"I would have liked to have seen that."

As a segue, I asked, "So what's the plan tonight?"

"We should—" Gabriel's thought was interrupted by the sharp ring of his phone. He brought the phone to his ear. He didn't verbalize a greeting, but listened intently. "Be there in ten." He snapped his phone shut and peered at Joshua. "You okay with babysitting?"

"Thanks," I muttered annoyed, rolling my eyes.

"You sure you don't need me?" Joshua inquired, leaning forward.

"You can drop me at Marie's," I chimed in, feeling like a third wheel.

"Nope. I am meeting Phineas and a Slayer with the Conclave. It may be best to go unaccompanied."

"Ah," Josh said as he leaned back in his chair again and relaxed. I was thankful. "Is Sebastian still setting up for the meeting?"

"Yes. I doubt we will see him until tomorrow. Van Heerdan is already over there."

"You need me to do anything?"

Gabriel picked up his duffle, shoved the files into it, and roughly tossed it over his shoulder. A tiny bit of dust puffed into the air from the bottom of his bag. "Just call if we have any unwanted guests."

"Will do."

He hollered as he headed out the door, "Have fun, kids," and snapped it shut behind him.

I looked at Josh. "I suddenly feel like I'm ten."

"I am very glad you're not."

"Me, too, actually." I stood there awkwardly. I realized that I had never asked Gabriel what the Concilium might ask me. He had given me background information on the people, but no prep on what they might ask, besides them wanting me to be the bait.

I felt like a witness about to go into court without practicing my statements with the lawyers. Didn't they usually get to do that? They always did on television. I still felt like the tidal wave of impending doom was going to squash me at any moment. I wanted to groan as the knot in my stomach returned.

I looked over at Joshua who had the book I had given him in his hand. He was leafing through the pages and was oddly quiet. His thick eyelashes cast a shadow on his cheek as he looked at the book. The warmth of the light made the bluish veins under his skin almost invisible. He looked more human tonight.

After many long moments had passed, I finally broke the silence. "Sooo?"

He raised his head to meet my gaze and smiled. The warmth in his eyes hit me like a wave breaking upon the shore. I took in a breath, almost startled.

"So?" he returned.

"Any plans for tonight?" I asked.

"I think you need to relax and get a good night's sleep. Tomorrow will be a very long day."

I broke eye contact, bent down, and pressed my face to the cool granite counter. "I don't want to think about tomorrow," I moaned.

"As I asked before, are you okay meeting with them?" he asked, his voice like velvet.

"Yes. It just makes me feel a little sick to my stomach is all. It's so overwhelming. I don't know what to expect."

He stood up, slid his cool hand into mine, and lazily pulled me towards the stairs. "Let's watch a movie. It will be a good distraction."

I followed his request without complaint. I would spend the rest of my days being with him if I could. I squeezed his hand, and he returned the gesture.

The great room was stuffy from being shut all day. I wrenched open a window on each side of the room to provide a crosswind. The white sheers billowed languidly as the breeze eased the heat from the room. I stood in front of the last window, breathing in the night air.

The fragrance of the orange blossoms lightly scented the air; my favorite smells would soon be gone for another year. Everything seemed temporary, even the perfume in the air. As I gazed at Joshua, the light from the television made his skin the color of alabaster. He caught me staring at him and held out his hand for me to join him.

He pulled me to his side on the couch, mindful of my rib. My anxiety melted away, and it almost felt like we were two normal people enjoying an evening together at home.

He kissed the top of my head. "Any movie preferences?"

"Yeah," I murmured. "Things need to blow up."

"Blow up. You got it." He scrolled through the menu.

I ran my fingertips along his forearm and watched goose bumps rise from his pale skin. I liked how he reacted to my touch.

He flipped through stations past infomercials, upcoming attractions, and drug ads. Happy jingles promised weight loss, cholesterol control, and allergy relief in one easy little pill. I giggled through the huge list of disclaimers on the last one. "May cause swelling of the hands and feet, or sudden death," I parroted. "Well, order me up some of that!"

"Are you sure you don't want the one that may cause bronchospasm? There's nothing sexier than a hacking cough."

"I don't know; the unwanted hair growth sounded much hotter to me."

As we were finishing giggling, we settled on a movie about Irish brothers that promised lots of action. I watched the film and leaned my head back on Joshua's chest. The lulling rise and fall of his chest drew me closer to sleep as he lazily rubbed my back. Each stroke made my body feel heavier. I slipped into the darkness of sleep, but being in his arms didn't save me from the nightmares.

My heart stabbed against my ribs. In my dream, I walked on a slope while a light blinded me from seeing past my lashes. I held out my hand as a guide, then my fingers dipped into cool air. I froze.

I was once again confronted with the wall of darkness, but this time, I knew what was on the other side. I could sense him just feet in front of me. I tried to scream, but my voice, as in many dreams, was absent. I tried to run, but my legs were planted in place like stone fixtures. I clawed at the air in front of me, thrashing like some helpless prey already caught in a hunter's trap. His voice felt like a feather brushing against my ear, but I was unable to decipher what he was saying. He was obscured behind the wall of shadow.

His icy hand seized my arm like an iron manacle, and I yanked against his hold, bruising my wrist against his impossible grip. I was being inched into the darkness, my feet scraping against the pavement. I could hear my clothes flap as I threw my body in the opposite direction. *I was going to drown in that darkness*, I thought as I drew in gasping breaths. With one final yank, I was plunged into shadow.

All at once, I screamed and tried to stand while thrashing to free myself, but I was locked against someone. Pain shot through my injured rib. Then, I let out a thankful gasp when I realized it was Joshua. He eased his hold on me as soon as he could see that my mind had caught up with reality.

"It's okay," he murmured.

Tears stung my eyes. A gust of wind blew through the room, smelling of rain. I glanced at the curtain whipping in front of the now clouded sky, the full moon eerily illuminating a layer of cloud. I shivered and felt the chill from the mist of sweat on my skin. Joshua held my face so he could peer into my eyes.

"I'm so sorry, love," he stroked my cheek with his thumb. "I wish I could take all this away."

My voice felt strangled as I finally whispered, "It was just a dream."

"Can you tell me about it?"

"I've had it before. I'm in a pool of light that's blinding; I squint to see beyond it, but there's only blackness. It's like there is literally a wall of darkness coming for me." I shivered again. "It's just...*he* was there this time. He had me, and I couldn't do anything about it."

"I'm sorry—I didn't know you were having a nightmare. You were so still. He won't get you. You know that, right? I won't let him."

I didn't respond. Maybe he would. What if I allowed them to use me as bait, and it went badly, and I lost everything? If they didn't catch him, how many more girls would lose their lives? Was he killing them because he thought they might be me, or just because he liked to kill? Would I be able to live with not stopping him? *No.* Not if I could do something about it now. I somehow felt better, my decision made. I would do whatever it took to end this. *Anything to help.* I let out the breath that I hadn't realized I had been holding.

I reached out to Joshua and touched his face and his chiseled jawline with my fingertips. I leaned in and pressed my lips to his. He let out a soft moan as he parted his lips and moved them with mine. I pulled back and looked into his eyes; the green in them was glowing.

"I love you. More than anything."

"And I you." He ran his hand over my shoulder and down my arm as he cupped my elbow.

"It's funny. I thought I was in love before."

"With Robert?"

"Yes, but it was a fraction of what I feel now. I've always loved you, but now it's a whole layer I didn't think possible. I know this sounds cheesy, but you are part of my soul. When you touch me, even hold my hand…" my voice trailed off.

"Soul mates," he murmured.

"Sorry, bad to bring up the ex, eh?"

"It doesn't bother me." But then he got quiet for a long time; he seemed to want to ask something. I questioned with my eyes, and he sighed. "I have no right to ask, and if you don't want to tell me that's fine, but I was wondering. You went out with him for almost three years. And there was that e-mail you sent about a decision you were trying to make. Did you…" He didn't finish. "Never mind." He shook his head as if shaking the thought.

"No. We never did."

He looked into my eyes for a long moment, a smile playing at the edge of his mouth.

"What about you and Skylar Simmons?" I asked before I could stop myself. I didn't want to know, but at the same time, I did.

She was tall with red hair and perfect peaches 'n' cream skin—pretty much every girl's worst nightmare for competition. I had heard she was doing modeling to pay for college.

I had always hated her. It occurred to me that maybe part of me jealous even then.

He laughed softly. "No, no, and no. She had a little bit of crazy in her. I knew better."

"Really? She always seemed so—"

"She was a mess in a pretty package. I got out as soon as I could. The first two times I tried to break it off, she threatened to kill herself. No one wants to be around that kind of drama. Trust me, stable is much more sexy."

"Hmmm."

"She was the only one I went out with more than a few times. I told you, I didn't really date after my parents passed, and in high school, I hardly had time to hang out with my friends after sports, school, and my job."

He pulled me to his chest, and despite his cool body, I felt warm all over.

"My true love was right across the street the whole time."

"My Mr. Knightly," I purred sleepily.

He chuckled. "I guess so." He paused for a long moment. "You should try to sleep again."

"I don't want to sleep," I slurred as I fought with my weighted lids.

He coaxed, "You need to sleep...I'm here."

I pushed my legs onto the couch and stretched out, putting my head onto his leg. He pushed a suede throw pillow under my head, and I nuzzled into it.

A horrible feeling washed over me again, my heart grave with hopeless thoughts, and the prickling in my eyes returned. "I don't know how I will survive when you have to leave." My tears spilled onto the pillow, my body heavy with exhaustion.

"I'll be here all night, and I'll be back again tomorrow."

I forced the words out weakly, "That's not what I mean. When this is all over, you will take half of me with you."

His body shifted slightly. "Let's just worry about the now."

I started to say something else, but I didn't know if it was coherent. He rubbed my back, which speedily made me lose consciousness. I prayed my dreams would be of Joshua and fluffy, soft things like kittens and puppies...yeah, definitely fluffy kittens.

No organized royal death force of vampires.

No Bowen...

Just fluffy...

17

CONCILIUM

My head was pounding as I woke in a dimly lit room. My labored breath echoed off my surroundings, and I realized that I wasn't at home. Instantly, I was on my feet, whirling around, terror gripping me—I was caged.

There were two concrete walls lined with empty metal shelves and two walls of bars. I clasped part of my cold steel prison and looked out into a blackened room, only able to make out the far-off edges of the room.

Then I noticed my arms. They weren't mine, but they were. They were as pale as paper with thin blue veining visible through my translucent skin.

I doubled over in pain, thirst hit me, and my insides wrenched in agony and desire. I was drawn to an unmoving mass on the floor in the corner of my cell.

It was warm and inviting. I approached, something in me clawing to get at...what? With horror, I backed away until the bars dug into my back, getting away from the breathing body of a teenage boy. The steel groaned with the pressure I was putting on them.

I frantically felt my arms. They were firm, thinner, strong. And then I felt my face. I trembled as I opened my parched mouth and felt my teeth. A wave of hunger hit me, my mouth watered, and my canines unsheathed and elongated.

I squeezed my eyes shut and chanted, "No...no...no," my voice hoarse and rasping over my dry throat. I wanted to throw my body at the warmth in the corner. I slid my back into the furthest corner of the small room, feeling my will weaken, the pull to feed crippling my mind, my body wanting to take action.

I gazed at the reflective metal surface next to the door and took in my image. I could make out my silhouette...and my eyes. Two feral, glowing lavender orbs looking back at me.

I screamed and sat up in bed, frantically feeling my teeth. I looked at my room. The first signs of sunrise were filtering through the window, outlining the mountain in the distance, the last of the stars fading from sight. It was early; I squinted at the blue digital numbers on my alarm: 5:40 A.M.

"Only a dream. Only a dream." I gasped, digging my fingers into my pillow. My rib was throbbing, and I was still breathing like I had sprinted around the block.

Dragging myself to the bathroom, I examined myself in the mirror. "Please be a dream." I pleaded, part of me still not believing that it wasn't real. I had *felt* it. I could smell the dirt and concrete and metal in the room. I *had* to have been there.

I checked my eyes. They were not glowing; just the same pale bluish-lavender as always. I let out a sigh of relief and dropped down onto the toilet, still looking at myself. I didn't cry over the fright of my dream this time. My tears seemed to have dried up.

The thought of losing my humanity terrified me more than ever. I knew many people would have given their souls to become a vampire. Immortality and power were seductive. But all I could see was a world without sunlight—a world without hope.

"Oh Joshua," I whispered, my voice wavering with the weight of my realization. He was trapped, hating himself for the monstrous desires that had been imposed on him. I could feel how much I had wanted the boy's blood. I shuddered and felt helpless. And yet I marveled at Joshua's ability to hold onto his humanity for the past two years and not fall prey to his vampire nature.

"Ali?" Gabriel's voice was outside my bedroom door. "You okay?" I realized it had only been a few seconds since I had screamed.

"Yeah. Yes, thanks."

I stood and splashed some water on my face, then went to the door.

"I just traded with Josh and heard you from the van." He glanced over my head into my room.

"You can check if you want," I invited, stepping back. "It was just another dream." He walked in, looking in my closet and bathroom.

"I did not sense anyone. Just wanted to make sure." He held his phone to his ear and uttered, "Just a dream," and ended the call without saying another word.

"Thanks. No boogeyman today. Was that Josh?" I started down the stairs.

"Yes, the sun is up. He..." Gabriel didn't finish. I could imagine Josh trapped by daylight, unable to get to me after hearing me scream. I felt weak for screaming because of a stupid nightmare. Gabriel interrupted my abstraction. "Do you want to get some more sleep? It is early."

A quiver ran down my spine. "I think I've had enough sleep." I didn't want one more dream about a wall of darkness, a prison-like cell, a panel of judges, Joshua being dragged away from me, or me being turned into a vampire. I let out a fretful breath. "It's time for coffee." I brushed by him and clomped down the stairs, my body jarred by each heavy step; he followed.

Within a minute, I had the French press prepped. I pulled myself onto a barstool and rested my head on my hand while I waited for the water to boil.

Gabriel was pacing in the front room. I cleared my throat, trying to rid myself of my froggy morning voice. "How was your rendezvous last night?"

"About as good as your dreams," he said gruffly from the other room.

"Wow, that terrible?" The kettle dinged, and I poured the steaming water into the press.

"Those parasites are smart. Private planes came into San Francisco, San Jose, and Oakland, as well as a private train car from Sacramento within twenty minutes of one another.

"We were set for two targets and did not realize it was four until it was too late. We have no idea who or how many came into the city. There were too many witnesses to engage any of the vamps we did see. They disappeared before we could mount an attack. They obviously had help on the ground."

"Oh." I looked down at my bare feet; my toenails had a purplish tint because of the morning chill of the tile.

Gabriel leaned on the doorframe, his brow furrowed, lips in a hard line. "I should not have told you. Do not worry about it; we have a handle on the situation now."

"I would rather know."

"Me too, but I seem to tell you too much."

I shrugged. "I'm used to it. I have that effect on people. Sometimes I feel like Nick Carraway in *The Great Gatsby*; everyone tells him their secrets, even though he doesn't want to hear them."

"Partly, I think it is that you remind me of my kid sister," he said thoughtfully, obviously seeing a vision of her as he looked at me. "Her complexion was a little darker. Her eyes were light like yours, except khaki green. Same build. Same stubborn streak." He smiled wistfully at the memory.

"Were?"

He became still, and after a long pause, he added, "She died when she was a little younger than you. It was a long time ago."

I sensed that the subject was closed, so I didn't ask any more questions. In fact, I felt bad for having asked anything, as his features were now cast in sadness.

My first impression of the taciturn warrior was now gone. It seemed like I'd known him for a long time, like he was the cool uncle you see a few times a year, intense, but in a good way. The normally quiet one who fills you in on all the family secrets you weren't supposed to know.

I eyed the clock, and four minutes had ticked by, so I pressed the coffee and poured myself a cup. "Decaf?" I held out the cup, offering it to Gabriel before I took a sip.

"Decaf?"

"I didn't think my nerves could handle the caffeine."

"Probably wise. Sure."

I handed him the cup and poured myself one.

"Gabriel?"

"Yes?"

"Has Joshua killed many vampires?"

His seemed reluctant. "Yes, he has. You would be in awe of him. He is a magnificent fighter, but Bowen is not your typical vampire and not as easy to kill."

"How do you kill a vampire?

"Just asking because you are curious, right? Not because you are going to try?" He stared at me.

"Scout's honor." I held up my hand and made up my own hand signal since I'd never been a girl scout.

He smirked at my fake hand signal and continued, his voice matter-of-fact, "Take the head or completely drain the body of blood, but the only way to be totally sure is to burn the body or to leave it in sunlight."

"What do you mean 'totally sure?' If they don't have a head?"

"There have been a few cases where the vampire's head was almost completely severed, but the vamp recovered. It took months to regenerate, but it survived. So, like I said, burn the body."

"Is that all that stops them?" I asked.

"You can paralyze or incapacitate them with a stake to the

heart or a blood loss of over fifty percent. The blood loss will give you an hour or so. Even if they are able to feed, it will take them at least fifteen or twenty minutes before they are strong enough to do anything."

"So, you incapacitate them before you go for the kill?"

"In general, they are faster and stronger than normal humans. And those close to the original bloodline often exhibit special abilities."

"That bloodline being the original cursed tribe?"

"Yes, the further away from that line, the weaker they are. All vampires get stronger with age, but some will never be as strong as others."

"You said *normal* humans."

A grin played at the edge of his mouth. "Yes, normal humans, unlike me."

"You get to be superhuman, eh?"

"Yes, but I am not the only human with enhanced abilities. Slayers have increased strength, speed, healing, heightened senses, and slower aging. Many have their own individual abilities, just like the vampires. We are their foil."

"Oh, is that all? But you forgot the ability to never sleep."

He looked out the front widow. "Actually, that is what I need to do now. This is what I was waiting for." He indicated a car pulling up outside. A blonde girl emerged from the driver's side and waved to Gabriel. He bowed his head in greeting as she moved out of sight around the side of the house. "Joshua and I will be sleeping in the van. Uriel will keep an eye on things."

"It's daylight. Is this really necessary?"

"It is just a precaution; some vampires use human

familiars to do their bidding during the day, and they are not bound by darkness."

"Is she a Watcher?"

He walked towards the front door. "No. Only the best for you." He tapped his Slayer tattoo, and then disappeared through the door.

My stomach made a small flip as I realized this was much more serious than he was letting on if they had sent another Slayer to casually hang out in front of my house.

As it always was when with anticipating anything significant in the future, whether good or bad, time seemed to move like sluggish rush hour traffic on an impossibly hot day. Except it wasn't hot.

The sky was foreboding, filled with charcoal grey clouds that loomed over the valley, and the pavement smelled wet from the plump drops of rain that intermittently drowned out the sounds of the city.

I think I was conscious of every minute that ticked by. About an hour before my chauffeur was scheduled to arrive, I curled up in the large wingback chair in the front room. I jumped when I heard a knock at the front door. I must have dozed off. My neck was stiff, but I felt better, more rested. I stumbled towards the front door and glimpsed through the peephole. The blonde Slayer, Uriel, was leaning against the side of the house.

"You ready, chickie?" she asked in a thick Australian accent with a bright smile. Her front teeth were a little large, but they gave her a quirky charm that worked. Her straight, blonde hair hung in long layers more than halfway down her back and cascaded over her shoulders. She wore a black top tucked into low-rise jeans with a wide belt that coordinated with her rubber-soled boots—the type of boots that looked stylish, yet could also do some serious damage if needed.

"Yeah, just let me grab my bag." I rubbed my eyes as I darted to the kitchen to get my things. I stepped onto the porch, then double-checked to make sure the door was locked. The sun was low in the sky, and the street was bathed in a beautiful, dusky light.

We paused at the back door of the van. "You know how to get in from the back?" she inquired.

"Yeah." I smiled weakly at her, still groggy from my accidental catnap.

"I'll be up front if you need anything."

I went in through the back door and shut it behind me, then turned and let myself in through the inner door. Gabriel stood behind Joshua with his hands on the bar of the overhead bunk. Joshua was hunched in front of a monitor as he examined some footage. He repeated about five seconds of the video, watching it over and over. I smiled shyly as it felt like I was interrupting something. Maybe it was too much testosterone in an enclosed space.

"You ready to go, kid?" Gabriel asked.

"Yeah."

"All right, let us get on the road."

I sat on one of the swivel chairs in front of the bank of monitors. Gabriel disappeared through the inner door within seconds, giving my shoulder a reassuring squeeze as he eased by. The engine fired up a few moments later, and then I was alone with Joshua.

"Hey," I managed.

"Hey," he replied softly, his eyes probing.

"Where's the meeting?"

"Saratoga. It should take about twenty minutes to get there."

"Okay." I exhaled. "Why do I feel like we're going to a funeral?" I swallowed, trying to force the saliva past the lump in my throat.

I wondered what was going on inside his head. I was certainly nervous, but he was about to walk into a room full of people who wanted him dead, or at least half of them did. I felt selfish being nervous. I reached out and took his hand. He laced his fingers through mine.

"It's going to be fine. They're just going to have you tell your story and ask you a few questions. They have already been meeting for hours. We should arrive towards the end of the dinner break."

"How are you doing? Are you going to be okay?"

He looked at me, his eyes sparkling. "Aren't I always okay?"

"Touché. Nice non-answer." I let out a humorless chuckle.

"Learned from the best," he quipped as he squeezed my hand.

We sat in silence for a long while, swaying from the moving vehicle, emotion thick in the air. Without warning, he pulled me onto his lap and wrapped me in his arms. I relaxed and pressed my forehead to his temple, nuzzling his cheek with my nose. His warm breath spilled onto my neck and raised goose bumps. We sat in that position almost frozen—I wanted to stop time.

I whispered, "Love you," in a barely audible voice.

"And I love you, more than my own life."

I tightened my arms around him. The van downshifted and began to slow; I looked into his eyes, saying nothing, then slid into my own chair while I clung to his hand, my breath uneven. The van eventually stopped, and we reluctantly dropped hands. I tried to look casual.

Gabriel came through the door connected to the cab. It was dark outside now. "Okay, kids, game on." All three of us exited the side door where Uriel awaited us.

The house was nestled in an exclusive neighborhood on a large plot of land surrounded by oak, pine, and birch trees. Up-lights at the base of the trees cast a warm glow on the surroundings. The slate driveway wound its way to the oversized Spanish-style home, which was ornamented with intricate wrought-iron work around the windows and had a decorative gate at the immense front doors.

Well-armed personnel wandered in and out of the shadows. The place was a veritable fortress. Though we were protected from the outside world, I wondered what menace waited within.

A small, unassuming man in a grey pinstriped suit greeted us in the foyer and ushered us into what looked to be an oversized dining room. It was filled with low voices of people in intense discussion. Sebastian was seated at the head of the mammoth oval table at the far end of the room. He was speaking with the man I recognized from the files as Van Heerden.

There was an oversized mirror on the far wall that reflected the candles displayed on the shelf below it. Sculptures and other museum quality pieces were placed throughout the room. Recessed lights at half-power lined the ceiling, casting amber pools of light throughout the space.

Uriel disappeared into the crowd of murmuring people. I stood with Gabriel and Joshua at my sides, desperately wanting to hold Joshua's hand. Gabriel cradled my elbow and urged me towards the vacant chair at the end of the table, but I didn't take a seat yet. He stood next to me, while Joshua hovered at the edge of the room.

I saw Phineas take note of our entrance; he circled around the room, then attached himself to the redheaded Conclave member and whispered something in her ear. *What was her name?* I couldn't remember.

She looked up from her files and greedily fastened her eyes on me. Her thin lips curled into a smile, and she glanced up at Phineas, then back at me. She looked more cat-like than she did in her photo, thin and sleek with large eyes. She reminded me of April's grandmother's feline. An amazingly beautiful Siamese, she was nice to you at first, but as soon as she decided she was finished with you, she would bite you and run off. I hated that cat.

I broke my eyes away from the redhead's gaze and looked at Phineas more closely. His face appeared scraped and bruised at his temple. I realized his scowl was directed at Gabriel, who turned and peered back at him. He was grinning at Phineas, but it wasn't a friendly kind of grin. He looked down at me and shrugged. I guess he must have had a *conversation* with him regarding my bruises when they had met the other night. I suppressed my own smile.

The small man who had greeted us at the door rang a bell and pushed his circular dark-framed glasses up further on his narrow nose. His slick hair shone in the overhead light. "Members, it is time to resume," he said in a calm, assured voice, then he bowed his head in a quick nod of respect.

A hush fell over the room as the leaders took their seats around the table. The six Concilium members were seated at the table on opposing sides: to my left, the Council, and to my right, the Conclave. Sebastian had already been sitting at the other head. There were a few chairs lining the walls. Gabriel and Joshua seated themselves a few feet to my left against the wall. Phineas backed into a chair against the right wall, nearest the redhead. I stood awkwardly, not knowing what to do.

All the other people, Watchers and Slayers I presumed, filtered out of the meeting place. Many of them exited through the large French doors onto a stone terrace, where they mingled in hushed voices. The city lights could be seen through the glass doors. Judging from the elevation, the home obviously lay in the foothills. The doors shut with finality, making me jump involuntarily.

Sebastian cleared his throat. "Members, may I introduce Aleria Elizabeth Hayes. She is willing to answer any questions you might have about recent events. Please, dear, have a seat."

I sat halfway back on the chair, my posture straight and my hands folded on my lap under the edge of the table. I arranged a pleasant look on my face and made eye contact with each of them. It made me feel more confident.

The redhead, Crina Rousseau—*at last I could remember her name*—reclined in her chair, leaning heavily on the left armrest. She ran the index finger on her right hand over her bottom lip, the greedy smile still playing on her face. "So," she purred, "this is the girl who captured a prince's heart? Lovely, isn't she?"

My eyebrows pinned in confusion. *Captured his heart? What is she talking about?* I opened my mouth to object, but Sebastian held up his hand to me. My mouth audibly snapped shut.

"Rousseau," Sebastian warned.

"What?" she said, her voice almost slithered. "She is; look at her. A young Elizabeth Taylor, don't you think? The dark hair, fair skin, and those *eyes*—violet, aren't they? A true rarity."

Her compliment made me feel like I needed a shower and a large scrub brush and bleach, lots of bleach.

"Blue, actually," I whispered, just to be contrary.

She smiled and leaned forward. "You don't need to downplay your uniqueness here."

"Rousseau," Sebastian barked. "Let's get on with this." She leaned back in a mock pout, not truly fazed.

Rory Van Heerden shot a disapproving look at her, and then looked warmly at me. He was the young one with the dark curly hair and olive skin. His right shoulder was slightly lower than his left. I wondered if this was from the injury that had barred him from combat. "Miss Hayes, would you mind telling us your story from the beginning? From your first meeting with Bowen Reynard? Details are important, so anything you can remember would be helpful." He encouraged me to begin.

And so I did. I recalled all the events with perfect clarity. Being harassed at the café, Bowen stepping in, the walk to the parking garage, his meeting me every evening for weeks, topics of conversation, and so on. I told the story in a calm and detached manner.

But then I paused because I felt uncomfortable about the next part of my story. My stomach tightened as I remembered how vulnerable I felt in Bowen's apartment. I felt like the air was being sucked out of the room, like the weight of his body was on mine again; my palms began to sweat. I could feel Joshua's eyes on me. I didn't want him to hear this part. About my stupidity. I felt ashamed and dim-witted for walking up those stairs into Bowen's place, and now I had to admit it publicly.

Sebastian urged me on. I took an uneven breath and described the walk to Bowen's apartment and how he had seemed different that night. I described what we had talked about, how I had clung to the doorframe, how his touch had made me lose my will, how I had weakened, and how he had half carried me to the couch.

The room was silent. I trembled and looked at my hands, unable to make eye contact with anyone. I continued by telling them how I had pleaded "no" and "please." Someone to my left shifted in his seat. Then I summoned up Bowen's words: "I think breaking you will be much more fun. I'll see you soon; tell him hello for me."

I risked my first look at Joshua, since Bowen had been referring to him. I could hear the crinkle of movement as everyone else looked at him, too. He sat still as stone. There seemed to be an ocean of emotion behind his controlled demeanor, but to me, his face was a mask. He wasn't breathing. Gabriel sat next to him, cleaning his nails with a small blade and looking only mildly interested, but his jaw was tight.

It got easier after that. I recollected how I was saved that night, how Bowen had tracked me to THE Lane, how Joshua had saved me, how Bowen had left flowers, and how he had been invited into my home by my friend.

And then I told them about my last encounter two days ago, how I had arrived home and found him waiting for me in my room. How he had asked me to choose him, the promises he had made. How I had made a feeble attempt to escape, and how Joshua had intervened yet again. I ended my story with Bowen's fleeing when Gabriel had arrived.

They asked for more detail of the more recent encounter only two days before. I skipped the physical parts and hoped no one noticed the omission. They asked for the exact wording of everything he had said. I did the best I could to recall it all. Then the room broke out into smaller discussions. I felt exhausted.

Sebastian stood. "Why don't we take a short break? Gentlemen, might you take Aleria out for some air?" He indicated to Gabriel and Joshua.

I stood, my legs feeling hollow, as we walked stiffly towards the French doors. Outside, I felt like I could breathe for the first time in an hour. The tension in my body aggravated my injury. Needing support, I leaned against the stone wall bordering the terrace. When Joshua didn't join me, I looked over at him.

Both Joshua and Gabriel were silent, their heads cocked towards the closed French doors. They could obviously hear something that I couldn't. I listened until the silence seemed oppressive, but there was nothing besides the crackle of the ground beneath the guards' feet pacing the grounds, the scurry of rats in the ivy below, the croak of frogs in the nearby pond, and the whir of cars speeding down Highway 9. All that noise, yet I could not hear a single distinct voice within the room fifteen feet from me.

Gabriel and Joshua looked at each other, communicating with their eyes. Josh's hands formed two hard balls, knuckles straining whiter than his skin, the veins in his arms standing at attention. He wasn't breathing again. Was someone talking about him inside?

The small man appeared at the doors and opened them, entreating us to enter. I returned to the room, mildly reluctant, and took my seat.

Sydney Sato, a member of the Council, tucked her sleek, asymmetrical bangs behind her left ear and held a curious look on her square face. "Thank you for your openness, Miss Hayes. We are almost done here." She paused for an instant, her light-grey eyes probing my face, before continuing, "I want you to think back carefully. Can you sense him? Can you sense when he is near? A premonition, gut feeling, or the like?"

I sat unnaturally still. I started to say, "No," but that wasn't true. I *had* sensed him, even before he bit me. I couldn't put the feeling into words, but even in my dreams, I could feel his presence, some connection. "I hadn't put it together before, but yes. But, it's not like an advanced warning. It's just when he is really close. Like in the next room, so no real advantage."

Blackthorne's voice was dark and endless, like a moonless night. "He did indicate that he would see you again."

Whenever I glanced at him, his presence seemed to suck the light out of the room. He was the leader of the Conclave, though this was the first time I had heard him speak. He had a well-kept beard like Sebastian, but I sensed no kindness in him. His face was lined like a cracked desert floor thirsting for water, and his small, dark eyes seemed to hold secrets that hovered behind his wire-rimmed glasses. He was much taller than I would have expected, a few inches over six feet. His hulking shoulders added to his imposing presence.

I replied, "Not exactly, just that he wanted me to choose him willingly."

"He wants her," Rousseau alleged with a sadistic glee.

I shook my head. "Not necessarily; he wants revenge. I am the last human connection Joshua has to the world. That's why all of this started."

"That may be how it started, but that's not what it is now," she countered.

"What do you think would be worse for Joshua: my death, or my choosing Bowen and losing my soul—becoming the monster he helps you hunt?"

Phineas scoffed and leaned in to whisper something in Rousseau's ear again.

Rousseau gave me a hard look. "No, my dear. He wants the girl *and* his revenge. You are the reason he is still here. You are the reason we will get him," she beamed. "With your permission, of course," she added, her eyes heavy-lidded like a cat eyeing its prey.

Joshua gasped. I looked over at him, and Gabriel was holding him in his seat by his shoulder, the strain between them visible. Gabriel hissed under his breath, "This is not the place."

Joshua broke his silence. He was still seated, but he thrust his finger accusingly at Rousseau and shouted, "She doesn't just want to use her as bait. She wants to sacrifice her! She has no intention of protecting her!"

"My dear boy, do you think you know my mind?" she jeered.

Blackthorne broke in, "Sebastian, control your charge."

She cut in again, "Do you not see—"

Sebastian boomed, "Crina, if he says it, it is so. He can't read your mind, but he can read your intentions." It was the first time I had heard him carry a harsh tone in his voice. Rousseau leaned back, jutting out her jaw in disgust.

"And you never tell me to control my charge when you can't control yours." Sebastian's eyes locked on Phineas. At the same time, Blackthorne's expression burned while he glared at Rousseau.

Did Gabriel tell Sebastian about my run-in with Phineas? I looked at Gabriel. He made eye contact with me, but his face was emotionless. Joshua followed the look between us.

"I don't know what you mean." She obviously didn't.

Phineas backed up and sat in the chair behind him. His nostrils flared, and he let out a huff. She eyed him over her shoulder and quieted as she saw his reaction.

There was a long pause. Nigel Abacha broke the silence and spoke for the first time, addressing me. He looked as kind as he did in his picture. "Despite some of my colleague's zeal, your safety would take precedence. Miss Hayes, will you help us?" he asked in a mild North African accent.

I cringed, not because of the question, but because I could feel Joshua scowling at me. I exhaled and looked at my hands again. "Yes. I will," I whispered. "May I go now, please?" I didn't want to see their faces. I wanted to crawl into a hole and hide. I had volunteered to be bait.

"Thank you, Miss Hayes. We will set things in motion yet this evening. We will give you the details you need tomorrow afternoon before sunset," Mr. Abacha said.

I nodded, still not looking at anyone. I heard the doors open and the voice of the small man. "This way, please, Miss."

I stood and strode out the door, trying to get out as quickly as I could. The door shut behind me, then quickly reopened. I turned to look and found Sebastian was standing there with his hand extended. I reached out and took it.

"You did well, child," he assured as he gently squeezed my hand. I felt a lump in my throat develop. "It will be just a few more minutes." He paused and with a proud look on his face, then repeated, "You did very, very well." With that, he dropped my hand and returned to the room.

I murmured, "Thank you," but I wasn't sure if he heard me.

When I reached the foyer, I spied a padded bench in a dark corner and sat down. Several minutes ticked by, and I was still alone. Sitting amongst the shadows somehow made me feel safer. I wasn't looking forward to my next conversation with Joshua. I leaned my head against the wall and closed my eyes and waited.

The meeting room door opened and shut harshly. I looked towards the hall, expecting to see Joshua emerge, but was taken aback by Phineas entering the room. Anger dripped from him as he paced back and forth. I pulled my legs up onto the bench and wrapped my arms around them to make myself as small and inconspicuous as possible.

After another minute, he noticed me and let out a revolted sound. I rolled my eyes. I was so not in the mood for this, and I knew he wouldn't dare touch me here.

"What is your problem with me?" I asked.

His face twisted into a sneer. "You have been corrupted by the thing you love." *Overly dramatic, aren't we?*

"Corrupted?" I asked.

"All vampires are soulless beings and should not be tolerated."

"Since when is the world black and white? There are always shades of grey."

"Not in this case," he said with a hiss.

I half laughed. "And what if you are wrong? What if all of them do have souls? What if there is still good in some of them? What if there is a way they can be saved?"

"That's impossible. The Devil can never set foot in heaven again, and vampires cannot find their souls."

"I'm glad the world is so clear for you," I bit out.

"You are the one not seeing things clearly."

I felt like I was having a junior high argument. He was listening, but not hearing me at all. Then I realized that there was more to this. I swallowed hard and decided to ask. "What happened to you? Or was it to your family?"

He seemed startled by my question. *Really? This wasn't exactly a shocking conclusion to draw.* He clamped his mouth shut and said nothing. I was about to ask another question when the door down the hall opened again. Phineas heard it and stormed out the front door.

The knot in my stomach returned when Gabriel and Joshua materialized from the hall. We walked outside to the van. Josh's silence was painful. Being a coward, I steered towards the cab, hoping to ride in the front with Gabriel, but my plan was thwarted when Uriel magically appeared from the shadows to return with us. I guessed her vehicle was still out at my place. I grumbled to myself and climbed into the back.

Fifteen minutes later, Josh still hadn't uttered a word. I felt like I would explode from anticipation. "Would you please say something?" I pleaded in a soft, pained tone while continuing to stare at my hands. I waited.

"What are you trying to do, Ali?" he finally asked.

"I need to do what I can to help."

"By letting them use you?"

"No!"

"Not all of them care about protecting you. The ends justify the means to the Conclave!"

I took a moment and gathered myself together. I needed to be logical. "Is Bowen a high priority target?" I inquired in my most reasonable voice.

"Yes," he said reluctantly.

"If he is captured, will it save girls my age?"

"It depends on *why* he has been making these recent kills, but probably."

"Will it help you?"

He didn't answer.

"I'll take that as a *yes.*"

"Don't worry about me," he said, his voice strained.

"Not what I asked. Will it help you?"

He gritted his teeth and spoke through them. "Yes."

"Might it keep my family safe? They won't be out of town forever."

He slumped his shoulders. He was losing this argument, and he knew it. He admitted "Yes," in a defeated tone.

Repeating his words from a few short hours ago, I looked him in the eye for the first time and said, "I love you, more than my own life."

"Not fair," he complained.

"Didn't we already cover that? Life isn't fair. And I can't let one more girl disappear when I can help. I can't risk losing my family or you. I just can't. Who am I to let that happen? I can't do *nothing*."

"The Conclave will sacrifice you without a thought."

"But the Council won't. Gabriel won't. Sebastian won't. You won't…"

"If something happens to you." He squeezed his eyes shut.

"It won't." I bent down on my knees in front of him and held his face between my hands. He kissed me with a fierceness he had never done before. In truth, it scared me a little, but I let go of my thoughts and kissed him back with the same fevered urgency.

18

SHOULD'VE

Gabriel and Uriel dropped us off and went to follow a lead. Joshua and I were left alone again. He observed the circles under my eyes and insisted that I sleep. I wanted to argue, but I didn't have the strength—a clear indicator that he was right. I sluggishly went through my nighttime routine. I eventually sat tubbed and scrubbed in my pajamas at the top of the stairs.

I was so relieved to have the meeting with the Concilium over, that offering myself as bait tomorrow didn't seem that bad. Maybe I was delirious. I knew Joshua was somewhere in the house, but I couldn't hear him. I blinked, and he was suddenly sitting in front of me on the stairs like he had been there the whole time.

"I thought you were going to bed?" he said softly.

I groaned and rested my hands in my lap. "I should. I need to, but I don't want to..."

"Convincing you to go to bed is the only argument I won

today."

"I just don't want to have bad dreams." I gazed at him pathetically.

He stood up and held out his hand, saying, "Come on." I took it. He led me into my bedroom, and I crawled into bed while he sat in the window seat, looking outside. "I'll stay close. Please get some sleep," he pleaded.

I whispered, "I love you," in a semi-slurred voice, already descending into sleep. I remembered starting to have a nightmare, but then I felt his weight on the bed, followed by his cool hand stroking my cheek, which lulled me back to sleep. He held the nightmares at bay all night.

When I awoke, it was already late morning. I had slept hard. My mouth felt stale, so I went into the restroom to brush away the nasty feeling. There was a note taped to the mirror in Josh's handwriting:

> *I love thee, I love but thee;*
> *with a love that shall not die;*
> *till the sun grows cold*
> *and the stars grow old.*
> *—William Shakespeare*

I smiled. *Look at him getting all mushy.*

I spent my day doing normal things, wondering who was lurking about to protect me. The van was a couple of houses down with different embellishments, a different sign and ladders strapped to the sides.

At 3:30 P.M., my cell rang for the first time in days. I raced upstairs, snagged it from my desk and breathlessly said, "Hello."

"Hey, chick, are you still going to the AP English meeting today?"

I had totally forgotten. I processed for a split-second. "Uh, yeah…yeah, I'll be there."

"Okay, just making sure. You've kind of fallen off the grid this week."

"I'd forgotten. Thanks for reminding me, Marie." I looked at the clock. "Could you save me a seat? I'll probably arrive just as it starts."

"No problem."

"Thanks, I'll see you in a few."

"Bye."

Crap! I ran in a circle around my room, frantically gathering my clothes. I jammed my legs into my favorite jeans and thrust my arms through the sleeves of a blouse. A second later, I checked the mirror, then pulled my silver locket on over my head before I tromped down the stairs.

I got to the door and realized I should write a note. *That's if I make it to my car before someone stops me.* I scribbled:

> At AP meeting from 4-5,
> back by 5:30 at latest. Have cell.

I burst the front door open and looked down the street. It was eerie, no one in sight. I loped two houses down and stuck my note under the wiper blades of the van, almost falling as I turned to sprint to my Mustang. I didn't want to be late. Mrs. Saunders was not tolerant of truancy. Capital N-O-T.

I sped through the neighborhood and hopped onto Highway 85. I hit 79 mph, trying to make up some time. I prayed for the streets to be clear of police as I roared to school.

I parked in the garage and took the stairs two at a time. I ran down the hall, stopping two classrooms down to catch my breath before walking into the room. I was flushed from the run, and my hair was sticking to the back of my neck. The weather had definitely warmed up today. I started to knot my hair in a bun and then remembered the stupid bruises on my neck.

I peeked into the room through the window; Mrs. Saunders hadn't started speaking yet. I slipped through the door, waving at some of my friends, as I strode to the back of the room towards Marie. She moved her bag off the seat she'd saved for me next to her and Peter.

Mrs. Saunders began speaking the moment I sat down. She was in her mid-thirties and feisty, known for her rigorous program and no-nonsense approach to teaching.

It took me a few minutes to focus on what she was saying. All I could hear was the pounding of my heart and the sensation of blood coursing through my body from the adrenaline rush of trying to get there in time.

She spent the next hour going over expectations for the class, warning the students who already had senioritis to drop the class and take the standard English class, and informing us that there would be a test on the first day of school over the summer reading. Groans escaped many of my classmates. I was unfazed by the workload.

She handed out what she called a "Literary Response Sheet," and explained how to use it while doing the summer reading. After a brief question and answer period, she wished us well and sent us on our way.

I walked down a flight of stairs, trailing behind Marie and Peter. Marie pointed to the doors one level down, and we stepped into the main lobby. "I need to turn some forms in to the office. Are you guys up to going out tonight?" She was asking both of us, but I knew she was more interested in Peter's response.

He looked at her. "I am eighty-six sure I am free. Text me when you get the plan together," he said, then looked at the time on his phone. "Oh, I have to pick up my little brother from karate." He backed towards the doors. "Text or call me," he added one last time, his voice echoing down the stairwell as he disappeared through the heavy metal doors.

I smiled at Marie. "Eighty-six percent sure he's free."

She beamed. "How about you?"

"I'm one-hundred percent sure I'm busy. Sorry."

"No problem. I'm sure that I can get a group together. A one-on-one thing would be too weird at this point."

"I think he might be interested, though." I playfully nudged her with my elbow.

"I think so, I hope so," she fretted, biting her bottom lip.

"You have chosen well, my friend. I'm sure it'll all work out. Peter is a catch, and so are you."

"So, you can't come for sure, for sure?"

"Nope, a friend is visiting from out of town." *And I am going to be vampire bait.*

"Okay, maybe tomorrow."

"Sounds good."

We hugged, and she headed through the glass doors to the main office, clutching her paperwork. I returned to the stairwell and almost bumped into April. Her arms were brimming with binders, books, and miscellaneous papers. She smiled brightly, her perfectly white teeth vivid against her golden skin.

"You got that?" I asked dubiously.

"Yeah, thanks. I never cleaned out my locker. They called me in to clear it out. How are you?"

"Great," I lied. "And you?"

"Good. I like my summer job so far. And we're going to head up to Clear Lake for a few days next week."

"I'm jealous." I loved their house on the lake. I thought of past summers sitting on the dock, hanging my feet in the water, feeling the warm breeze on my skin, hearing the lap of the waves on the shore.

"My parents said everyone can come up in July. The basement will be ready by then."

I was about to reply with excitement when I heard metal doors slam shut and scuffling feet paired with boisterous male laughter up the stairs. I could hear Hunter Williams and Ryan Johnson slamming into one another; they must have been in the football meeting. They came into view with their dark blue jerseys and athletic shorts on. Ryan jumped down five steps, narrowly avoiding Hunter's intended body slam. April and I flattened against the wall, the handrail cold through my shirt. Ryan spun and scarcely avoided us, letting out a delighted chortle while holding a cell phone in his hand.

"Give it back," Hunter bellowed, but there was amusement in his voice.

"Give it back," Ryan echoed in a girly voice. Hunter ran past us, but accidentally tipped the edge of one of April's binders, and they went flying. Papers fluttered down an entire flight of stairs, a veritable snowstorm.

"Sorry, April!" Hunter yelled, not slowing down. "Ryan, you are going to die! Give it back." The cacophony abruptly stopped when we heard the door at the bottom of the stairwell crash shut.

We stood in disbelief, looking at books, binders and papers splayed all around us.

"Wow, that was—"

"Irritating," she finished. I couldn't disagree.

"I'll help." I set my shoulder bag on the ground and started gathering.

"Thanks." We talked while we picked up the sea of papers and stacked them on the bottom step.

I picked up my bag, then slung it over my head to free up my hands. "Let me take half this time," I offered.

"You sure?"

"No problem. Not in a hurry." We walked to the bottom floor of the garage, and I helped her put everything in her trunk.

My car was one flight up, so I opted to take the ramp because it was closer. I hugged April and walked leisurely to my car, soaking up the sun. I heard the hum of her engine as she drove off. The sun was halfway to the horizon and shining directly in my eyes when I reached my floor. I had to almost close them as I shuffled towards my spot. And then my world stopped.

I backed into the guardrail as I stared blindly into the garage. It was my wall of darkness. And *he* was here. I could sense him watching me. I stood there in the sun, knowing that I was safe. Well, at least until sunset, because of the way garage was designed, there was no way for me to leave and stay in the sun. I was trapped. *How did he get here in daylight?*

I turned and looked over the rail. Maybe I could jump? There was about a fifteen-foot drop onto some uneven ground, but it was doable. *Sort of.* I stepped up onto the cement curb and got ready to swing my foot over the rail, eyeing the rocks jutting from the golden foxtail weeds and the clay-like soil. This would hurt, even if I didn't break anything.

"I wouldn't do that," he advised coolly.

I looked towards the voice. "It's better than the alternative," I challenged.

"But Peter will be so lonely," he pouted in a tragic voice.

I halted. "You didn't."

"You know I did. And I know you won't leave him here. And there's nowhere for you to go without serious bodily harm."

"Yes, but you intend to harm me, too."

"No, I already told you what I want."

I paused, thinking, then finally said, "Kidnapping, really? I thought a vampire would be a little more creative." I was surprised by how even my voice was.

"I'm a fan of the classics," he bantered. "And creative enough to avoid your little Watcher plot."

"And I walked right into your scheme." I kicked the rail with my heel, feeling like an idiot once again. I was the stupid person in the horror movie who wandered off on her own, knowing good and well there was a knife-toting psycho in the neighborhood.

I bit my lip and looked over the rail again. I carefully took out my phone, blocking my action with my body. *No signal! Of course. A little help, please!*

He made an exasperated sound under his breath. He was right: I wouldn't leave Peter. And I couldn't send up the bat signal for a rescue either. I wanted to curse as I cautiously gave up and walked into the darkness. I saw spots for a few moments until my eyes adjusted to the shadow.

Bowen was in the darkest corner of the garage, coolly leaning against the side of a black Mercedes, the windows as black as the paint. The trunk was open, and a small amount of light illuminated the unconscious body of Peter. I gasped, rushed over, and took his pulse. Bowen didn't so much as twitch while I counted heartbeats. It was strong. I sighed in relief, and oddly enough, I didn't feel frightened.

"What do you want?" I asked, acid dripping from my voice.

He unhitched himself from where he was leaning and walked towards me. He stood close, his body skimming mine as he reached up and closed the trunk without a word. I held my ground, resisting the urge to dive back into the sunlight. I knew it wouldn't do any good to leave.

He bent down, almost touching his cheek to mine, and whispered, "I would like you to get into the car, please."

He reached around and put his hand on the small of my back to guide me to the door. I repressed a flinch when he touched me. He opened the back passenger side door and motioned for me to get in.

I deliberated for a moment before consenting. He blurred with movement, and I felt a light brush against my hand; a warning went off in my head. I patted the side pocket where I keep my phone. It was gone. I looked at him, and he flashed a crooked grin as he dropped my phone into the chest pocket of his shirt.

I tossed my bag into the car and crawled inside, feeling defeated. The automatic locks clicked the second he closed my door, and he was almost instantaneously behind the wheel. I checked the handle, despite knowing that I was locked in. I was powerless.

Part of me expected him to toss me a blindfold, but he didn't. He was controlled, but there was a recklessness in his eyes that I hadn't seen before. In the dark garage, the only light in the car came from the buttons on the dash. I touched the window and felt an odd coating. I tried scratching at it, but it was like Teflon. *Figures. A special vampire-mobile.* I sat there, stewing in emotion, but I couldn't actually conjure up a single adjective to describe how I felt.

When he pulled into daylight, I could see out the windows with perfect clarity, but the color was bleached out of everything. The coating on the windows blocked much of the spectrum. He drove to an industrial area in Campbell not five minutes from my home. *He had been camped out minutes away this whole time.*

He flipped open the glove compartment and pulled out a small black remote with a flashing LED light. He thrust it towards the tinted windshield and impatiently clicked the button. A large steel door strained and growled open. My head was jerked back and forth as the car lurched over a bump and into the cavernous warehouse. He clicked the remote again, and the closing door eclipsed all the late afternoon light.

The headlights automatically came on when we entered, and I saw that every window and crevice of the place had been sealed with some dark material. When he cut the engine, the lights went out, and we were plunged into utter darkness.

My breath hitched in my throat; I couldn't see anything, no matter how much my eyes strained. I heard the driver's door open and close. I sat in the back seat of the pitch-black car, the air stuffy, for an immeasurable amount of time.

I closed my eyes, even though I couldn't see anything. Joshua's image came to mind. I could see him gently smiling at me and pulling me close, his body pressed against mine. I imagined leaning in to press my lips to his. At that moment, I was overwhelmed with sadness. I wanted to be able to say goodbye, but it wasn't going to be possible. *Be strong.* I sucked in a hard breath. *Be strong.*

My mind drifted to a future that Bowen's entrance into Joshua's life had destroyed. I imagined a world that could never be, of walking down an aisle in a white dress embellished with lace and a long satin train trailing behind me, my father putting my hand in Joshua's with confidence. My yearning was almost palpable.

I flashed forward to having children, my belly round, expectant with child, of growing old and being surrounded with grandchildren. I pictured how distinguished Joshua would look with salt-and-pepper hair like his father before him. But Joshua would never age. We could never have children or the white picket fence. Maybe it was 1950s of me, but that's what I wanted. My lip trembled at the fleeting nature of my dream, a dream that could never be realized.

My awareness shifted, and I could almost smell the incense from the church. I spoke a single word aloud, tilting my head in supplication.

A single prayer, pleading, as I begged, *"Please."*

19

COME ALONE

I heard movement outside of the car. Bowen flung open the door and reached in to unfasten my seatbelt before I could even drop my hand to the buckle. He wrenched me from the car. I felt a twinge from my rib and gasped. He moved around the back of the car, dragging me with him. There was something colder about him.

He opened the trunk. Peter's body was in the same exact position I'd remembered. Bowen removed Peter from the trunk and tossed him over his shoulder like a rag doll. Then, he grasped me under my arm just under the shoulder, his iron hand cutting into the muscle. There was no point in straining, as there was no hope of breaking his hold. The existing bruises on my arm ached with each step.

A light became visible in the corner of the building as we moved towards it. It was some type of cage with steel bars and a large weave grate welded over the top like the ones in warehouse stores protecting high-ticket items.

I ground my teeth, feeling like a helpless child again, angry at being unable to fight against the supernatural with any efficacy.

He shoved me inside, obviously irritated with me, and dumped Peter on the floor. As soon as I heard the heavy metallic clank of the door, I felt both petrified and relieved; Bowen was locking us both in and leaving us alone. In less than a second, he disappeared into the darkness.

I rushed to Peter, checking for a pulse again, but I couldn't feel it using his wrist. I pressed my head to his chest. He felt cool, but I could detect his heart rate, as well as his shallow breathing. Something shiny caught my attention under one of the shelves. Keeping on all fours, I crawled over and investigated. It was a shard of metal edge several inches long. I palmed it and stowed it in my back pocket, then returned to Peter.

Bowen appeared again at the door and opened it. He placed my bag and a bottle of water in the corner. I stood up to face him. He didn't seem irritated anymore; in fact, his whole demeanor had changed. In an instant, he wrapped his arms around me in an embrace, but I stood with my arms at my sides, unmoving. He held me there for a moment, pressing his cheek against mine. He buried his nose in my hair, breathing me in.

His raw emotion made me wonder if there was some shred of humanity in him, if some part of him truly cared about me or if he was entirely a monster. He was born to this life. Could he feel love? Or was I simply a means to an end in some twisted design? He abruptly disappeared, the door clanking behind him. *That was weird.*

I slumped to the floor next to Peter and twisted my hands in his shirt, wanting to cry. Did I want Peter to be aware of this world? Or would it be more merciful to let him sleep through this?

The smell of metal and dirt, coupled with the cold cement, made me even more miserable. I could see no way out. No way to save my friend. I wanted to peer into Bowen's head and see his plans, but I couldn't. I was human and unable to fight against something so strong.

I sat in silence and prayed that Joshua wouldn't be able to find me, that he would stay safe. I clutched my locket hidden underneath my shirt. Maybe Bowen would get frustrated and just finish me off. But then I looked at Peter. He would be doomed with me.

Bowen wanted some kind of confrontation. The French Coven wanted to retrieve their rebellious lost son, and he was out of time just like me. *How could I have been so stupid?* I reached for my phone, forgetting that I didn't have it.

"It's not there."

Ice ran through my veins as I looked towards the source of the voice. I hadn't realized that he had returned.

He swiped the screen of my phone, and the ghostly light illuminated his features. I saw him search through the directory. He smiled at me as he raised the phone to his ear. He stalked towards me like a prowling cat sure of victory.

He paused, triumph in his eyes. I could hear Joshua's voice imploring an answer on the other side of the phone. Bowen curled back his lips to reveal his canines. "I'm afraid she is unable to come to the phone right now."

I could only imagine Josh's response.

"Shhhhhh. There is no reason for threats. She's fine." He leaned against the bars of my prison. "Not to sound like the cliché villain, but she will remain that way as long as you do exactly as I say." He grinned at the response, then held the phone up to the cage. "Say hello, Aleria."

I shook my head no. His lips pressed into a thin line. I wasn't going to lure Joshua here. He ripped off the grate that was welded to the heavy bars and tossed it behind him with a horrible clamor, then thrust the phone through the bars, towards me again. I backed away from him until I hit the wall.

He let out an impatient gust of air, unlocked the door, jerked it open, and walked straight to Peter's motionless body. I screeched before he could touch him. He knew exactly how to control me. He handed me the phone.

"I'm here."

"Are you all right? Did he hurt you?"

"No, I'm fine, but he has Peter too." Bowen took a step towards me. "Josh, don't do anything, leave me—"

Bowen ripped the phone from my hand.

"You know as well as I do that you will not leave her here." He smiled again and instructed Joshua to come alone before giving him the address. He finished with, "I'll see you after sunset then," and ended the call. He did something to my phone and tossed it onto my bag. "You could save him, you know."

I looked at him, confused.

"The offer still stands. Come willingly, and I won't harm him."

"I don't believe you."

He glanced into the darkness of the room, and then back at me. I felt like he wanted to roll his eyes when he spoke again. "I have only lied to you twice, Aleria. And that was about attending San Jose State and my age. I have never lied about anything else, nothing important."

I thought about that for a moment and realized that, to my knowledge, he hadn't. "Hmpf. I see you are a noble villain. You just want me to join the dark side." I thrust out my chin in defiance.

"I'm afraid Luke Skywalker is not going to save you."

"Luke Skywalker used his powers for good and defeated his more powerful father, didn't he?" I retorted.

He only replied with an icy smile.

Then I realized that I was alone again.

A few minutes later, some bluish lights flickered to life from the high ceiling. The building was larger than I had initially thought. Naked steel beams every twenty feet or so held up the sagging roof. A catwalk hung overhead that had fallen into disrepair long ago.

Ancient-looking machinery stood dormant, caked with gritty dirt and spider webs. I wondered what had once been produced here. An elevated foreman's room was at the back of the building placed to oversee the majority of the space. There was a narrow set of stairs leading to it and a path that cut through the dust, showing recent use.

Bowen reappeared, and the force of his emotion made me stumble back a couple of steps. Words seemed to burst from him with a sudden urgency and were tinged with anger, or maybe desperation. I had never seen him drop his cool demeanor like this. "You can have everything you want if you are with me."

I blinked. "How do you know what I want?" I snapped.

His tone softened, and he looked pained. "We spent weeks talking to one another. Do you think that I didn't glean some of your desires from our conversations?"

I could feel my face burn, but not from embarrassment. "Really? What am I thinking now?"

"Be nice."

I shook my head in disgust. "You have nothing to offer me."

His expression was unreadable. "I think I do. The safety of your beloved, perhaps?"

"Maybe this isn't sinking in. I. Don't. Trust. You."

"I can offer you a life beyond your imagination. Immortality is just a piece of it. You can have everything you want. An extraordinary life. You told me you wanted to travel, to experience life, to have children, to have a legacy. You can still have that with me. You can have everything you desire."

"I thought the *undead* part took the *life* part out of it?"

His lips curled downward in frustration.

"And I thought vampires couldn't have children," I said in disbelief.

"Not all vampires can."

This stopped me short. "I don't understand." *Why am I having this conversation with him?*

"It depends on the bloodline and where you are in the genetic tree. Did your precious Watchers tell you about the *Rephaim*? (Hebrew: Terrible Giants)"

I had tried to absorb so much information in the last

couple of days, I racked my brain for more; the term seemed familiar.

He continued, "The original vampires are different, stronger—their bodies capable of change. If you are born a vampire, or if someone sires you within the first three generations, the bloodline is strong enough. Anything beyond that, and a vampire is sterile, incapable of doing anything but siring other vampires. Some genetic glitch that makes them like mules, mere foot soldiers of our kind. *Rephaim* are part of the ruling class whose origins are true royalty, the *Radix*. The root, the origin, the foundation for us all."

I looked at him blankly. Biology was not my strongest subject, but it reminded me of Pottenger's cats that we had learned about in biology class. They were fed cooked food instead of raw food for an extended period of time, and after a few generations, they became infertile, aggressive, and uncontrollable. Even the cats' appearance was altered; they became mangy.

It made me wonder if the diet of only blood was a natural way to keep their numbers down. Maybe the monster-like vampires that the Slayers routinely hunted were a result of being too far down the genetic chain, producing feral vampires. True monsters. I looked at him. "So, you really are a prince."

He gave me a single nod of confirmation. But he had an odd look fixed on his face, like he wasn't proud of it. Like it was a burden or a secret source of animosity.

He returned to the subject. "If your beloved decided to keep you forever, you would be barren for all of eternity, never able to experience what you desire."

"I have no plans to become one of you, and *he* would never turn me."

"You think he can bear to watch you grow old and die?"

"Yes, that is how it is supposed to be."

"Maybe."

"It is," I insisted angrily, my eyes piercing.

"If you were mine, I wouldn't be able to bear it."

"*You* will never have that problem."

He was silent for what seemed to be ages. He unlocked and entered the cell. I backed against the wall. He towered over me, looking down at me pleadingly, like he wanted to reach inside my head and alter my mind. He caressed the side of my face, and I twisted away from his touch.

He sighed, "I will only offer this to you once more. When I do, know it will be the last boon I bid you." Then he left abruptly, and the door clanked shut and locked automatically behind him. I didn't know if making him angry was wise, but part of me really didn't care.

I sat down next to Peter and immediately began to shiver. I wrapped my arms around my knees and rocked back and forth, trying to soothe myself. When that didn't work, I picked up Peter's unmoving hand and held it. His breath was shallow as his chest moved, almost imperceptibly. I was overcome by an ominous feeling that pressed in on me, wanting to crush the life out of me. I couldn't understand Bowen's motivation any longer.

He seemed more human. It made me ill to feel any softness towards him. He was plotting to kill me or turn me into a vampire. I tried to hold onto my anger. But he seemed altered. *Could his motivation for wanting to turn me have really changed? Or is he that good of a liar? Is he actually capable of change?*

Somehow, I could feel Joshua getting closer. I bowed my head and repeated my single word prayer...*Please.*

20

GUESTS

Joshua would arrive at any moment. I sat helpless, waiting. I was the bait all right, just not for whom I had expected. I played different scenarios over in my head, but what truly haunted my mind were tragedies.

I wanted a happy ending. I wanted Ferdinand and Miranda to live happily ever after and for Caliban to be banished. But in our story, Caliban was more powerful. There wasn't going to be a *deus ex machina* ending for us like I had learned about in school. In our story, there was no magical spirit ready to set things right so Miranda and Ferdinand could be together. Life was so much more difficult than fiction.

The familiar, tragic stories like *Romeo and Juliet* burned in my mind, stories where the protagonists could only be together in death. Or the more modern story of *Gatsby*, where the heroine traded her happiness to be with a despicable man and ended up being despicable herself. And of course, in that story, the hero died.

I started to plan, but every option seemed to lead to a different kind of death, or maybe I was being melodramatic. I drummed my fingers on my knees.

My head started to buzz, so I pressed my fingers into my temples, waiting and waiting. Peter shifted a little and murmured something. He wasn't conscious, but he was becoming more active. I reached down and held his hand to comfort him, but I think it comforted me more.

Sensing something, I stood up, walked to the door of my cage, and grasped the bars. At the far end of the warehouse, sparks started spraying through the oversized metal roll-up door in a perfect rectangle the size of a standard door.

In a flash, a dramatic array of light danced throughout the building. I looked up at the upstairs office, expecting to see Bowen racing towards the impending breach, but the room was still. The light faded, and the cutout piece of the door toppled onto the cement with a ghastly *clank*. Smoke billowed into the building—an entrance worthy of an action hero—but no one entered.

At the same time, a shadowy figure dropped without a trace of sound from the catwalk directly above. They landed inches from me outside the cell. My eyes bulged as I staggered back a half step. It startled me so much that all I could do was draw in a breath. I didn't have the air to scream.

In one single movement, a hand reached through the bars and snatched my wrist, pulling me closer, while the other hand covered my mouth. With utter joy, I realized the intruder was Joshua.

Once he saw I had contained my panic and recognized him, he released me and examined the door. I shook my head. There was no silent way to get me out. Bowen had the key, so tearing it from the hinges was the only option.

He cringed, then grabbed onto the door with his right hand. He mouthed, "Get ready," to me. I picked up my bag and knelt down next to Peter, pushing him into a seated position so we could get him up faster.

When I looked to Joshua for instruction, he froze for a second before raising his hands in surrender. Bowen was standing two feet behind him with a Durateus sword pressed into his back, ready to pierce his heart.

"I enjoyed the fireworks. What are you going to do for the second act?"

"I was thinking about making you disappear." Josh spat.

"Oh, that's been done before. In fact, I saw the Statue of Liberty disappear once. You should think of something more original."

Joshua cringed as Bowen pressed the sword harder into his back.

"Now, get on your knees," Bowen commanded.

Joshua looked at me warily as he dropped down, his profile to me. Bowen backed up a few steps, then took the blade away from Josh's back. I could see blood seeping down between his shoulder blades where the skin had been pierced.

Bowen stalked back and forth, keeping the blade angled at Josh at all times, tracking his every movement. I could see the wheels turning in his head.

"You going to do something, or am I going to die of old age first? Oh wait, I can't," Josh provoked.

"You do want to die?"

"Just get to it," Josh said, no amusement left in his voice. "You have me. Take your revenge. Let her go."

"What would be the fun in that? I have more interesting options."

"Of course you do, you sick—"

"Tisk, tisk. There is a lady present."

"Yes, and you obviously know how to treat a lady."

"Well, aren't you spunky. I didn't know you had it in you after listening to all the tender moments between the two of you."

I locked my eyes on his face. *How did he know about the Watcher's plan? How would he have heard Josh and I speak to one another?*

Josh glanced at me. He was thinking the same thing.

"I'm a regular Renaissance man," Josh quipped.

"So, your task is simple. Drain the boy, and after a little while, I'll let you go." Bowen smiled.

"And if I don't?" Josh responded.

"You won't like that option. Of course, you won't be around to see the consequences. Although, you could give her to me, choose your own life over hers. You could walk away right now—I would even let you take the boy." Bowen backed up a few paces, giving the illusion of some privacy.

"Josh, just take Peter and leave," I whispered desperately. Neither one of them were going to die for me. Not for me.

"I won't leave you with him," his voice broke. "That's not an option. Ali, he intended for Peter to be your first kill. He doesn't mean for Peter to walk out of here alive. That's why he took him. To control you and then to feed you. No one is walking out of here."

"Peter is innocent. He had nothing to do with this." I pleaded, "Please, take him and go."

"I will *not* leave you. I'd rather die." End of discussion.

But then it occurred to me: I could save *both* of them. Bowen wouldn't let them walk out if it was Joshua's choice. But if *I* chose him, he would. Calm washed over me.

I sank to my knees next to Joshua's side and looked at him through the bars. I loved the hollow under his cheekbone, the curve of his jaw and the fullness of his bottom lip. He met my gaze. I admired his thick lashes and the gold flecks in his intense green eyes. Time seemed to stand still for a moment.

I was just about to stand and offer plan B, but Joshua was already on his feet. Two blades dropped from his forearms, and he flung them at Bowen with deadly accuracy. Everything happened in the blink of an eye. Bowen knocked the blades from the air with his sword and threw Joshua against the bars, the steel bending to the shape of his back.

Joshua launched himself at Bowen. The sound of tearing metal split the air as their bodies smashed through some of the machinery. I could hear blow after blow, a body being tossed into one obstacle and then another. They were on the catwalk above. Dirt rained down and scattered on the ground with a crackle. The walkway screeched from the tumult. Joshua landed a kick with such force that Bowen went through the rail and plummeted to the ground. I could hear machinery give way as he landed. I held my breath and waited.

Joshua dropped from above and disappeared into the

shadowed area where Bowen had fallen. The room was eerily silent. Trying to desperately see into the darkened corners, I clenched the steel with such ferocity that my arms went numb. Then suddenly, Joshua's back was against the bars directly in front of me.

I recoiled, screeching, "*No!!!*"

Bowen's dagger plunged into Joshua's heart—I could see the tip of it through his back. He fell sideways and landed flat on his back with a slapping sound as his body hit the floor. Unable to control his fall, his head bounced. The Durateus dagger stuck unnaturally out of his chest like a tombstone.

Bowen held his sword above his body, positioning himself to make the kill. Blood was dripping from his mouth, past the curve of his chin, onto his fitted white shirt. A thin trail of blood ran down the back of his left arm from his shoulder. He fumed, seeming shocked that Joshua had done so well against him.

He was about to take the final strike when I screamed, "No, please! No!" He stopped short and looked at me. I looked into his wild eyes and promised, "I will never forgive you, in this life or the next." I prayed that I did have the power over him that the Watchers had said.

He growled, then uttered what sounded like a curse in another language. He looked at me with an unfathomable expression, like he had volumes that wanted to spill out of him, but they were locked tight. His arm dropped to his side as he abruptly turned on his heel and disappeared.

Joshua let out a gasp, and his body shuddered. His arms were limp at his sides. Crimson liquid inched across his shirt and ran down to the floor. He closed his eyes and became like stone.

I helplessly watched the blood flow out of him. I reached through the bars and took Joshua's hand, holding it like it was my lifeline.

I wasn't sure how much time had gone by, and I wasn't sure how long Bowen had been watching me. He was staring at my hands clasped around Joshua's hand. His expression was solemn.

21

MAMAN

The slow click of high heels broke the silence. Bowen's head perked up. He tilted his head to track the sound.

"*Bonjour, mon fils,* (Hello, son)" greeted a voice from the darkness. It wasn't human; I could tell that without seeing the being to whom it belonged. Her voice was sensual, strong, and captivating. It seemed as if two voices were speaking in unison, blended in perfect harmony and melody to make her voice otherworldly. She was speaking French; I recognized the words as a formal greeting.

His body didn't move, but he bowed his head acknowledgment. "*Maman,* (Mother)" he replied without inflection, his eyes trained on me.

I struggled to understand. I'd taken French freshman and sophomore years, but in the past year, I'd already forgotten so much. I concentrated, willing myself to comprehend the words.

The voice moved closer behind him. "*Il est temps de rentrer, mon fils. Il est temps de prendre ta place avec—* (It is time to come home, son. Time to take your place with—) I could only pick out words and phrases to get the general context.

He cut her off with surprising ferocity. "I'm done being a puppet for your regime, Mother. You should know me better than that." He looked me in the eyes as if he wanted me to understand.

She replied, her French accent thick, "This little rebellion of yours has lasted three hundred years. It is over. The world has changed; nations have risen and fallen in your absence. These petty humans should be worshipping at our feet. We should not be hiding in the shadows. We should be ruling as we once did."

"That is *your* wish, Mother."

"You are a prince; you should know your station."

"*My* station…" He let out a single knife-like laugh. "You mean, under your thumb."

"You leaving to find your own way is one thing, but taking your brother with you—"

"*Taking* him?" he replied incredulously. "I never asked him to come. He made his own choices."

"You knew what he would choose."

"I told him to return home when he found me. I sent him home."

"You should—" She stopped short as if she had just realized she had an audience beyond her son. Her blue eyes flashed red for a brief instant as she turned her icy stare on me. Maybe she hadn't realized I was here, due to her attention on her wayward son. I guessed if my son had run off for three hundred years, I might have been singularly focused too.

Or maybe I hadn't been worthy of her attention until now. Regardless, I didn't want it. I wished I could melt into the industrial floor. She was the scariest thing I'd ever seen. I'd sooner face a volcanic eruption or an act of God than her.

She was exactly as I had imagined from Gabriel's description: statuesque. Her perfect, white skin cast off a glow from the light, almost giving her a visible, iridescent aura. Her blonde hair was tightly pulled up into large barrel curls on top of her head with a crystal-encrusted ribbon crisscrossed through it. Her grey suit was ultra high fashion, regal, elegant, and over-the-top. The embroidered corset bodice and fitted suit jacket with a dramatic fur-lined collar were designed to intimidate.

She stepped forward to speak to me, her stiletto boots clacking on the cement. Her brilliant eyes turned blacker than midnight, as if her pupils had devoured every trace of color from her iris, as she purred, "Sleep, child, there is no need for alarm. You will be at peace soon."

I wanted to ask if that meant 'dead soon,' but this was not a vampire I would have chosen to irritate. A subtle wave of energy pulsed from her body that seemed to distort the air as it moved towards me. When it engulfed me, I felt exhaustion slither from the crown of my head to my toes. Part of me wanted to succumb, to let it all be over. I glanced at Joshua and Peter and firmly thought "No." The feeling receded. I seemed to have more command of myself than I thought.

Her delicate nostrils flared. "Sleep, child, sleep." She was trying to lull me, and her fervor increased.

"It's no use, Mother. It doesn't work on her." Her eyes

released me and fastened on him, looking as if his words stung.

"Impossible!" she exclaimed, her French accent making her sound even more superior.

"Mother, I have to touch her before it works, and even then, it's momentary. I have only encountered a handful of people able to resist us in all my years."

She looked at me again like she wanted to squash me, but there was a trace of something else...admiration? "So, is this why you have stayed here so long? Why we were able to locate you?"

I could see him deliberating. A shadow stalking outside the open door caught my attention. The silhouette looked to be clad in leather and well armed. *Most likely part of the famous royal guard the Watchers had mentioned.*

The queen approached my cage with an outstretched arm. "Don't, Mother," Bowen warned.

She didn't like his interference, but stopped in her tracks. I had the feeling that no one had ever said "no" to her. Power emanated from her entire being.

"Son, it is finished." She petulantly waved her hand towards me while looking at him, and another distortion sprang from her hand. This one knocked me backwards, and my head hit the ground with a crack.

"My Queen, if you are ever to have me back, it will be on my terms. I am my mother's son," Bowen said as he bowed his head in what seemed to be reverence, but could have been sly mocking.

She responded in French again, her tone passionate.

Bowen retorted in kind, but they were speaking too quickly for me to follow now.

I felt angered that a piece of me had started to understand Bowen. I could imagine him ruling alongside his gluttonous, power-hungry mother. She controlled every aspect of his life. One day, he had had enough. I wondered if the catalyst was a woman—maybe an arranged marriage? Whatever it was, he had disappeared. He was ruled by rebelliousness and fed by his anger. He lashed out at the world, cashing in on petty grudges to occupy his empty existence. A prince without a country. A wanderer rejecting his birthright to make his own choices.

I didn't want to understand him. Or feel anything for him. I held onto my fury and tried to focus on all of his offenses—I would allow him no sympathy. He had taken Joshua's human life from him. He planned to kill me. He planned to kill Peter. A creature like that was not capable of love. Then, all of the moving pieces came into focus.

Free will.

Choice.

That was what everything came down to, didn't it? Bowen wanted me to *choose* him of my own free will. To be bound to him for eternity. She, the Queen, wanted him to *choose* her and his duty—to go home and rule with her.

I was overcome with hopelessness.

If I choose him to save Joshua and Peter, will I lose my soul for sacrificing myself? Will I be strong enough to keep from killing innocent people? Bowen certainly won't help me from doing that. He'll encourage it to strengthen the bond between us. If I make that choice, will there be any way to go back? Will there be any way to still be me? Or will it be like I was told: I'll cease to care about anyone but my mate and the bloodlust? The connections to my human life being so easily severed.

They lapsed into English for a moment. "End this, my son. I will not leave without you. Loyalties have shifted; we have made alliances with some of the other ancients. We will join with the Italian and Spanish Covens. We will rule!"

"I'm surprised you haven't allied yourself with the animals in the Carpathians, Mother," he sneered and turned his back to me.

At that point, they switched back to French, their voices racing. I inched back across the floor towards Joshua, my head throbbing where it had met the concrete. They didn't notice my movement. I strained my arms through the bars until pain ripped through my shoulder and my rib ached like someone had jammed a thumb into my torso.

I managed to wrap my fingers around the hilt of the dagger and pulled. Joshua's entire torso raised with the effort. I realized that it was wedged between two ribs, pinched between the bones. I held my breath, and my lungs burned for air as I yanked on the blade as silently as possible. It came free suddenly, and I hit my knuckles on the bars with such force there was a dull twanging sound. I bit my lip and tried not to yelp, but instead, let out a ragged breath as quietly as possible. Thankfully, I had managed to maintain my hold on the knife and not drop it.

They were so wrapped up in their heated debate, they hadn't noticed the sound. Joshua let out a faint moan. He'd lost so much blood. I wondered how long it'd take for him to recover and if he'd be able to recover without more blood.

He'd lost so much of it already. I got choked up when I took in how far the pool of blood had extended across the floor. I tucked the bloodied weapon underneath the edge of his body, obscuring it from Bowen's view.

I retreated back into my cell and sat exactly where I'd been when the queen had knocked me backwards. I looked at my hands. They were covered in Joshua's blood. I carefully wiped them on the back of my t-shirt so it wouldn't be visible.

I re-examined my hands. No blood. No cuts that his blood could have seeped into. Then I started listening to the conversation again. They were back to English.

"Turn her or end her. I have lost patience with this. You *will* come home. Leave a corpse or bring a bride. Your choice. I will use force, if necessary."

"My Queen, *Maman!* (Mother!)" he implored.

"This. Ends. Now," she declared with finality.

He pursed his lips and glanced towards the door. I followed his gaze and saw a line of at least a dozen guards waiting by the door. He bowed his head as the largest one broke rank and silently drew closer.

I think he was the most massive man I'd ever seen in my life. Hulking, broad shoulders that said his body was designed for destruction shifted under his leather coat. A menace emanated from him that equaled—or even surpassed—the queen. His dark hair was long enough that it cast shadows over his eyes, which I guessed were dark as well. He had an olive complexion, but he seemed to transcend nationality. His features could have been anything.

He stopped several feet behind Bowen and glanced over at me for a split-second, and then back at the queen. A moment later, I felt his eyes on me again. Then slowly, the look of puzzlement was replaced by what appeared to be recognition. I was bewildered, but the queen began speaking and drew my attention.

"I will leave you. There will be a contingent of my guard left. There is a private jet awaiting you at the airport." She looked past Bowen. "Dagan, please prepare for our departure."

The gigantic man disappeared through the door with the stealth and quiet of a vampire, but there was something different about him. And the queen's tone was very reverent when addressing him, despite her words being a command. But maybe I was overanalyzing. I looked back over at Bowen.

He sighed, appearing heavy, beaten. "Which airport?"

"San Francisco. You have two hours."

He turned his back to her—in the movies this is something you never do to the queen. And then she was gone. She moved so quickly, it was as if she had turned to mist. He stood there for a long while without moving.

I furtively looked at Joshua and noticed the gaping hole in his chest was almost closed. His lips twitched as if he were talking with someone. My hands itched to touch him. Peter murmured something and drew his arm to his face. Whatever Bowen had done to him was wearing off. I scrambled to his side, wringing my hands in his shirt out of nervousness.

Sitting on my knees, I touched his face and bent down towards his ear. "Peter, it's Ali. Can you hear me?"

He slurred something incoherent. Part of me still didn't want him to wake up. Only horror awaited him.

"Peter, take your time. I'm here." I avoided saying

everything would be okay, because for all intents and purposes, it wouldn't. He cringed, and I grasped his head.

"What happened?" he whispered, finally lucid.

"Um…" My mind was spinning. *How do I respond to that? A vampire prince in hopes of seeking revenge kidnapped you, to control me, in hopes that he could crush Joshua and run away with me. Is that what's happening? That is, not to mention Watchers, Slayers, Keepers, and vampire alliances threatening the world as we know it. Add a few aliens and the abominable snowman, and we'll have a real party.*

Peter nudged me, and I realized I still hadn't answered. "We were taken," I said softly. "I'm trying to figure a way out."

He moaned and rolled on his side away from me. I rubbed his back, trying to give him some comfort.

"Why?" he croaked.

"I, uhh, I…" I didn't want to lie, but on the other hand, I didn't want to give him information that would get him killed.

Bowen was still playing the part of a statue with his back to me. I wondered if he was paying attention at all or if he was locked in his thoughts.

"Just relax, you have a pretty big bump on your head," I told Peter.

He started to make some sort of reply, but it came out as, "Mmpfth."

I leaned down to his ear again. "I want you to save your strength. When the time comes, you will need to move fast."

He replied, "K," and relaxed his body.

I stood up and moved to the edge of the cell, holding onto

the bars, and looked at Bowen. He cocked his head slightly, acknowledging me.

"I'm out of time," he said like he was hollow.

"I guess that means that I am too."

He circled towards the cage, not noticing that the sword no longer adorned Joshua's chest. I concentrated, keeping my eyes on Bowen so I wouldn't draw attention to Josh.

He stood a foot from the cage with a ghostly look on his face. All I could think was that he appeared broken. This wasn't the confident creature I had come to know. He seemed *hopeless*.

"I have never been human. I was born into this. I never had a choice. When I escaped, I could have improved myself in some way, tried to make myself worthy of something better, but I didn't. I felt disdain for every living creature. I even hated you. But then, I wondered why he cared about you, why he would keep your picture.

"Out of boredom, or maybe curiosity, I spent time with you. I didn't realize that I felt differently about you until I felt," he paused, like he didn't want to say the word. Then he explained, "Jealous. But it was too late. You already hated me. You had seen my emptiness." He clenched his fists into hard balls and flexed his jaw. "I have no right to you. I know that, but I can protect you if you choose to come with me. If you choose me, I can offer you—"

"Offer me what? Choose you or die? To let people I care about die? What kind of offer is that? The moment your mother walked in here, all other options were gone. She isn't going to let any of us walk out of here. The second you leave this place, her guard is going to destroy us. Or are you going to claim otherwise?"

"I can protect you. I *want* to protect you."

"That's not enough for me. Or can you protect them, too?"

He didn't answer my question. "In a little while, I am going to make my offer to you one last time." He paused, his face pleading. "Please consider it. I'll leave you alone to deliberate."

"Would you please let me out of here while I think about it?" He didn't respond. "Where am I gonna to go? You are faster and stronger than me. Her guards are outside. I'm not stupid enough to think I could get away. All that an escape attempt will do is make my end more painful. Plus, you know I wouldn't leave them behind."

He frowned, unlocked the door, and was gone. I heard the office door on the second floor click. Then, I heard what I thought might be talking or arguing upstairs, but I couldn't be sure. Was he on the phone?

I crept out of my cell towards Joshua; there was so much blood. It looked like there was a crimson flag sailing from the left side of his body, flowing away from him on the slightly sloped floor. Even with his healing abilities, he wouldn't be able to recover without help. Half of his blood must have pooled out onto the concrete.

There was about a foot between his body and the wall of the cage. I stepped to his right side and lay down on my left next to him, glancing one last time at the blood pool on the other side of his body. I pressed my face to his cheek. He was so much colder than normal, almost icy, and he was so still.

The movements he had been making with his lips had vanished. I kissed his forehead, his cheeks, his chin, his lips, wetting his face with my tears. His eyelids fluttered. I pressed my mouth to his ear while cupping his face with my trembling hand.

I kept my voice so low that I could barely hear it. I didn't want to chance Bowen hearing it upstairs. "Can you understand me? If you do, please blink twice." I raised my head to watch.

He very slowly, but deliberately blinked twice.

"Did you overhear anything that happened? Did you hear the queen?"

He blinked twice.

"I think we're out of options." My voice cracked.

He blinked twice.

"I love you. I love you. I love you." I whispered as if they were my last words and kissed him on the mouth. His lips twitched in response.

He blinked twice.

"I'm so sorry, love. I'm going to do some things. I pray you'll be able to forgive me someday. If I survive the first, you need to get Peter out of here."

He blinked once.

"I don't think you're in any position to argue."

He blinked twice.

"And you say I'm stubborn. I hate to tell you this, but I'll win this round."

He blinked once.

"Please know that I love you more than anything in this world. No matter what happens. Don't blame yourself for any of this. You survive, you hear me? And please, please forgive me."

His eyelids fluttered rapidly. I reached into my back pocket and secured the shard of metal that I had found. I knew this was a long shot. The only hope to save both him and Peter would be to have Joshua somehow get them out. I pressed the sharp edge of the torn metal into my wrist.

When the blood started flowing freely, I used my other hand to open his mouth and then placed my wound inside. He was motionless. The blood pooled in his mouth for a moment. It seemed as if he was trying not to swallow, but then he did, and there was an almost immediate change.

His lips molded to my wrist, and I could feel him take some weak pulls. He let out a small gasp, and then I felt his fangs plunge into my flesh. It hurt for a second, but then it felt good—really good. My body relaxed, and I rested my head on the floor. I remembered how much it had hurt when Bowen had bitten me; this wasn't the same. Joshua had told me that Bowen had done that on purpose, that they can release a hormone that makes it pleasurable. I didn't think this was a bad death. He weakly raised his left hand, sluggishly sliding it up his body, and touched my wrist. His pulls became greedy.

I hovered there in euphoria. He could have it all. I would let him take it if he needed it. I'd known that was a risk. He was young and might not have had enough control to stop. My mind started getting fuzzy. I liked the idea of my blood in him. In a strange way, I would now always be with him; although, this was not how I'd pictured my life ending.

I watched his face. He squeezed his eyes shut hard and shuddered, then feebly pulled my wrist from his mouth as he gasped. He drew my arm back for a brief second, then licked the gash, and it stopped bleeding almost instantly. Then his arm flopped lifelessly at his side. His body felt a little warmer, and he started to breathe more regularly again. I drew myself up on my elbow; my head still a little light. I cupped his face, and this time, he was able to look into my eyes.

I whispered, "I love you," and kissed him again. His lips responded sleepily. "I know you're angry with me right now. Please understand this is all I can do to save you. I have to be *terrible*." My tears started to spill over onto his face. I wiped them away, apologizing.

"This is so hard," I whispered. "Please don't hate me. You need to get Peter out of here. Don't come after me. I need to know that you are okay. That you're out there somewhere. I may not be *me* anymore. I don't want you to see that. I'm so sorry." I kissed him once more, spilling as much of my soul into him as I could. I put my hands on the floor on either side of his face and drew my knees underneath me.

He wobbled his head back and forth, making protests in short gasps. I could hear his heels scraping the floor weakly. He grabbed my wrist, but I could easily break his grip. He was getting stronger by the minute, but I'd have just enough time to save him. There was no chance of getting out of this in a fight.

I stood to my feet, and his fingers grabbed at my shoe. "Forgive me," I whispered, one last time as I walked away from him.

Forever.

22

CHOICE

My legs were so shaky they felt foreign under my body. I stood in full view of the upstairs office, strong in my resolve. I could taste the metallic twang of my blood from Joshua's lips. With so much of his blood in the room, I wondered if Bowen would notice the addition of mine. I looked at my wrist; there was nothing left but a furious line. I intentionally bit my lip, drawing blood to give a reason for the scent of my blood in the room.

After a few minutes, the door creaked open, and Bowen materialized in the doorway from the darkness. He glanced back over his shoulder into the office before descending the stairs, looking like someone headed to the guillotine. I couldn't understand his expression. *Wasn't I the one about to lose everything?*

He stood motionless in front of me, not even breathing.

I drew in a deep breath to steady myself. The dusty smell

of the warehouse assaulted my senses. Everything seemed overwhelming.

"Will you come with me? Will you *choose* me?" he asked in a blank voice.

My mouth suddenly felt dry, and my throat constricted as if I had been wandering in the desert. My body was revolting against my decision. "I will, but I have one condition."

His nostrils flared. "Condition?" he asked hoarsely as he tensed infinitesimally.

"I'll go with you. I'll *choose* you, if you promise me their safety. You won't let the guards touch them. Lie, if you need to. Do whatever it takes. Do that, and I'm yours."

He looked relieved. I was sure he thought I would rather choose death over being with him. He didn't understand that being with him was going to *be* death. I could feel his emotion shift, the darkness in him recede. "I give you my word no harm will befall them."

Hesitantly, I added, "Wait. I have one more thing to ask."

His lips flattened into a hard line.

"Please." My eyes were glossy tears, ready to streak down my cheeks. "If you're going to turn me, it can't be here—it needs to be somewhere else."

"Agreed," he answered, but his voice was hoarse.

I can do this, I thought. Maybe I was just trying to convince myself. He took a step towards me, and I sucked in a breath involuntarily. I could still feel Joshua on my lips, smell him on me. Bowen caressed my cheek with his fingertips, then touched the bite mark on my bottom lip as he explored my face. I closed my eyes and pictured Joshua behind my lids.

He hesitated for a moment, and then I felt his cool arms

envelop me. He pressed his forehead to mine, breathing in my scent. His hands explored my back, one between my shoulder blades, the other caressing the bit of skin revealed at my waist. A chill raced up my spine. He ran his nose across my cheek, his breathing irregular. Every touch was a test. There was an element of wonder, like this was the first time he had touched me.

My breath hitched in my chest as he pulled me closer. My arms bowed out like a ballerina's, hands at waist level so not as to touch him. When I remained unresponsive, he dropped his arms and looked into my eyes again. Two glowing glacier blue eyes peered into my very soul. He was obviously frustrated with the robotic way I held my body. He could sense the empty shell of me.

He pressed his lips to my ear. "I don't believe you."

With trembling hands, I put my arms around his neck and grasped his collar, trying to keep myself in place. I wanted to put my fingers around his neck and choke him. I felt anger surge through my body, my nerves a network of sparks. *Can he feel my contempt?*

I retreated inside myself, relaxed my body and responded to his touch. He pressed his parted lips to mine, and I reacted this time. He pulled me closer, touching the tip of his tongue to mine tentatively, tenderly. I shuddered, and a tear toppled over the edge of my eye. He wiped it away with his thumb while still kissing me. Joshua's presence a dozen yards away was burning into my back. I wondered if he could see me. Bowen drew away enough to look into my eyes, but didn't say anything.

"They will be safe," I confirmed in a whisper. "Whatever

this grudge is, it is forgiven." Both declarative statements, not questions.

"Yes," he replied, serenely running the back of his fingers under my jaw, completely engrossed in me.

"Okay," I said, unwinding myself from his embrace. "Let me grab my bag." He assented, and as I walked over, I noticed my cell phone battery on the ground; that was why it hadn't worked. I leaned down as if to tie my shoe and palmed it.

I stood back up and continued to the cage; my bag was slumped between two of the bars. I glanced into it as I popped the battery into my phone and roughly zipped the bag shut, and then paused. I reopened it and examined the contents more closely. There was a small Durateus knife, much smaller than the dagger with which I had practiced. The size of a hunting knife you would stick in a boot. The silver gleam of the hilt made me smile. *Did Gabriel put this in here? Maybe I have a third option.* It would be a death sentence for sure, but I felt oddly comfortable with that.

I stepped towards Bowen and avoided even a glance at Joshua, afraid I would lose my resolve. Bowen smiled at me, a genuine smile. He looked exultant. I smiled uncertainly in return, but of course, I was thinking something far different. *I will end you. You will never have me, and if the Watchers can trace my cell, they can take out the guard too.*

The next moments seemed to happen in slow motion, though they really took mere seconds. I was listlessly moving towards Bowen, conspiratorial plans consuming my thoughts. When I was just a few yards away from him, I sensed something pass through the air, preceded by a faint metallic click on the far side of the warehouse.

I glanced at the origin of the sound, seeing nothing but a dim light through the hole in the roll-up door. I swung my head back around and focused on Bowen. He was still as a pillar, looking down at himself in disbelief, his arms bent and hands held up awkwardly at shoulder-height, like a surgeon who had prepped his hands for surgery. Suddenly, his crisp white shirt was washed with scarlet. He collapsed to his knees and stared at me pleadingly as he fell backwards, paralyzed.

I stumbled away from him, as the fire from automatic weapons cut through the night air, both outside and on top of the building, shattering the silence. I flinched as some of the windows broke out, and a bright flood of light spilled in through the new fissures in the building. There was an odd mixture of intense light and utter darkness throughout the building, each shaft of light crisp and clean, though not shedding much illumination into the recesses of the room.

Backing away several more feet, I looked at Bowen's immobile figure once again. Then I slipped on Joshua's blood and crashed to the cement floor, cracking my elbow on the hard surface. I sucked in a startled breath and gritted my teeth from the throb of pain that ran up my arm. I clutched my elbow fiercely and rolled to my side, then to my knees. Josh ineffectually moved one of his legs.

"Can you stand?" I questioned.

"Working on it. Check Peter," he said, his voice labored.

I dashed into the cell, weapons' fire echoing in the cavernous building. I slid on my knees to Peter's side, like a baseball player sliding into home, seized his shirt, and shook him. He opened his eyes, looked around wildly, then fixated on me.

"Peter, I need you to get up!"

"Thought you'd never ask."

"Help me with Joshua," I urged.

We pulled him to his feet, and he swayed back. He was recovering faster than I thought he would, but he still couldn't move under his own power. Peter gaped at the blood all over the ground as he placed one of Joshua's arms over his shoulders, and I moved to do the same.

Suddenly, I heard booted steps approaching swiftly behind me. I whirled around, almost toppling Josh over, as I grabbed for the dagger on the ground and thrust it towards the approaching danger. Headlights from a car outside blazed through the hole in the roll-up door, silhouetting the oncoming person. I gripped the dagger with a steady hand.

And at the exact moment I thought all was lost, I gasped in joy and relief when I recognized Gabriel. He was sprinting towards us, a black crossbow in one hand, the other held up in peace.

"We are evenly matched outside, but it could go either way. Let us go." He pushed me aside and pulled Joshua's arm around his shoulder.

As we started moving to the side door, we were stopped in our tracks. I saw a flicker in the office, and then, there abruptly appeared before us, a battle-ready figure with a sword in one hand and a dagger in the other, legs spread a shoulder's width apart like a god of war ready to defeat an army.

All of us stood aghast at the carbon copy of Bowen towering before us.

23

IDENTICAL

E verything fell into place at once. *There were two of him.* That was why he often seemed to be in two places at once and was able to get across town in minutes. Bowen seemed to have such a gift for evasion because he had a partner looking out for him and vice versa.

They were dressed identically. Save the hole in Bowen's chest, it would have been all but impossible to tell them apart. Although, the one who stood before us was different—colder —crueler.

He looked at me with utter contempt. His eyes swept over our group, lingering on Joshua's sagging body between Gabriel and Peter. A merciless smile twisted his features. "Son," he acknowledged.

My eyes shot to Joshua. His mouth fell open as the information registered. Bowen was not his sire.

I then realized that I had seen his eyes before, and my heart crystallized. *He* was the one in the apartment. *He* was the one who had attacked me. The worst offenses did not belong to Bowen.

Had the twin killed the girls, too? Was Bowen trapped in his sadistic brother's game after he had tried so hard to escape his mother? Bowen was by no means innocent, but this changed everything—and yet nothing.

My Shakespeare dream came flashing back at me. Together, the twins were Caliban, embodying the two opposing sides of his character. Caliban wasn't just a monster; he was given the most beautiful and touching speeches in the play; his love for his island was unparalleled.

The twin took two steps to the side and dropped down on his haunches next to his sibling. He pulled the arrow from his brother's chest, using his thumb and index fingers, while keeping hold of the sword at the same time. He tossed the arrow at Gabriel's feet as if spitting at him.

Bowen moaned and started stirring, like a wild beast after the tranquilizer dart starts wearing off. His blood loss was minimal, so it wouldn't be long until he regained his strength.

More shots echoed in unison with loud screams, the type of screams one would utter while making a last stand, when seeing the reaper coming with his reddened sickle.

"The screams: them or us?" I whispered.

"Them." Gabriel grinned. He shrugged out from under Joshua's arm, and Peter took on the extra weight, though Joshua was able to bear some of his own weight now. Gabriel never took his eyes off the twin as he pressed the crossbow into my left hand and took the dagger that was locked in my right. Once he had the dagger, he reached above his head and unsheathed the Durateus sword he had strapped to his back.

Bowen's twin moved a few steps away, and Gabriel tracked with him, now equally armed. I wasn't sure if he could he go up against a vampire that old? Gabriel launched himself towards him, and there was a terrible clang of metal sparks flying in the dim light. One of the twin's swords skittered away, scraping the cement like nails across a chalkboard.

Gabriel skipped back a few steps, and his adversary circled around for another pass. He flew at Gabriel and knocked him to the ground as he flipped to retrieve the sword he had lost. The twin's eyes flashed red, then became black like his mother's had. He made a punching motion towards Gabriel, and a ripple pierced the distance between them, tossing Gabriel into the wall. Dust rained down from above with the impact.

"Cheating already? Cannot handle fighting a human," Gabriel challenged.

The twin hissed through his teeth. His face no longer held the cruel smile. "*Semideus* (demigod)..." he scoffed. "I don't think you qualify as human." Then they hurled into battle again, but it wouldn't last long. Gabriel was moving with inhuman speed, but his opponent was faster.

I had been so captivated by the battle that I had almost forgotten the crossbow. I hoisted it up and took aim, waiting for a good shot. They moved fast like dragonflies clashing, making it difficult to track them. There were flashes of light sparking from their swords as they fought on. I finally found a clear shot and fired, but I missed; however, it distracted the twin for a fraction of a second while he evaded the shot.

He spun around and looked like he was going to come at

me, but Gabriel landed a blow, hitting the twin's sword. A shower of sparks flew when the metal of their swords connected. The twin engaged him again, then they broke apart. Gabriel had lost his dagger in the last scrimmage.

"You have a name, or you just use your brother's?"

The twin didn't reply, but he smirked. It seemed that Gabriel was trying to figure out his origin. They circled back and forth, swords poised, ready for attack.

"You afraid to tell me?"

"My vanity is not so great that I can be baited."

"This is your chance to gloat and let us in on your villainous plan."

"I leave the scheming to my mother."

"Okay, no entreaties to your vanity. Just tell me your name."

"I go by Tyran ᵗ⁻ᵉᵃʳ⁻ᵃⁿ. Would you like me to spell it for you?"

"That is not what I meant. Your *real* name."

"I'm aware of what you meant." He grinned, then attacked again.

I reloaded the bow, took aim once more, then waited for my shot. I fired and struck Tyran in the back of the leg. He growled, but it didn't slow him down. I reloaded, noticing there were only two arrows left.

Yanking at the zipper on my bag, I pulled the knife out to hand it to Peter. A cold hand took my elbow and relieved me of the knife—Joshua. He wobbled, but he was standing on his own.

Another loud clash drew my attention, and Tyran plummeted backwards towards us. His arms were wide as he tried to regain his balance. He took both Peter and Joshua to the ground. Tyran quickly popped up like a martial artist, his back to Peter and Joshua, who were still on the floor. I looked at Gabriel. His shoulder was weeping blood, his body soaked in sweat, and his hair pasted to his forehead like wild black sea grass. He was holding his own, but he was tiring fast.

Something grazed me, and at that moment, Joshua was on Tyran's back. Josh cinched Tyran's neck in the crook of his arm as he plunged the blade into his back, striking the heart. Tyran went limp and collapsed onto the ground, Joshua beneath him.

Josh shoved the body off him as Gabriel approached, chest heaving, sword raised to take the Tyran's head.

"Stop!" a voice thundered through the building.

Simultaneously, a cold blade slid under my chin. An arm looped around me from behind, binding my arms uselessly to my sides. My gaze flew to the place on the floor where Bowen had been, even though I knew where he was now—right behind me.

I cursed myself for not shooting Bowen with an arrow to keep him down. I felt like an idiot. Peter was still on the ground, motionless beside me, his face frozen in horror as he watched. His arms were wrapped taut around his torso. I tried to see why he was on his side so awkwardly, but Bowen turned towards Gabriel, Joshua, and Tyran, blocking my view.

Gabriel stood with his weapon poised over the twin, debating, his face warped into a grimace.

"Do it!" I screeched.

Bowen pressed the blade harder into my neck. I wasn't exactly sure when it happened, but I was ready to die. I could feel blood trickle down my neck, tickling my skin like an insect crawling on my body.

"No!" Joshua yelled as he replaced his hand on the dagger in the twin's back and twisted it.

Tyran's body convulsed, though he had no control over it. The only sound I heard was labored breath and fighting outside. We were at a standstill.

Bowen finally broke the silence. "I see you dishonored our agreement and brought a few friends along." He dug the blade in a little, and I let out an involuntary whimper. I pressed my lips together to keep them from making another peep. This wasn't like the movies; the adrenaline coursed through my veins until it was painful, my heart strained. Every cell in my body ached.

"No, I didn't," Josh replied and shot a look at Gabriel.

Gabriel shrugged and addressed Joshua, "I may have put a tracker under your collar when we found Aleria had gone off on her own."

Joshua reached back, investigated under his collar and peeled off a minuscule device, then flicked it to the floor.

"So where do we go from here?" Joshua questioned Bowen. As if to emphasize the seriousness of the situation, he twisted the knife in the twin's back again, a new torrent of blood gushed from his body, and his skin paled to the hue of snow. Tyran grit his teeth, but didn't make a sound, his fangs digging into his lips. "It seems we have an impasse, of sorts."

"A standoff, it is."

Eyes were darting back and forth, assessing one another's weaknesses. It was unbearable. I struggled against my captor. He lowered his head and pressed his lips to my ear. He spoke so softly that not even another vampire could hear. "Please don't make me hurt you. I beg of you."

I swallowed and let my body go slack, forcing Bowen to take on some of my weight. I felt so tired all of the sudden, the adrenaline burning me out, leaving me ragged.

He kept his mouth next to my ear. A thought occurred to me, and I turned my head to speak in his ear. He stiffened and seemed leery, but allowed me to speak. "This is your chance to be free. You escaped your tower, but not your brother. He has never allowed you to be free. You could live a good life and not have to clean up his messes anymore. You could find meaning again."

This assumed his brother was the one killing the girls. My gut told me I was right.

I turned my head away from his ear. Bowen's breathing became rough, and his body shifted. He pressed his cheek against mine and buried half his face in my hair. Joshua's jaw flexed at seeing the intimacy of our pose. I wished I could see the expression on Bowen's face, as his body seemed to be struggling. He drew his face back to my ear, his cheek caressing mine.

"He's my brother," he rasped, inaudible to the others.

"A monster," I whispered, not putting my mouth to his ear this time.

"I—" his voice cut off with emotion.

Gabriel leaned forward a few inches, and Bowen tightened his grip on me. Gabriel rocked back on his heels. I cautioned him with my eyes.

"Free," I murmured. I offered the word like it was a hand

being offered to a spent swimmer. It almost felt like he was trembling. He pressed his body even closer to mine.

"I...I can't. He's my brother," he answered, but there was an edge of hopelessness.

Worried about his refusal, I felt the blood drain from my appendages. My head felt light and my hands cold.

He pressed his face back to my ear, and his next quiet words were not what I expected. "I am Belenus of the Celts, my brother Taranis. Know this: you will not be safe here. Your world, as you know it, is gone. You must leave this place. Use your Watchers; my brother will not forget." He paused.

I had no idea what he was planning, but his body seemed to hum like sound waves were building up deep in his core, yet there was no sound. His breathing was strained. I wondered what special abilities he had hidden.

"In the favored language of your Watchers, *Eris semper in corde meo* (You will always be in my heart)."

I repeated the phrase over in my head, trying to remember it. I knew something was about to happen.

A horrific sound came from above and usurped everyone's attention. The body of a woman smashed backward through the glass of the skylight, sailing like a missile and landing on the catwalk. Two vampires with glowing yellow eyes clad in black leather body armor bent down and peered through the jagged window. They moved like jungle cats, their eyes cutting straight through the midnight backdrop.

One of them hurdled himself onto the catwalk, landing next to the female without a sound. He seized her by the back of the neck and raised her up towards his gleaming fangs. I recognized the blonde mop of bloodied hair as he neared her jugular, her arms flailing weakly. It was the Slayer, Uriel, and she was losing as I stood there helpless, unable to do anything.

I tore my attention away from the scene above, and everything seemed to move in slow motion again. The humming from Bowen stopped. Gabriel raised his sword to take Tyran's head, as Joshua released his grip on the dagger and soared towards me.

Bowen pushed me onto Joshua with enough force to knock both of us to the ground. I landed on top of Joshua and watched as Bowen went diving towards his brother, grabbing his twin's wrist, and sliding him to the side.

Gabriel's sword arced through the air and struck the cement floor with such force, the blade stuck in the floor. Gabriel immediately strained to free the weapon. When he did, it glistened with blood. He'd made contact with Tyran. I glanced back, but Bowen and Tyran were gone like vapor. There was no way to confirm if Gabriel had made the kill.

The concussion of an explosion outside rocked the building. The firefight had been going on for several minutes now and had to have drawn the attention of the Campbell PD. I doubted they would know to focus their fire on the vampires and not the Slayers. This was going to get even messier.

When the explosion went off, Joshua rolled over and shielded me from the debris. He popped up and pulled me with him in one smooth movement. I looked down, and Peter was lying on the ground in the same spot he had been earlier. I panicked and ran towards him. Gabriel beat me there and hoisted Peter over his shoulder. Peter wasn't moving. Gabriel motioned up to the catwalk. "Get Uriel," he commanded to Joshua.

Josh took a step back, and with one graceful leap, lighted onto the catwalk next to her. He gingerly scooped her up, and then dropped to the ground, his body coiling to absorb the impact.

"Is she alive?" Gabriel asked.

"Barely." Joshua's eyes glowed, reacting to her blood-soaked body.

"Can you handle it?"

"Yes, let's go," he snarled.

We ran towards the roll-up door, away from the gunfire outside. Gabriel, Joshua, Peter, Uriel and I burst through the opening, emerging into the night air.

There were a few skirmishes, but the path to the van appeared clear. The side door slid open, and Sebastian's deep voice boomed, "We're pulling back."

Sebastian slid into the driver's seat, and the engine sprang to life, idling while we climbed aboard. The van had already begun moving as I heaved the door shut.

Gabriel placed Peter on the bench seat and opened the back cabinet. Some of the contents tumbled to the floor as he rushed to pull out the med kit. He ripped open the side of Peter's shirt and exposed a four-inch gash oozing with dark blood just above his abdomen. The surrounding skin looked bruised and red. He doused it with some type of powder and pressed a heap of bandages on the wound before wrapping a stretchy bandage around him.

Meanwhile, Joshua followed the same procedure on

Uriel's neck, but he didn't look hopeful. After he'd finished the field dressing, he carefully put her on one of the bunks.

I felt helpless as the van flew down the road away from the warehouse, sirens getting closer by the minute. It felt like we had pulled down a side street, then the engine cut off. I heard what sounded like dozens of emergency vehicles pass on the adjacent street. Once the riot of sound sped by, Sebastian fired up the engine and drove back onto the main road.

Gabriel called me over. "Put pressure on this." My hand replaced his, and he cut through to the cab and opened the front door. "Where are we headed?" he asked Sebastian.

"We have an emergency surgery center set up at the Saratoga house," Sebastian replied.

"We are going to need it," he said, grim. He then crawled into the passenger seat in the front and closed the door.

Joshua sank to his knees next to me and put his right hand on top of mine to help me keep pressure on the wound. After a moment, he put his free arm around me, and I leaned into his side.

When I worked up the nerve to make eye contact, I turned my head, and he kissed me with intensity. He appeared to be both relieved and furious. And frankly, he had every right to be both.

I closed my eyes, knowing there was a serious talk coming in the near future.

24

MENDING

We swayed as the van pulled into the steep driveway of the temporary compound. When we slowed to a stop, the van doors burst open, and emergency personnel rushed in to extract both Uriel and Peter from the van, Joshua helping them. I pressed myself to the side to get out of the way.

Afterwards, I stumbled from the vehicle in a fog, feeling responsible for everything. Other cars and such cluttered the driveway. Some people walked under their own power, and others did not. Both Joshua and Gabriel disappeared into the house.

I thought of Peter, probably under the knife at that moment, and felt like I was going to be sick. I broke out in a sweat, ran to the bushes, dropped to my knees, and puked over and over. Only bile came up. I hadn't eaten in so many hours that there was nothing much to throw up. Acid burned my throat, and my mouth was putrid. A breeze picked up, and I started shivering from the sweat.

When the heaving stopped, I twisted around and sat on the ground alone, watching the swirl of people move urgently around the courtyard. Crickets called into the night as the rest of the world went on as normal. There was a hint of skunk in the air, as well as chimney smoke. I gazed up at the clear night sky, the Big Dipper blazing above me. I wondered how many more times I would see this familiar horizon.

Bowen's voice echoed in my head: "You will not be safe here. You must leave this place."

My mind drifted back to Peter, and so I did the only thing I could think of. I bowed my head in a plea and prayed—*really* prayed—for his life. I would gladly have traded places with him if I could.

The world that seemed so clear to me weeks ago was now a huge palette containing variations of grey instead of just black and white.

I was so deep in thought that I was shaken when Gabriel sat on the ground next to me. The dry leaves crackled beneath him, and he smelled of sweat and blood. He looked exhausted. My stomach churned as I searched his face for news.

"How's Peter?" I croaked, my throat sore from dry heaving.

"Still in surgery. He was bleeding internally."

I nodded, my lip quivered.

"He is in good hands." He paused for a long while. "How are you holding up?"

"I'm always okay. Didn't you know that?"

"You need to be a better liar for me to believe you."

I shrugged and sat there in silence until I remembered something important. "Oh, I think I know something that you want."

"Pray, tell."

"I know Bowen and Tyran's real names," I answered.

"How did you find that out?"

"It was one of the things he whispered to me," I stopped to swallow, "when he had the knife to my throat." His eyes tightened at the memory.

"He said his name is Belenus of the Celts, and his brother is Taranis."

He exhaled. "That cannot be."

"He never lied to me. Well, about anything other than attending State and his age." I took a steadying breath. "Tyran was the one who attacked me the day you rescued me from that apartment. I knew it the moment I saw his eyes."

"I guess I should know by now that anything is possible," he replied.

I looked at him questioningly.

He shook his head sleepily. "I will tell you later."

"Do you think Tyran is dead?" I asked, remembering Gabriel's bloodied sword.

"Never believe a vampire is dead unless you personally burn the body."

"I take it this is from experience?"

"Unfortunately. Have you not learned that from the movies? Villains are hard to kill. They always return in the last act."

I debated for a moment, but decided to ask. "Umm,

Gabriel, Bowen said something else to me. I think it was Latin. Would you please tell me what it means?

"Of course."

"*Eris semper in corde meo*. I think." He blinked without saying anything for a moment. "Did I get it right?" I questioned.

"You seem to have a strange impact on vampires," he said with an odd smile on his face.

"I don't understand."

"He said, 'You will always be in my heart.'" He sat motionless for a long while as we watched the commotion in front of us. "Do you know what your last name means?"

"No, I didn't think it really had a meaning."

"It is an Irish name, meaning 'fire.' Fire is beautiful and mesmerizing. It has the ability to illuminate things and chase away the darkness, leaving warmth. But if there is one errant spark, it can burn down the world around it.

"That impact you have on vampires, on Joshua, you are like fire." He hesitated. "You can shed light on truths and help bring focus. But to those brothers..." He let the words hang. "Vampires never forget." He reached over and squeezed my shoulder. "I will go check on things inside, and...go easy on him." He indicated a dark area next to the house and disappeared through the front doors.

I rubbed my eyes and focused on where Gabriel had indicated. Joshua was sitting in the shadows on a bench beneath a trellis heavy with wisteria. He was watching me, looking troubled.

I stood and stretched. So many places on my body complained: the back of my head, my rib, my elbow, the list went on—sitting on the ground for so long hadn't helped. Exhaustion set in as I walked over to Joshua and sat tentatively next to him. There was a faint sense of déjà vu. It reminded me of sitting in the gazebo the night he had told me he was a vampire. It seemed like years ago. I wondered why Gabriel had said to go easy on him. *Aren't I the one in trouble?*

"Hey." *Wow, my big opening.*

"Hey."

"Ummm. So, are you talking to me?" I asked.

He let his breath out in a gust. "Shouldn't that be the other way around?"

"Why wouldn't I talk to you? I was the one who…It doesn't matter." I suddenly felt a thousand years old.

"I will acknowledge it. I felt betrayed when you walked away from me. The thought of him touching you. I…" He stopped for a moment. "Aleria, I know why you did it. And almost losing you repeatedly today has put things into perspective."

"Then if you aren't mad at me, why are you sitting over here in the dark?"

"Als, I have stolen your life. You have to leave everything because of me. I've told you this before."

"When are you going to get it through your thick skull that it isn't your fault? The blame lies with a pair of twin vampires. Well, I suppose most of it may squarely rest on Tyran's shoulders. And I thought I was the one with the guilt complex."

"I thought you might be lonely in the land of the guilty," he said lamely as he examined his shoes.

I leaned, bumping his shoulder playfully. "You know, brooding vampires are *so* last year."

"Sorry, I didn't get the memo." A grin crept onto his face when he looked over at me.

I continued, "You should really look into that. Secure your passwords, maybe buy a locking mailbox."

"How about lovesick vampires?" he smirked.

I smiled. "They are *always* in fashion."

25

EPILOGUE—ACCEPTANCE

"Sebastian?"

"Yes?"

"This is going to work, isn't it?" I asked.

He smiled and rubbed my shoulder reassuringly. "I will do everything in my power. I promise, within a week's time, we will have a resolution that your parents will not question."

"When I leave, you really think my family will be safe?"

"I believe so, but of course, we will keep them under observation for as long as it takes," he assured, as he looked me square in the eyes.

I let out a sigh of relief and gave him a spontaneous hug. He chuckled and returned the embrace, patting me on the back.

"Thank you." That was the phrase I needed to hear more than anything else—*as long as it takes*. When I finally let go of him, his eyes sparkled with warmth.

"Be assured, your story is just beginning."

My family returned from my grandmother's on Sunday, as scheduled. It felt like I hadn't seen them in months rather than just nine days. I tried to enjoy every moment I had with them.

Later that day, Sebastian called my cell to let me know that the Council had decided I had three weeks at most before I should leave. Three weeks was all I was given to neatly tie up all the loose strings of my life in California. I sighed heavily.

I was wondering how they were they going to satisfy my parents; my curiosity was growing rampant. I should have figured it out.

Two days after my parents returned, Joshua dropped by for an evening. They were so excited to see him that they'd hardly commented on how pale he'd become. He wove a tale of his life in college at Penn State and of his upcoming year of studies abroad. He informed all of us that he was going to be in London for the next academic year.

I looked at him with the appropriate expressions as he spoke. I smiled, nodded, and asked questions about his life at school, as would be expected. But the moment he mentioned London, I felt like I was doomed—like we'd be separated by an ocean that would drown my heart. When worry distorted my face, Josh winked at me, but I couldn't figure out what he was up to.

I wanted to walk him out to the car alone, but my whole family trailed behind, so I couldn't quiz him like I wanted. My family had missed him, too. I wondered when I would see him next. I had never thought of myself as impatient, but the days were ticking by at a torturously slow rate. I was sure it was because there was too much of the unknown looming over me.

Three days later, I received a large, priority envelope posted from London. I furrowed my brow as I examined the outside. *Signum Academy.* It sounded important, but I had never heard of it. My mother entered the kitchen as I started to open the envelope.

"What do you have there?" she inquired pleasantly.

"Um, something from Signum Academy," I answered, intentionally vague, as I tried not to betray my ignorance in the situation. I pulled out the contents of the envelope and raised the cover letter to read it.

My mom started to ask another question, then decided to read over my shoulder instead.

> Miss Aleria Hayes,
> We are pleased to accept your
>   application to Signum Academy in
>   London. In addition to your
>   acceptance, you have been bestowed a
>   full scholarship for one year.
>   Graduation from our educational
>   institution will give you priority at
>   many of the top universities in the
>   world...

And the letter continued, complete with brochures, dorm assignments, and every detail of which I might only dream. I could hear my mom breathing behind me, but she said nothing. It was impossible to tell if that was a good thing or a bad thing.

My mom finally broke the silence; I hadn't been able to utter anything, since I was still shocked by the letter. "I didn't realize that you had applied to this place."

I hated lying. "Uh, yeah. It was just for fun. I never thought I'd actually get in. They only accept a few Americans each year." *That sounded convincing, right?*

"Wow," was all she responded with. She took the letter from my hands and read it again, then proceeded to go through the additional information. After perusing the packet, she made a surprised sound. "Classes begin in less than three weeks! It looks like there's a tour for parents in one week." She hesitated, and almost under her breath said, "I wonder how much airline tickets would be?"

"Really? So soon? They don't give you much time, do they?" I replied. There was another long silence. "Mom?"

"Yeah?" She had an unreadable expression.

"Do you think you and Dad will let me go?" I figured asking from the weaker position would be better.

"This is really big, Ali. We'll discuss it." She paused and smiled. "I'm very proud of you. This seems to be a big honor."

"Thanks." Of course, those words burned my conscience. I hadn't really earned my way into anything. I groaned internally. This was killing me.

And then it happened. She turned back towards me and asked, "Didn't Joshua say he was going to be in London?" *Bingo.*

"I think so."

"I wonder how close he'll be and if he knows anything

about the school. It would make me feel a little better knowing he was around."

I shrugged, trying to be casual. "We can ask him. I'm pretty sure he's around for a couple of more days. I'll try to call him."

"Great, see if he'll come for dinner tonight," she offered, smiling.

"Sure." *I hope we are serving type O positive.*

I dashed upstairs and called Josh to invite him to "dinner." He said he'd been expecting my call and that he'd be over just after sunset, too late for dinner, and of course, to let my mom know that he'd have eaten by then. I reacted in false surprise.

I heard my parents discuss Signum Academy in their room behind closed doors. Sneaking into the hall, I tried to hear as much as I could. From the tone of their voices, it sounded good. But my mom had already been lamenting the fact that I only had one year left before going away to college. Now, she was being robbed of that year—so was I.

She had been gathering applications for schools no farther south than Los Angeles and no farther north than Portland. She wanted me to be able to come home for all the breaks. Despite her desire for me to be closer, I couldn't imagine her keeping me from this opportunity.

I heard their conversation wrapping up, so I crept out of the hallway, avoiding all of the squeaks successfully. I rounded the corner just as they opened their door, making me jump. Two seconds earlier, and I would've been caught, not that it would have been that big of a deal.

Just then, there was a knock at the front door. I tiptoed over and yanked it open to reveal Joshua with a box of my mother's favorite chocolates. He tapped the box with his finger, and we smiled conspiratorially at one another.

With Joshua's help, everything was settled by the end of the evening. Not only did my parents approve of my going, but they were pleased that Joshua had someone like family to be nearby. I was amazed at his persuasive abilities, especially since they were so subtle.

I woke slowly the next morning, huddled in my quilt, and I felt better than I had in days. I had slept in longer than I'd intended to. Maybe something about having my course set had allowed my brain to finally rest. Then, I realized that my family was not the only set of people I had to tell I was moving.

Fiddling with my cell, I dreaded my next move. After several minutes of procrastination, I sent a group text to the girls asking if we could get together. The whole group agreed to meet me at Breanna's house. I ran over different scenarios in my head and practiced my answers. Anxiety unfurled in my stomach, making me feel a little green. I knew that most would be happy for me, but both Marie and Kaela wouldn't like it—at all.

I pushed my legs through my green khaki shorts and pulled on a black tank top. I decided that I should enjoy my shorts as much as possible for the next two weeks, as I doubted I would need them much in England. After I was ready, I drove over to meet everyone. When I arrived, I took inventory of the cars outside, and as planned, I was the last to arrive.

After everyone was seated, I told them my exciting news. Breanna and April jumped up and exclaimed their congratulations, giving me hugs. As suspected, Marie and Kaela were quiet with tight smiles. They tried to be happy for me, but I could see and feel their disappointment.

For the next few hours, we all hung out by the pool. I borrowed a bathing suit from Breanna. It looked pretty ridiculous on me, but I was glad I'd stayed. I was the first to leave, but I heard the front door shut again quickly behind me. I turned, and Kaela was quickly closing the gap between us. I swallowed hard because I knew that expression.

When she didn't stop me, I continued to walk to my car, but my passenger door opened as she slid into the seat. I turned on the engine to get the AC going and shifted in my seat towards her.

She furrowed her brow a bit, and then asked, "How did you bruise up your elbow?" I was surprised no one else had asked earlier, although my news may have distracted them.

I shrugged. "I fell. I slipped on something and landed on it." I left out the slipping in a pool of blood part.

She nodded, but didn't say anything. The silence became awkward as I sat there listening to the drone of the air conditioner. "You didn't get a scholarship, did you?"

"Uhhh. Yes, I did." *True, the Council is giving me a free ride the Watcher academy, which is apparently more rigorous than university.*

"I just don't remember you applying for anything, and you would have mentioned it. I have this feeling that you *have* to go. That something bad happened and that other bad things are going to happen. Are you gonna be okay?"

How in the heck does she do that?

I didn't look at her. I rubbed a dried droplet of coffee off the center console with my thumb while I thought through my answer. "Yeah, I'll be fine," I finally replied. She would see right through me if I tried to lie to her, not that I wanted to.

"You won't be alone, will you?"

"No, I won't." I couldn't help but smile a little.

"I'm going to miss you," she said, and they were her last words to me.

"I'll miss you, too."

She scrambled to her knees and hugged me over the center console with such ferocity that I couldn't breathe for a second. Then, she got out without another word, making me feel a little whiplashed.

I sat there, my car still idling, missing all of them with such intensity it made me doubt everything. In addition to my friends, leaving my family was going to be a thousand times worse. I couldn't shake the melancholy feeling that had overcome me during my conversation with Kaela. The tidal wave was no longer threatening me; I was being swept out to sea. Everything was going to change.

I went home and had dinner with my family before retiring to my room to pack up some of my stuff. I wasn't going to take very much, but I wanted to go through my things and get rid of as much as possible.

Night felt like it would never arrive, and my body throbbed with fatigue from what seemed to be the never-ending day. Telling my friends I wouldn't be there for senior year had been mentally exhausting. I realized it was finally dark outside, so I checked the clock on my nightstand. It read 10:00 P.M. I was losing time. I sighed and sank into the chair in my room. I'd hoped to see Joshua today. At that moment, my phone vibrated with a text.

It was from Joshua: "Patio behind gazebo if you can."

I quickly replied: "see u in 2 :o)," my excitement barely contained. I crept down the stairs and out the back door with barely a whisper.

I walked through the yard and used the slate stepping-stones that skirted the outside of the gazebo to reach my favorite place in our yard. There was a 15' x 15' flagstone pad completely obscured from view in the far corner of our massive yard. My mom had planted beautiful blooming hedges, shrubs, and vines on all sides, leaving only a small pathway to enter the patio. There were only three items on that concrete slab: two oversized lounge chairs and a small table. It was the perfect place to read during the day or to watch the stars at night.

I stepped through the narrow entrance, and Joshua was waiting with his back turned to me. He turned, and a breathtaking smile spread across his face, an unguarded grin that was never allowed in the presence of others. I don't know if my feet hit the ground those last few steps before I flew into his arms. We stood there for countless minutes, locked in an embrace that I never wanted to end. He finally leaned back enough to kiss me.

"I feel like I haven't seen you in a long time," I whispered.

"I feel the same way, and we haven't been alone in, what, a week?"

"Eight days, not that I'm counting," I replied, looking innocent.

He gently tilted my head up and gazed into my eyes with a dark expression. He made some small circles on my chin with his thumb as he seemed to be gathering his words.

I waited and waited.

I finally broke the silence. "I'm obviously not going to like what you're about to say, so please stop torturing me and just say it."

He grinned. "Am I that transparent?"

"Only to the trained eye," I responded.

He sighed. "I'm flying out tomorrow."

"Oh." I tried not to seem too disappointed, but unhappiness about being apart was radiating from me like... well, like I was the sun. I cringed.

"Don't worry. I'll see you in two weeks. I'm leaving with Sebastian to help with some reorganization in the training center outside of London. You won't actually be at the London facility, but about twenty miles outside the city. Gabriel is staying here to oversee you getting out okay."

"Two weeks," I groaned.

"It'll fly by—promise."

I grumbled.

He took my hand, led me to one of the lounge chairs, and pulled me down with him. I curled next to him on my side and rested my head on his chest. He rubbed my back as he spoke. "Gabriel has a fairly elaborate exit strategy for you."

"Really?" My interest was piqued.

"Well, it's very important that you are *seen* moving, but we don't want them to know where you are going. Decoys, fake

IDs, disguises—all the cloak and dagger you've ever dreamed of. The location given to family and friends will not be your actual whereabouts. Like I told you before, we will be in a suburb far from the city. Decoys will be seen periodically in the other locations."

"Hmmm. I was just picturing having to switch planes a bunch of times."

"I thought *I* was overprotective of you, but compared to Gabriel…" His words trailed off. The protectiveness did make me feel infinitely better. "The Council has training centers in New York, Paris, Rome, Prague, and Bucharest, in addition to the one in London. Gabriel is seeing to it that they have to scour every major city in Europe if they want to find you. A veritable needle." He didn't finish the cliché, opting to give me a little squeeze instead. I sighed.

I shifted so I could see his face, and the lounge chair cushion crinkled. I examined his ghostly profile in the moonlight and watched his chest rise and fall.

"Are you happy?" I stopped for an instant before adding, "I know that's a loaded question."

He drew in a few more breaths, then casually rolled to his side so we were nose-to-nose. He ran his index finger over my lips while he contemplated his answer. His eyes were dark as emeralds in the shadowy light, but they still sparkled.

"I think I am. For the first time in…" He closed his eyes for a long moment. "Since my parents," he finally said, and the melancholy that had seemed to be a permanent fixture on his face was replaced with contentment.

I took the hand that was still on my lips and kissed it. "I'm glad," I murmured.

"It's you. You know that, don't you? You've changed everything." He indicated the horizon, so I peered over my shoulder. One star was brilliantly outshining all of the others. "You're my North Star."

I felt a lump grow in my throat. I didn't know how to express my feelings into words. He'd been there for me my entire life. And now, the love I felt for him—it dwarfed everything else. My bottom lip quivered, and my eyes pricked with approaching tears.

"I..." My voice choked off, making me feel like a stupid schoolgirl. Still unable to speak, I grabbed his shirt and pulled him those last few inches to my lips. His arms encircled me, and my heart started to pound so hard, it felt like my body was pulsing with each beat.

I gasped, "Can you hear my heart?"

I could feel his smile as he continued to kiss me. "It has to beat twice as hard, because it's beating for both of us."

He kissed my cheek, then my jaw, under my jaw, my neck, my collarbone, and then my neck again, where he abruptly stopped. He stopped, and his body became rigid. I had my hands knotted in the back of his shirt. His breathing was hard, his cool lips pressed against my skin.

Then reality hit me—I was making out with a vampire, and he was struggling for the first time. Being close to me had never seemed to bother him, but then again, we hadn't been in this exact situation. He rolled onto his back and closed his glowing eyes.

"Are you okay?" I whispered.

"Just give me a second." After a little time, his breathing returned to normal. He shook his head. "I'm sorry."

"Don't apologize."

"It's hard not to."

"I know there's nothing I can say that'll make you feel better." Although I kept trying to think of something to say that would, I changed the subject instead. "Will I get to see you tomorrow?"

"I'm afraid not; we leave on a private plane at sunset. Sebastian and I are leaving with the remaining members of the Council and Conclave, including Blackthorne."

"Really? Blackthorne is willing to be on a plane with you?"

"He seems to have realized the value of working with the Council and me. We'll see. Because of him, it looks like they'll give reforming the Concilium another try."

"This is huge, isn't it?"

"Yes."

We continued talking for a few minutes about the details of his departure, and then he had to go. I tried to keep my chin up when we kissed for the last time for two weeks. I somberly walked back to my room and noticed a card and a carefully folded piece of red tissue paper on my pillow.

I opened the card; he had written a few partial lines from my favorite e.e. cummings poem:

> i carry your heart with me(i carry it in
> my heart)i am never without it...
> i fear no fate(for <u>you are my fate</u>...)

After reading the lines several times, especially the underlined phrase, I unfolded the tissue paper. There was a silver chain with a small charm dangling on it. I smiled. The charm was of the North Star.

The next two weeks were a blur of packing and preparation. The afternoon before I was set to leave, I received a package with the clothing I was to wear to the airport, down to the shoes and underwear. Every detail was being looked after.

The day of my departure, San Francisco was unusually cold. I stepped out of my parents' van, the sounds swirling around me and echoing off of all the cement and glass. Cars were honking and revving impatiently. People rushed from cabs. Others bid their loved ones farewell. The smell of car exhaust, both diesel and regular, hung like steam in a too hot bathroom, clinging. But I wasn't in a hurry to move. I stood there on the curb, regarding everything quietly, feeling the finality of it all.

Joshua was just fifteen hours away; I touched the charm on my necklace, hidden under my shirt, and drew strength from it. I looked up as a plane flew low overhead, its jet engines screaming. I hugged my family like I would never see them again, while tears flooded my cheeks. They wanted to walk me to the security checkpoint, but I convinced them not to. I watched them drive off, and as their vehicle disappeared from sight, I realized just how much I was leaving behind. My heart felt so, so heavy.

I wiped away the last of my tears and forced myself to concentrate on the task at hand. I checked in, passed through security, and entered the restroom as instructed. I found the handicapped stall in the corner, and when I was alone, I softly knocked at the door, and it opened. I was shocked to see Uriel in front of me. She grabbed my hand and pulled me into the stall with her.

"You're okay!" I exclaimed softly as I gave her a hug. I didn't know her well at all, but I felt overcome with happiness to see her.

She squeezed me back. "Slayer healing abilities," she replied in her Australian accent. "I need your hat, jacket, and scarf," she listed with a fairly excited gleam in her eyes.

She seemed to enjoy the cloak and dagger. I removed the aforementioned clothing and handed it over. She swirled her blonde locks into a wig cap with amazing speed, put on a brunette wig my exact shade, and pulled it through the back of the baseball hat as I had been wearing it. She took off the scarf she'd had around her neck and the silvery-pink scars from the battle were still apparent on her neck. She handed me a bag with new clothes, and I got dressed as she finished putting on my outfit. I hadn't realized that we were built the same until now.

The fabric of the black, velvety blazer with silver buttons was expensive. Uriel reached into the bag and pulled out some red hairpieces and clipped them into my hair, then proceeded to apply some makeup. After, she then twisted my hair into a chignon and handed me a pair of dark-rimmed glasses. I transferred the contents of my backpack into a leather messenger bag.

"Your new passport and tickets are in the front pocket of your new bag. Make as little eye contact as possible. Put in your ear buds and listen to music so no one will talk to you, but keep the volume low or off so you can still hear everything around you." She continued listing directions with lightning speed, and then knocked twice on the stall door.

A voice from the other end of the bathroom responded, "All clear."

Uriel grinned. "You ready, biscuit?"

"Yeah, umm, yes."

She swung open the door, and I got the first glimpse of us in the mirror. She looked remarkably like me. And I didn't look like myself. I looked like an ivy-league college student on my way to my law class. The red highlights she had clipped into my hair looked absolutely real.

She wagged her eyebrows. "Good huh?" she asked, indicating the new look.

"Amazing," I agreed.

I looked down the row of stalls and noticed a girl at the end of the bathroom. She was dressed in the same outfit as Uriel. She waved at me. Uriel looked at her. "Gentry, wait five before you go." The girl saluted and disappeared into a stall. "Ashley, please wait ten," she added.

"Will do," came another voice from another stall. She sounded British.

"Okay, Ali, go ahead and get to your plane."

I gave her elbow a squeeze as I went for the exit. I put my earphones in, but didn't turn on the music. I waited at my gate and read a book, trying to be as invisible as possible. I was utterly relieved when I was able to board the plane. I took my seat and prayed that no one would be next to me.

Finally settled, I allowed myself to listen to music and closed my eyes. The air started hissing through the vents overhead as the last of the passengers were finding their seats. It was so close to take off that I thought I was going to get to sit by myself, but then I felt someone slide into the seat next to me. I kept my eyes shut. I didn't want to look at whoever was stealing my privacy.

The flight attendants started the take-off monologue. I pulled the earphones from my ears and shut off my music before they asked me to, still unwilling to open my eyes.

As the engines wound up, nervousness hit my stomach. In all the excitement, I had forgotten how much I hated flying. I let out a long breath and clutched one of the armrests, holding onto both my locket and North Star charm in the other hand.

A warm hand covered mine on the armrest, startling me. Bewildered and half-scared, I opened my eyes and turned my head to look at the person next to me.

"I heard that you got nervous on planes, but I wouldn't have believed it," he said.

I was so shocked, I sat there without responding, as I blinked my eyes over and over again, looking through his disguise.

"Peter? What..." Without finishing my sentence, I leaned over and embraced him as well as I could while being belted to my seat.

When I let him go, he responded, "It seems there was some activity around my house. Sooooo, they thought it best..." He didn't need to finish the thought.

"I'm so sorry." I could feel my face twist tragically. This was how Joshua must have felt when he realized that my life would never be the same.

"Are you kidding me? This is exciting," he said in earnest.

"But you…"

"This is our second life, Ali. Like the movies, but for reals."

I couldn't help but grin at his excitement. "Okay then." I let out the breath I had been holding and felt oddly better.

"Just one thing."

"Yeah?"

"Please don't puke on me."

I laughed. "No promises," I said, elbowing his arm. I leaned back in my chair again and stared at the back of the seat in front of me. I'm glad you're here, Peter," I said softly.

"Me too," he agreed. I could hear a smile in his voice.

A second life.

I liked that. I closed my eyes and let all my anxieties melt away.

26

THE NEXUS: CHAPTER ONE

A SNEAK PEEK AT BOOK TWO

"You are acting awfully cavalier about my pain," I scolded in mock irritation.

He tried to stifle his grin. "Cavalier?"

"You know, indifferent, offhand, uncaring, thoughtless, *condescending*. You need another synonym or two?"

"No, I know what it means. I just wanted to see how many you could come up with. Five is quite impressive for such a mentally challenged person."

"Urgh!" I tossed my book at him.

Peter ducked and let out a roar of laughter.

"Not all of us were born with the foreign language gene. You're impossible." At some point, I started getting genuinely upset. I popped out of my seat and began thrusting my books into my bag.

"No, no, no, no. Sorry, sorry. Please sit back down. I promise to help."

Glaring at him through narrowed eyes, I measured his sincerity. "Fine, but I've reached my teasing limit today." I exhaled hard and sprawled back onto the sofa. I started to laugh, feeling a little stupid for my tantrum, even though it was partially justifiable. Peter had been teasing me *a lot* all day.

He settled back onto the other couch again and was fanning the pages of the book I'd flung at him. His light brown hair was sticking up all over the place in a serious case of bedhead. His skin had grown pale without the help of the California sun. He used to spend so many hours in the pool playing water polo that he'd radiated a golden glow even in the winter. Now, his natural blond streaks were almost gone. Our relocation to England had altered him dramatically.

"You know you are remarkably good at most of this stuff," he said. His expression was earnest.

I sighed, feeling conflicted, but appreciated the olive branch. "Not as good as you, genius boy."

"Everyone has their strengths and weaknesses."

"And Sebastian seems to know mine. This is my own personal hell—not one, but *two* foreign languages. I think my head may spontaneously combust one of these days." I dramatically reclined, pressing the back of my hand to my forehead.

"At least you wouldn't have to conjugate anything in Latin."

"Or French."

"Don't worry, I would write a nice epitaph for your tombstone. Something like:

> *Here lies Aleria Hayes.*
> *She has seen better days.*
> *In Latin and French, she was no good.*
> *Too bad she never understood."*

"I'd better not combust if that's the best you can come up with."

"I was on the spot."

"And poetically gifted you are not."

We both laughed. Bad poetry aside, Peter kept me grounded. He'd been a close friend for over three years, but here in exile, he was my best friend. Besides Joshua, he was now the only person in my life who'd known me for more than a few months.

While I pondered in silence, he grew thoughtful.

"You ever get homesick?" he asked, raising his dark brown eyes to meet mine. It was the first time he'd voiced that question.

It'd been four months since we'd fled here to protect our families. Of course, the parental units were under the impression that we'd earned scholarships to an exclusive academy in London. They didn't know that the academy was actually not in London and was run by the Council, which was part of the Concilium of Watchers. Nor did they know about vampires and their conflict with the aforementioned Watchers and how we mere mortals had been swept up in the middle of it.

"Yeah, sometimes, but we're always so busy that I don't really think about it that much." I frowned. "I guess that makes me kind of heartless, doesn't it?"

"I've always thought you were a little heartless." His eyes widened, and he put up his hand before I could react. "Sorry. No more teasing, really."

"It's fine. I was just being a baby." I paused for one beat. "No comments; I know I just opened myself up *again*."

He laughed.

"It's going to be hard being away for the holidays, isn't it?" I questioned. I thought about my thirteen-year-old brother, dressing up in his Halloween costume, stuffing his cheeks with too much turkey at Thanksgiving, opening Christmas presents with religious zeal—all without me.

If we couldn't solve some very serious issues with the

French coven, it would never be safe for me to go back. I would have to "die" in an accident while abroad and disappear.

I studied Peter for a second and felt miserable. He'd been kidnapped and used as a pawn to control me, thrust unwillingly into the vampire world, nearly dying because of it. Well, he actually had died in surgery for about sixty seconds.

"Yeah, it'll be hard to be away, especially at Christmas."

"Do you regret it? Choosing to come?" My voice sounded thicker than I had wanted it to.

"Sometimes."

My heart clenched, and guilt flooded in. I tried to be still and not react.

He rolled onto his stomach and gathered a throw pillow against his chest, resting most of his weight on his elbows. "But I know it's better I'm here. I just couldn't risk my family. Part of me is really excited. I love learning about all this, and I actually like England. I can't wait to be a Watcher out in the field. It's this whole world that I would've never known about." He paused thoughtfully, chewing on what he had said. "No, I don't regret it. I like this life."

My heart started beating regularly again, and I tried not to exhale in a noticeable gust. I didn't want him to realize I'd literally been holding my breath, awaiting his answer. I looked at the antique grandfather clock next to the entrance of the common room. "It's 5:40. We'd better get changed. Sunset is in twenty minutes. We are supposed to be in the mat room by 6:10."

"I guess the break is over." He stood, stretched, and let out a long groan. "Time to get our butts kicked."

"Speak for yourself. I plan to do the kicking."

"See you in thirty, I—" He cut himself off when we heard someone frantically running down the hall.

Gentry emerged, visibly shaken, her red hair wild and skin so pale it was almost translucent. "Meeting in room 110 right now; grab anyone else you see. Go now," she commanded, then sprinted down the hall.

Peter and I looked at one another for a split-second, then simultaneously sprang up and ran to the stairs. I could hear Gentry behind us as we sped down the last hall. The large classroom was already full. All faculty, staff, and students— about twenty in total—were abuzz with nervous energy. Peter found a seat in the front.

I surveyed the room for a place to sit. Leslie motioned to me from the back and slid over to make room for me on the table where she was sitting. When we'd first met, I'd wondered how she could possibly be a Watcher in training. She appeared to be more supermodel than stealth. The whole leggy, blonde thing had really intimidated me, though she was nothing but welcoming. She and Gentry had helped me adjust to life in the Watchers.

I shuffled through everyone on my way to the table. It was so tall I had to jump a little to seat myself next to her. Leslie looked at me; instead of giggling from my lack of grace getting up here, her grey-blue eyes were apprehensive. A horrible feeling gripped my stomach. I nudged her shoulder with mine, and she smiled thinly at me while we waited.

Sebastian entered the front of the room like a gust of wind

and stood before us. Gabriel and Joshua arrived behind him and stood to the side, both leaning against the wall. Sebastian's shirt was misbuttoned and his tweed jacket rumpled. I'd never seen him with even a hair out of place.

He launched into the briefing: "I am ordering an immediate evacuation of this facility. You have thirty minutes to pack your things. Bring only what you can carry. Destroy anything personal that you are not taking with you. Pull hard drives if you cannot take the computer. Leave nothing that can be traced.

"Three days' worth of clothing will be required. You will get wet leaving here, so wrap anything that needs to stay dry." He surveyed the faces in the room, but it seemed like he looked at me a split-second longer than everyone else.

Out of the corner of my eye, I saw Gabriel stare at me with a peculiar expression, but I kept my focus on Sebastian, wanting answers. Gabriel's eye contact made me realize that Joshua had kept his gaze *away* from me, without wavering. He had stayed focused on the front of the room. *Am I imagining this?*

I wasn't surprised when Ian, one of my classmates, raised his tattooed arm and started to ask a question. He was never afraid to make extra inquiries, even if that meant having someone irritated with him. But somehow, his cool factor and intelligence seemed to keep his constant questioning from getting annoying. "Sir, why do we need—"

Sebastian held up his hand and exhaled noisily. "We have lost contact with all of the other academies in the last three hours. Four experienced Watchers have gone missing; they are presumed dead after the message we decoded from one of them. We are out of time. Go now. No more questions. Meet in the basement. Leave the lights on, so it appears to be business as usual."

With that, he left the room. Everyone seemed frozen for a moment, reeling from the information. Then, with a purpose, everyone erupted from the room.

I lingered for a few seconds as the last few rushed off. Reality seemed to slow and sounds became indistinct and hollow as though I were trapped under water. In this daze, I was only vaguely aware of Gabriel stepping out with a grim expression. When I realized I had lost sight of Joshua, I started to leave the room.

Then, suddenly, he was behind me and gently caught my arm. He turned me to face him, holding both my arms firmly. "I need you to promise me something. Can you do that?"

I nodded mutely, still feeling numb.

"When we evacuate, I won't be with you. You need to stick with Gabriel. No matter what. Don't leave his side."

"I can't ask him to babysit me. Everyone needs—"

"Promise me." His green eyes were blazing into mine.

I wanted to argue, but I couldn't. I couldn't shake the feeling that I was somehow involved in what was happening. "Okay," I agreed hoarsely.

He pulled me against his chest and kissed the top of my head. "You should go pack," he said as he released me. I started to turn and head for the door. "Ali, wait." He looked at the door warily, then grabbed my wrist and spun me back towards him.

He took my face in both hands and kissed me urgently. I wrapped my arms around his waist and pulled him as close to me as humanly possible. A calm pulsed through my body as his cool lips moved with mine.

"Sorry, but you'd better get packing. I'll see you in a few minutes."

"Love you," I murmured.

"I love you, too," he breathed. His eyes were warm, but his expression was fixed with worry.

I turned on my heel and dashed up the stairs, then barreled into the postage stamp-sized room that I shared with Gentry. We had only known each other a short time, but she was already a trusted friend. I had seen her briefly in San Francisco the day I had moved to England.

We looked enough alike that she had been one of the decoys for my extraction. All it took was a pair of sunglasses, temporary hair dye, and a curling iron. Even my parents would have had to do a double take. Having Gentry around was kind of like being able to have my friend Kaela with me; somehow she always knew how I was really feeling, even if I put up a brave front.

When I entered, she already had most of her things packed; I had thought I was efficient until I had started rooming with her.

"You're done already?" I asked, knowing the answer. I started putting my things in the oversized Ziplocs she had left on the dresser for me.

"Of course, darlin'. *I* didn't feel the need to hang about after the meetin'," she teased in her adorable Irish accent.

"I didn't 'hang about', Gentry."

"Sure ya didn't. You *needed* to talk to the hot vampire. I get it." She winked and started forcing the air out of some of my bags, sealing them, and loading them into my backpack for me.

My romantic relationship with Joshua was a secret. It was becoming increasingly hard to keep it that way since everyone in school was being trained to be observant. I think most dismissed it since Joshua and I'd known each other all our lives. They expected there to be a close relationship. Gabriel had had it figured out since the beginning, but he'd always turned a blind eye.

I put on some dark clothing that would dry quickly and sat on my bed for a moment, trying to think of anything I might've missed. "Gentry..." I hesitated, wondering if I should ask.

"Time is a tickin' here. What's on your mind, love?"

I sighed. "Was it just me? Or did both Gabriel and Sebastian...never mind." I remembered my journal. That would be disastrous to leave behind. I reached under the mattress to procure it and sealed it in a bag.

A funny look twisted itself across her face. "Now that ya mention it..." Her words hung in the air.

"I didn't mention anything. It's fine," I said, shaking my head as I stuck a knife in my boot.

"They both looked at you more than the rest of us. I had disregarded it, but..."

I sighed. "Which means that they think that Bowen's coven is most likely to blame." I dropped my head into my hands.

"Time to go, love," she prompted, then strapped on her backpack. I agreed and did likewise. We left our room for the last time and navigated our way to the basement.

Gabriel appeared with a pack over his shoulder and a

canvas bag in his hand. He unlocked a door marked "Storage" with a brass key, then ducked into the room for a moment to light a torch on the far wall.

We all strained to see inside. Instead of an industrial room lined with shelves and stacked with dusty boxes, the large space was empty, and there were ancient looking stone walls befitting a castle. A murmur went through the room as we looked at one another in surprise. Gabriel opened the canvas bag and handed Ian a compact electric lantern as he motioned him into the room. As each of us filed in, he handed us a lantern.

The room was cool and smelled like some of the medieval cathedrals I'd visited while heavily disguised on my days off. The odor resembled dust, wax, incense, and a hint of iron. Joshua arrived with an odd shaped pry bar and some ornamental looking metal object about the size of my hand. He tossed the metal item to Gabriel, who walked over to a decorative design chiseled into the wall. He pressed the object into the center of the design, and it fit snugly. Then he proceeded to twist it clockwise.

There was a sound of sliding stone beneath us and a clank, as if something had unlocked. Everyone instinctively moved to the edges of the chamber. Joshua bent down and lodged the pry bar into a deep groove that must have appeared after Gabriel twisted what I then realized was a key. I expected him to try to lift the stone, but instead, he pulled it down like a lever, and the entire section of the floor sank down a few inches. Gabriel twisted the key counter-clockwise in the wall, and a mammoth stone in the ground slid to the side. Only blackness could be seen beneath.

Joshua stepped into the gaping hole in the floor and disappeared. I listened for him to land, but there was nothing. *Of course, he's a vampire, so that doesn't mean anything.*

Light began to glow from the opening. Joshua called up, "Okay, I'm ready."

Gabriel walked to the edge of the hole and looked down. "Good." Turning to us, he spoke quietly. "Toss Joshua your bag, then follow. He will help steady your landing. Quickly, go."

One after another, members of our group disappeared through the opening. Within a couple of minutes, I turned and looked around. It was my turn; only Gabriel was left. He motioned me towards the entrance with an open hand and a grin. He seemed to enjoy the adventure of this much more than anyone else, or at least he wanted it to appear that way to me.

There was some murmuring drifting up from below. It sounded muted, like the others were in a passageway a little farther away from the room beneath me. I peered over the edge—there was about an eight-foot drop down to a stone platform of some sort.

I dropped my bag and sat down at the edge, dangling my feet into the hole like a small child. At that moment, I felt like I was five years old, sitting next to my mom on the piano bench, wishing I was big enough to reach the pedals.

Sliding off the ledge, I hit the ground hard enough that my feet tingled. Joshua steadied me when I arched backwards. If he hadn't been here, I would've toppled off the ledge onto my head. I noticed that we were essentially alone and that everyone had moved down the hallway because the room was quite small. He gently kept hold of my arms and projected his voice to Gabriel. "Is that it?"

Gabriel looked down at us. "Yes. You ready?"

Joshua shrugged, and then looked at me with the same concern he had shown earlier.

Then I realized we were missing someone. "Where's Sebastian?"

Gabriel nodded to Joshua and disappeared from view.

Joshua kept his voice low. "He wants everything to appear like business as usual. I am going to escort him to his weekly meeting with the Concilium in London as I usually do when Gabriel isn't attending. Well, it will look like we are heading that way from Signum's main campus. We have an alternate exit plan."

I opened my mouth to say something, but he squeezed my elbow and glanced towards the passageway. All within a second, I slumped my shoulders, set my jaw in protest, then exhaled in defeat. I already knew he wasn't leaving with me. He looked towards the murmuring, gave me a quick grin, kissed my forehead, and jumped up through the opening above with ease.

"Take care of her," Josh said above.

Gabriel reappeared, and I scrambled off the platform. At that moment, I realized we were actually in a tomb, and this was the entrance to a network of catacombs. Shelves were carved into the south wall where bones rested, crowded together. Gabriel landed on the lid to the crypt and strapped on his pack. As the ceiling started to close, I looked up and watched Joshua until the room went dark. Gabriel handed me the lantern I had left on top of the crypt, and then urged me forward.

The last expression on Joshua's face—the worry—and something else, was burned into my vision while my eyes adjusted to the darkness. Sensing the urgency, I caught up to Gabriel, his presence making me feel better. But the other part of me kept thinking about the sound of that sliding stone sealing us into the catacombs—sealing us into a tomb.

GLOSSARY OF TERMS & LATIN PHRASES

- **Concilium**—the original unified group of Watchers. Their duty is to watch and document the lives of vampires. If an immortal begins to cause undue harm to humanity, they dispatch a Slayer to eliminate the deviant.
- **Conclave**—the group of Watchers that separated from the Concilium, believing that all vampires should be hunted down and exterminated. They believe that the ends justify the means, so human casualties are an acceptable consequence of the war.
- **Council**—the remaining members of what was once the Concilium. They document the lives of vampires and other immortals. Their motto is that they only interfere if absolutely necessary. If a vampire begins to kill indiscriminately, the Council dispatches a Slayer to stop the threat to humanity. They believe that all life has value.

- **Durateus Sword**—durateus is the Latin term for wood. Slayers developed a specialized sword with inlaid wood to make it effective on vampires.
- **Familiar**—a human that serves a vampire. This may be in the form of performing duties or willingly allowing the vampire to feed on them.
- **Semideus**—half-divine or a demigod.
- **Sire**—the vampire that brings another vampire into existence, a parent of sorts.
- **Slayer**—they work with the Watchers to keep vampires in check. They are the vampires foil and have the supernatural strength to combat them. They are human and therefore age, but at a much slower rate.
- **Watcher**—a member of the Concilium, Council, or Conclave. See "Concilium."

ACKNOWLEDGMENTS

First of all, I need to say that without the patience and encouragement of my husband, I wouldn't have been able to complete this novel. You have put up with going to bed alone when I stayed up half the night and given me time to get out of the house and write without the distractions of home. You amaze me every day.

In addition to my better half, I need to thank a host of other people. Two people in particular that have helped me in the editing process more than I can express. They have been willing to read and reread the entire novel and mark every page if need be. Katie Isaacs, I appreciate your ability to be both brutal and encouraging at the same time. Alexis, thank you for pushing me to do better. Your memory is amazing and still blows me away. You are a rock star.

And yes, there are still others: Judy, Jeanette, and Irene for helping with translations. Rachel for being the continuity police and for being willing to read all three books and track all the threads for me. My brother, Chris, for helping me talk through my mythology in the very beginning. Lily Fry and James Stewart, for going through a draft and editing supplementary material. Thanks to Sonia, Karen, Lisa, Rebecca, Rachel, Myra, Nancy, Roy, Jessica, Danielle, Giselle, and Jessie for giving me some great feedback. And to many of my students and former students, for enthusiastically being my focus group.

Vera Walker, for taking the horrible clipart rendition of the Slayer tattoo I designed and turning it into something beautiful. And of course for designing and illustrating the cover. You have an amazing amount of talent! You are gold!!

And to Mom and Dad, both of you have always urged me to stretch my legs and try out new things. Thank you for encouraging me to always explore.

An additional thanks to Beth and Tamar for spending so much time on the second edition. I appreciate your dedication and attention to detail.

BOOKS IN THE WATCHER SERIES

Chronological Order

0 — 1 — 2 — 3 — 4 — 5 — X

For ultimate suspense, read
the prequel after book two.

Extras can be
read along
with the books

The Watcher Series

Allure: A Watcher Series Prequel

The Unintended: Book One

The Nexus: Book Two

The Sacrifice: Book Three

The Fallen: Part One: Book Four

The Fallen: Part Two: Book Five

Light & Shadow: The Watcher Series Shorts & Extras

Storm and Solace: A Beauty & the Beast Retelling

In this *Beauty & the Beast* role-swapping mashup, Saxa is stripped of her powers and cursed by her two sisters. She has twelve weeks to change her ways or lose everything—including her life.

Brandr, shipwrecked after a terrible storm, is swept into the world of gods and goddesses. When he trades his life for his brother's, he sentences himself to a world he knows nothing about.

When their paths collide, nothing is as it seems. Who will survive this game of immortals?

CREATIVE WRITING BOOKS

Large Work

Prompt Me Novel: Fiction Writing Workbook & Journal

General Inspiration

Prompt Me: Creative Writing Workbook & Journal

Prompt Me More: Workbook & Journal

Prompt Me Again: Workbook & Journal

Genre Specific

Prompt Me Sci-Fi & Fantasy: Workbook & Journal

Prompt Me Romance: Workbook & Journal

Prompt Me Horror & Thriller: Workbook & Journal

Prompt Me Mystery & Suspense: Workbook & Journal

Reading Log

Prompt Me Reading Log & Analysis

ABOUT THE AUTHOR

Robin Woods is a former high school and university instructor with two and a half decades of experience teaching English, literature, and writing. She earned a BA in English and an MA in Education.

In addition to teaching, Robin Woods has published seven highly-rated novels, an award-winning creative writing series, and has multiple projects in the works.

When Ms. Woods isn't chasing her two kids around, she's spending time with her ever-patient husband, or sitting in a coffee shop wondering how vampires like their lattes.

For more information, an extended bio, free writing resources, links to social media, and free extra scenes, visit her website at www.robinwoodsfiction.com

Thank you for reading.
If you enjoyed this novel, please take a moment to write a review. It is the best way to help the authors you love.

www.ingramcontent.com/pod-product-compliance
Lightning Source LLC
Chambersburg PA
CBHW060357260626
47160CB00006B/2344